ALSO BY AMANDA FLOWER

FARM TO TABLE MYSTERIES
Farm to Trouble
Put Out to Pasture
In Farm's Way
Crime and Cherry Pits

NATURAL BARN KILLER

A FARM *to* TABLE MYSTERY

AMANDA FLOWER

Copyright © 2025 by Amanda Flower
Cover and internal design © 2025 by Sourcebooks
Cover illustration by Marco Marella

Sourcebooks, Poisoned Pen Press, and the colophon
are registered trademarks of Sourcebooks.

All rights reserved. No part of this book may be reproduced in any form or by
any electronic or mechanical means including information storage and retrieval
systems—except in the case of brief quotations embodied in critical articles or
reviews—without permission in writing from its publisher, Sourcebooks.

No part of this book may be used or reproduced in any manner for the
purpose of training artificial intelligence technologies or systems.

The characters and events portrayed in this book are fictitious or
are used fictitiously. Any similarity to real persons, living or dead,
is purely coincidental and not intended by the author.

Published by Poisoned Pen Press, an imprint of Sourcebooks
1935 Brookdale RD, Naperville, IL 60563-2773
(630) 961-3900
sourcebooks.com

Printed and bound in the United States of America.
KP 10 9 8 7 6 5 4 3 2 1

*In memory of Bill Faust
and in honor of Liz and Emily Faust*

Chapter One

"Shiloh, there are times when I think you purposely make your life harder than it has to be," Chesney, my farm manager, said as she flipped over a folding table onto its feet.

I shook out the autumn leaf–printed tablecloth and smoothed it over the tabletop. "How should I respond to that?"

"With acceptance," Chesney said with a smile as she set folding chairs around the table. "You have been a mess for days over this Thanksgiving Day meal when you could just have eaten pizza and taken a nap."

"Pizza doesn't sound very Thanksgivingy."

"*Thanksgivingy* is not a word, and I have had pizza on Thanksgiving more times than I could count. It's been a bit of tradition for Whit and me." Her voice was typically cheerful, but she looked away.

I frowned and wondered why Chesney was on edge. I had sensed some tension between her and her sister, Whit, the last several weeks. However, just an hour before our guests were to arrive was not the time to ask her about it.

Instead I said, "You should have said something when I

sprang this idea on you to have Thanksgiving here at your house."

"It's your house, Shi. We are just living here, and we're grateful for that. Besides, who would turn down a Thanksgiving meal made by Jessa?"

I winced at the sight of the chairs as she set a third one around the table. "Is that the best we have?"

"See," she said as if I had made her point. "You're making your life hard, but since I knew this would be a concern, I bought cushions and chair covers. The guests won't even know that they are sitting on old metal folding chairs."

I laughed. "You do think of everything."

"That's why you hired me," she said with a grin.

She wasn't wrong. When I left my television producer job in Los Angeles and came back to Cherry Glen, Michigan, with the goal of saving my family farm nearly two years ago, I hadn't realized what a big job I was taking on, nor did I understand that I needed help. Both of those things became crystal clear very quickly. Chesney had been an agriculture graduate student at the closest university, in Traverse City, and was looking for work in her field for experience. When we met, I hired her on the spot. Thankfully, when I came into some family money, I was able to hire her full-time and let her and her younger sister live in a farmhouse on the property for very low rent. Now I didn't know what I would do without her. Both she and Whit had become like little sisters to me, so I found it especially hard to know that there was any kind of rift between them.

Huckleberry, my faithful pug, had dived under the table

as soon as the cloth had been placed, as if he believed it was a fort built just for him. Chesney and I might be frantic getting ready for the Thanksgiving meal, but Huckleberry was having the time of his life.

My little pug got a piece of the tablecloth in his mouth and pulled with all his might; the cloth fell to the floor.

I put my hands on my hips. "Huckleberry! You can't be doing that when the table is set."

He cocked his head at me, pretending he didn't know what I was talking about. Suddenly, as if his curly tail burst into flames, he ran to the window and started barking. I followed him to window. Diva, the top chicken in the henhouse, and her band of angry chickens stood outside squawking and carrying on. I didn't doubt for a second that Diva put up a fuss just to aggravate Huckleberry. Annoying the little pug was one of her favorite pastimes. That and tormenting the other living creatures, including the humans, on the farm.

Recently, we had moved the chicken coop from the next to the barn by my father's farmhouse to Chesney's side of the farm. The reason for that was that Diva and her flock of killer hens had gotten it into their bird brains that the small colony of orange barn cats in the big barn were public enemy number one. The chickens terrorized the cats to the point the felines stopped eating and refused to leave the safety of the hayloft. Something had to give. Rather than move the innocent cats, Diva and the chickens, who were the troublemakers after all, had to be relocated.

Diva and her hens settled into the coop by Chesney's house immediately and gave the impression that it had been their plan all the time to move. I knew she was just a chicken, but Diva had a way to spin everything to her advantage. It was a skill I'd never held, so I had respect for her in that regard.

Huckleberry took offense to how Diva and her gang treated his cat friends, so he barked at her at every chance he got.

The large white hen flapped her wings and glared at Huckleberry through the window.

"It's almost like she is saying 'Come at me, bro,'" Chesney said as she peered through the glass.

"It's exactly what she's saying. That chicken is out of control," I said.

Huckleberry wiggled his bottom and barked again.

His high-pitched yip did little to intimidate the chicken; she began pecking at the ground like she didn't have a care in the world.

Before this could escalate too far, I scooped up the pug. At this rate, with the two animals taunting each other, we weren't going to get any work done, and we only had forty-five minutes before guests started to arrive.

This called for reinforcements. "Go in the kitchen and get a snack from Jessa."

He cocked his head when I said "Jessa" and "snack." The two words were synonymous in Huckleberry's world. It could be because my friend Jessa owned Jessa's Place, the most beloved eatery in the small town of Cherry Glen, and because she was much more likely to slip the little pooch a piece of bacon or a chunk of cheddar cheese than I was.

Huckleberry adored her. He loved that she never skimped on the fat or sugar in her recipes. That is how the pug felt he had the right to eat each and every day.

Meanwhile, I fed Huckleberry low-fat organic dog food. It was no wonder he liked her cooking better. He waddled off to the kitchen with the anticipation of a delicious treat.

I picked the tablecloth off the floor and smoothed it over the table again. The table was twenty feet long, and it would seat our party of sixteen comfortably. When I decided to host Thanksgiving at the farm, I invited everyone who had supported me in my journey to save Bellamy Farm, which was finally back on its feet. I could see a future where the farm could not only be self-sufficient but actually make a profit. I had so many ideas on how to expand our offerings and outreach, and for the first time, I felt we would able to achieve them.

I picked up the set of pumpkin-shaped place mats that I had purchased for this celebration and began setting the table. I prayed that Huckleberry didn't get in his head to pull on the tablecloth again. I'd hate to have to lock him in a bedroom during the meal. He loved turkey, and then there would be the howling.

Chesney and I were just about done setting the table when Whit came down the stairs.

Whit attended school at the university in Traverse City. It was the same school I had attended decades ago. I had been a film and television production major, while she was in the theater department. However, those two departments in the small university overlapped a lot with faculty and coursework. I liked to ask her about what classes she was taking and who was teaching what. Most of my old professors were retired or close to it, but a few remained, and it amused me to hear her stories about my old teachers that proved that the older faculty hadn't changed at all.

Whit's clothing, to me, always looked slightly uncomfortable. She either wore something skintight and revealing or a baggy jogging suit or sweats. While her sister did nothing much to her hair, Whit dyed hers black with streaks of bright colors. Today it was black and orange, perhaps a leftover look from Halloween. I actually didn't know what her natural color was, as I had never seen it.

Chesney on the other hand, was very simply dressed all the time. She was either in jeans and a flannel shirt or jeans and a hoodie. She always wore her brown hair up in a ponytail, and the glasses that she wore on the bridge of her nose gave her an intellectual look. That was fitting since she was always studying and learning something new, even though she had achieved her master's and was no longer in school.

"There you are," Chesney said. "I thought you would come down earlier to help us get ready for Thanksgiving."

Whit glared at her sister with so much animosity, I took a step back.

"I never said that I was going to do that," Whit snapped. "I didn't make these plans. I wasn't asked if I wanted to have Thanksgiving here."

Chesney winced and glanced at me as if she was ashamed of her sister's rudeness. I gave a slight shake of my head to show it didn't bother me. It did surprise me, however; I had never heard Whit speak to her sister or to anyone else that way before.

"Happy Thanksgiving to you too," Chesney quipped.

Whit rolled her eyes and slung her giant black leather bag over her shoulder. "I'm going out."

"Out?" Chesney asked. "It's Thanksgiving."

"I know that."

I sidestepped toward the kitchen. I didn't know what was going on between the two of them, and frankly, I didn't want to know.

"You should stay home," Chesney said. "We have a great day planned. It's a day for family," Chesney said.

"Family? What family do we have?"

Chesney gave a sharp intake of breath. "The Bellamys are family to us."

"To you, maybe. I said I'm going out, and I am. You're not my mother. You can't tell me what to do. Besides I'm an adult now. Even if I had a mother, she couldn't tell me what to do either," she snapped.

Chesney jerked back as if she had been slapped.

I bit the inside of my lip. I knew how much that statement would hurt my friend. She and Whit lost their parents in an accident at an incredibly young age, and Chesney, who is nine years older than her young sister, took it upon herself to raise Whit the best that she could. She was just a teenager when she essentially became a parent to Whit—regardless if Whit agreed with that title.

"Whit, what has gotten into you?" Chesney asked.

"Nothing. I have things to do." She dug the toe of her black combat boot into the rug.

"On Thanksgiving? What do you possibly have to do on Thanksgiving? Everything is closed."

Whit glared at her. "Why do you even care?"

"Because I'm your sister, and you live here with me, and I have a right to know what is going on with you." Chesney's volume rose with each word.

"Maybe I want to move out."

Chesney blinked. "Move out where and with what money? You work for pennies at Michigan Street Theater, and you're going to school. You're neck deep in student loans without enough in your pocket to buy a cup a coffee at Jessa's Place, much less pay rent."

"I can live with friends. I can't live with you forever, Chesney."

Chesney took a sharp intake of breath.

I had to get out of that room, but I was on the wrong side of the Thanksgiving table and didn't want to move for fear of drawing attention to myself. This was one fight I wanted nothing to do with. I had enough family drama of my own, thank you very much. Since I was stuck there, I kept smoothing the same spot on the tablecloth in front of me like I was petting a cat.

Chesney went back to setting the table. "Fine. Go. Dinner is at three. If you're here, you're here. If not, there may be leftovers."

Whit stomped out of the house.

I looked up from my overly smooth tablecloth. "You okay?"

She shrugged. "Living with family isn't always easy."

I knew that better than most.

She shook her head. "Whit's just being dramatic. She'll be back by dinner. She would never miss Jessa's turkey," Chesney said, but she looked worried as she stared out the window, as if she wasn't entirely sure that was true.

"I'm going to go grab the candles from the pantry," I said, relieved that I was finally able to make my exit from the room.

Even if I didn't know the layout of the house, I could have easily found the kitchen by following my nose. The heavenly aroma coming from the center of the house led the way. I didn't know if what I was smelling was the turkey or the sides or just that divine combination of the two, but I hoped everyone arrived at the meal on time because I couldn't wait to dive in. I'd skipped breakfast that morning with the intention of eating double at the Thanksgiving meal. As my tummy rumbled in protest, I wondered if that had been the right choice.

Jessa stood at the stove stirring a large pot of gravy with a whisk. With so many people coming, we would need a lot of gravy. We were Midwestern after all, and everything went well with gravy, but nothing went as well with it as Thanksgiving dinner.

Jessa hummed while she worked. She was a woman of average height and build, but those were the only things average about her. Somewhere between the ages of fifty and seventy, Jessa had long white hair that, when it was loose, fell halfway down her back. At the moment there were long teal streaks running through her hair, which she had pulled back in a ponytail with a turkey-print bandanna tight around her head to keep her hair out of her face.

Jessa had been dyeing her hair bright colors for decades, long before Whit had been born. She was a trendsetter through and through.

Esmeralda, my long-haired part Siamese and 100 percent queen of the farm, watched Jessa with a level of admiration that she dared not bestow on any other of her subjects. Esmeralda hoped and prayed for just a spoonful of Jessa's gravy, but it looked to me as if Esmeralda already had several dollops, as was evident by the small bowl on the floor that had been licked clean.

Huckleberry stood on the other side of Jessa with the same expression on his pushed-in face. They really were a pair.

The cat scowled at me as I interrupted her continued appeal for gravy. I had a suspicion that Huckleberry and Esmeralda would sleep very well that night in a turkey coma of their own.

"How much gravy have they had?" I asked.

"Was I supposed to be measuring it?" Jessa chuckled.

I groaned. "Cut them off now," I said. "People are going to slip them so many treats at dinner. I'm afraid they might get sick."

Jessa sighed. "How can I? Look at those little faces."

On cue, the cat and pug looked at me with the most pathetic expressions I had ever seen.

I folded my arms. "Sorry, kids. No more gravy."

Huckleberry lowered his head in sad acceptance while Esmeralda gave me a view of her backside and sauntered out of the room. I would pay for that decision later. Esmeralda knew how to hold a grudge.

"I'd watch my back if I were you," Jessa said.

"I'm used to it." I shrugged and picked up a piece of cream cheese–stuffed celery from the charcuterie board. One of my very favorite snacks.

Jessa went back to stirring her gravy. "Everything is just about ready. The turkey has another forty minutes and will have plenty of time to rest and be ready at three. Do you expect everyone to arrive on time?"

"I asked them all to be here by two, so I expect the stragglers will wander in just before three."

"You're a smart woman." She stopped stirring and lowered the heat on her pot. "Did I hear shouting coming from the dining room? I was dying to run in there and see what was going on, but you just cannot leave gravy on the stove. It will either congeal or burn. What's the tea?"

"Whit and Chesney had an argument," I said. "I think it's normal sister stuff."

Jessa raised her white eyebrows at me as if she wasn't so sure. "You know I don't like to poke my nose in other people's business."

I laughed because poking her nose in other people's business was her main occupation. Because of her diner, Jessa knew everything about everyone in Cherry Glen. She might not go out of her way to learn another townsperson's business, but rest assured she knew about it.

"What do you know? Is Whit okay?"

Jessa wiped her hands on a tea towel and flung it over her shoulder. "She's going through something. I don't know what. She's been in the diner a lot more often in the middle of the day than ever before, and she's typically not alone."

"Not alone?"

"She's with a guy who is old enough to be her father."

"Oh," I said. "Like a date?"

"I don't know, but I do think she at least is enamored with him. Every time they meet, it looks like she is hanging on his every word. He's a little harder to read."

"How old is he exactly?" I asked.

"Your age, I would guess."

"I'm not old enough to be Whit's mom."

"You are technically." She shrugged.

I didn't know how that made me feel, but I was more concerned about this news about Whit than I was about Jessa making a point of my age.

"What's his name?"

"She introduced him as Rhett."

"Like *Gone with the Wind*?"

She laughed. "I don't think that would be a reference that Whit would know."

"Does Chesney know?" I asked.

She shook her head. "Whit told me not to tell her. She said that she would tell her herself she was ready.

I arched my brow. "But you're telling me?"

Jessa shrugged. "She never said not to tell you, and if something is going on with her, you can relay the news to her sister. Just because I made a promise doesn't mean that you did."

Great. I loved getting involved in family drama. It was my favorite.

Chapter Two

"Let me take your coats," I said to my best friend, Kristy, and her husband, Kent, as they came into the house. Each of them had a toddler in their arms. Kristy's twin daughters were just about the most beautiful children I had ever seen. They had their father's blue eyes and their dark hair and tanned skin from their mother.

Kristy put her daughter down, and she attached to my leg. I knelt down to give her and her sister a hug, and then I helped them out of their coats and hats. "I made a play area in the corner of the living room just for the two of you."

The girls beamed at me and then took off for the toys.

Kristy smiled as she removed her coat. "Thanks for doing that. It will keep them occupied for ten minutes…eleven if we are lucky. Seriously, toddlers are no joke. I thought I was tired when they were newborns, but now they can run away from me. At least as newborns they couldn't escape."

"So I have heard," I said.

She turned to her husband. "Honey, can you get the covered dish from the car?"

"You brought your taquitos?" My mouth watered just

thinking. Kristy's taquitos were my very favorite food—better than any I had when I lived in California, where it felt like there was a Mexican restaurant on every street corner.

She grinned. "Of course, I did. My *abuela* would come down from heaven and slap me upside the head if I didn't make them every Thanksgiving. We're going to Kent's parents for another Thanksgiving tonight, so I made a double batch. No one wants to be haunted by my *abuela*, especially not me."

I put their coats in the study, which Chesney used as an office and exercise room. Her fancy exercise bike with its giant TV screen stood in one corner. It made a great coat hanger.

When I came back into the living room, I found that my cousin, Stacey, and her date had arrived.

I went over to greet them. Stacey gave me a pleasant smile. "It's quite strange to be back in this house after living here for so long." She looked around the room. "I'm impressed with the updates."

"I can't take credit for that. The previous owner made them," I said.

She nodded. "I thought as much. It's a very modern farmhouse. I don't know that that is your style."

I wanted to ask my cousin what she thought my style was but thought better of it. Some of Stacey's opinions of me I didn't have to know. Like all of them.

I held my hand out to her date. "I'm Shiloh."

"Rhett Lumberly," he said.

I froze as I shook his hand. Rhett? Could this be Whit's

Rhett? I could not imagine that there would be more than one Rhett running around Cherry Glen. This did not bode well if Whit, who worked for Stacey at the theater, had a crush on her boss's boyfriend. Stacey had been mixed up in more than her share of messy love triangles over her lifetime—the most recent one being just this summer.

Rhett gently removed his hand from mine. I had not realized that I continued to hold it as a million thoughts ran through my head. I dropped my hand to my side.

Stacey arched her perfectly plucked brow at me. My only cousin was ten years older than me, in her late forties, was naturally blond, and had the perfect hourglass figure, sparkling blue eyes, and a sharp tongue that could slice a person in half.

She was a former Broadway actor and one of the most beautiful people that I had ever seen in real life. That was saying something since I had worked in Hollywood for over a decade. In LA, I was surrounded by beautiful people on a daily basis. Stacey could outshine all of them, and that afternoon she glowed. Her long blond hair was perfectly styled, her makeup was flawless, and she wore a form-fitting sweater dress that hugged her curves.

Rhett was equally handsome. He was tall with dark hair and eyes. He watched Stacey with an appreciative smile on his face. She appeared to be just as enamored with him as she gazed at him from under her flashy eyelashes. No matter what, I knew she considered this to be a serious relationship or she would not have brought him to Thanksgiving. Stacey was secretive about the men she dated. That was how she had gotten into awkward entanglement with her last boyfriend over the summer. If she had been more open then about who she was dating, she might have learned earlier that he wasn't who he claimed to be.

Rhett looked down at Stacey. "This is the house you grew up in?"

She nodded. "I must say I am pleased that it's back in the family. Shi might not believe this, but it was an exceedingly difficult decision for me to sell my half of the farm so that I could pursue my dream and save Michigan Street Theater."

This was news to me. Stacey had always given me the impression that she didn't care about the farm. Maybe I had misjudged her.

"It looks a lot better than it did back then. It costs a lot to do this level of a remodel. The house is over one hundred years old, and these old buildings always have a surprise or two up their sleeves. I know that from renovating the theater. I had my share of surprises when I did that job."

Rhett smiled at her. "I admire all your hard work. I wish I'd known you then. I would have helped."

Stacey blushed. *Blushed.* I had never in my life seen my cousin blush unless it was on stage and called for in her role.

"How did the two of you meet?" I asked.

"I came to a performance at the theater in the summer and sought her out to let me know how impressed I was with the production, considering it was held in a small town on a limited budget. Knowing that Michigan Street Theater would be a perfect fit for the project I was working on, I introduced myself." He smiled at Stacey. "It was adoration at first sight."

A blush appeared on my cousin's cheeks for a second time.

They seemed to be perfectly happy with each other, but I wasn't going to stop digging just because Rhett appeared to be a nice guy. "What's your project?"

"I'm a historian and am on sabbatical from my university this year to write a book."

"A book about what?" I asked.

He cleared his throat. "I don't like to talk about it much. It's a history piece, but I can't tell you much more than that."

I frowned.

"Call me superstitious, but I'm constantly afraid that someone will swoop in and steal my ideas." He forced a laugh.

Stacey shook her head. "I don't even know what his book is about, but he promised me that I would be the first one to read it when the manuscript is complete."

"I can't think of a better person to share my masterpiece with." He smiled down at her.

I wrinkled my brow. If my boyfriend was writing a book and didn't tell me what it was about, I would have a problem with that. Why so secretive? To me, it wasn't the best foundation on which to build a lasting relationship. However, I would never give Stacey that advice. If I told her what to do, she would always do the opposite. Maybe Rhett was just a superstitious writer. Maybe.

"Has he met my dad yet?" I asked my cousin. "If he's into local history, Dad would be the one to talk to."

She shook her head.

"Does your father have an interest in history?" Rhett asked.

"Most definitely. He is more of an amateur historian and a collector."

"At times those are the people who know the most because of their laser focus on one topic," Rhett said. "I'm looking forward to meeting him."

Stacey clicked her tongue. "Don't let him hear you call him an amateur." She placed a hand on Rhett's arm. "You are going to love Uncle Sully. I know the two of you will have a lot to talk about." She looked around the room. "Is he here?"

"Not yet," I said. "Quinn is bringing him."

Stacey slipped her arm through Rhett's. "Let me show you around the house. Maybe this will give you some inspiration for a setting in your book." They walked off to the kitchen together. From my first meeting with Rhett, I didn't see any red flags, but I did have my concerns in relation to Whit. Why would he be having lunch with Stacey's employee at Jessa's Place multiple times a week? More importantly, why wasn't Stacey with them?

I went to the front door just as my boyfriend, Sheriff Milan Penbrook, parked his SUV on the lawn next to Kristy's minivan. I watched as he climbed out and hurried over to the passenger side door. He reached his hand inside and helped a petite woman with cat eyeglasses and a regal demeanor out of the car. She looked like she was in her sixties, but I knew his mother, who liked to be called Miss Charity, was much closer to eighty.

I clenched and unclenched my hands. I had met Milan's

mother a few times, and she was a no-nonsense lady. I still wasn't sure if she approved of me. From what I had heard, she loved Milan's ex-wife. A new girlfriend could be a problem. Milan insisted that Miss Charity liked me just fine, but I believed that he said that to put me at ease.

Miss Charity was beautiful, and it was clear to me where Milan got his good looks. He had his mother's coloring and her bright eyes. He also wore glasses that gave him a distinguished look. He caught me staring and winked.

My stomach was instantly in knots. Why in the world had I gotten it into my head to host Thanksgiving for this odd assortment of guests? Yes, they were all connected to me, but how was Stacey going to get along with Chesney or my father with Miss Charity? The biggest question of all was how my neighbor Quinn Killian would interact with Milan.

This was truly going to be a disaster.

I held the screen door open for them. "Please come in. Miss Charity, it's so nice to see you again. I was so glad when Milan said that you would be joining us for Thanksgiving."

She glanced up at me. "Since Milan's heart was set on coming here, I didn't have much choice in the matter. It was either your house for some turkey or spend the day alone." She looked around. "This is your house, isn't it?"

"Sort of. I own it, but I rent it out to my farm manager."

She sniffed. "If you are the one throwing the celebration, why aren't we eating at your house? I find this all very strange."

"I live in a little cottage in the woods. There wouldn't be enough room to host a big party like this there."

"You own this big beautiful farmhouse, but you live in a cottage in the woods?" She held her pocketbook closely to her chest. "That doesn't make sense at all. You should be living here, and the farm manager can be in the cottage. It's only right."

I forced a laugh. "I've lived in apartments most of my adult life. I don't need much space. My farm manager and her younger sister live here. It works out very well for us all."

"If you get married, you might have to move things around. You can't expect a man to live in a cottage. That would be a blow to his ego. You're not Snow White, and your future husband is not a dwarf, and that's especially true if you got it into your head that you're going to marry my son." She narrowed her eyes at me. "And children. What about children? Don't tell me that you are one of those liberated ladies who wants a career and not children. You may say that now, but when your biological clock goes off, you will feel much differently. Believe you me. I speak from experience here. I was nearly forty when Milan was born."

My heart skipped a beat. Who said anything about getting married? Milan and I had only known each other for nine months. Had he said something to her? And children? I didn't know how I felt about that with Milan or anyone else. I liked my life just as it was. I finally had stability at the farm. I didn't need a new obsession, like concern about my biological clock.

I forced another laugh. "We aren't thinking anything of the kind."

"Then why are you seeing each other? I'm a Christian

woman, and people go steady to marry, not for mere amusement. I know that's what the young folks do nowadays, but you and Milan aren't that young. You need to think about the future. At your age, it's get married or get off the pot. There's no time to waste." She pointed her finger at me and sniffed. "I need to powder my nose. Where's the ladies' room?"

I pointed down the hallway. My hand shook a little. "Just down the hall and to the left."

She handed me her coat and shuffled down the hallway with her pocketbook still pressed up against her chest.

Milan grinned at me. "Happy Thanksgiving." He kissed me on the cheek and wrapped me up close in a hug. "You did great."

I looked up at him. "Are you kidding me? What's with the marriage talk? And kids? *Kids?* Did you say something to her I should know about?"

He laughed and tugged on my hand, pulling me outside onto the wraparound porch. The screen door slammed behind us, and I was grateful for that. I didn't want any prying ears to overhear our conversation.

"Not at all," Milan said, finally answering my question. "She just wants me to settle down with the right person, as she says, and have a few babies. It's nothing to worry about."

I swallowed. "What's a few babies?"

He laughed.

"She doesn't see me as the right person?" I asked in a whisper.

"I never said that, and she never said that." He hugged me again and spoke into my hair. "Mom is a pistol. She always has been and always will be. She likes you. I can tell." He let me go. "She gives people she likes a hard time."

I wondered what she did to people she despised.

"Is everyone here?" He peered through a window and scanned the room as he removed his jacket.

I shook my head. "We are just waiting for Quinn, his daughter, Hazel, and my dad." I could have mentioned Whit too, but I had a feeling she wasn't coming back. I couldn't help but wonder if she had been in such a rush to leave the house because she knew Rhett Lumberly, Stacey's historian-writer boyfriend, would be there. If she really had a crush on Rhett, like Jessa suspected, I imagined it would have been difficult to sit across the table from the couple. Whit worked for Stacey, and she worked more closely with her than anyone else in the company. She would have to know about Stacey's relationship with Rhett.

"I will be happy to see Hazel and your dad," Milan said with a twist of his mouth.

I noted that he didn't say that he would be happy to see Quinn. I had hoped over the last several months that the two of them could let bygones be bygones and stop being rivals, but it appeared that wasn't the case. I had also insisted to Milan hundreds of times that Quinn no longer had any feelings for me, nor did I have any for him. In fact, I didn't know if Quinn ever really cared for me in that way, or I was just the only eligible single woman in his age bracket in all of Cherry Glen. If I was being honest with myself, I thought it was the latter.

Milan kissed me full on the mouth, and I felt my toes curl

inside of my boots. I wondered how, after kissing dozens of toads, most of which lived in LA, I got so lucky to be with a man who clearly cared about me so much. If I had known that I would find him by coming home, I would have left Hollywood a whole lot sooner.

Sadly, the smile on my face was short-lived as a pickup truck came down the driveway. I knew the truck well. It was Quinn's, and I could tell by the look on his face when he jumped out of the cabin that he had seen the kiss.

This was going to be one awkward Thanksgiving indeed. Just like Chesney said, I had a knack for making life harder for myself.

Chapter Three

To my surprise, my father didn't climb out of Quinn's truck.

As Hazel and Quinn walked up to Milan and me, I asked, "Where's my dad? Is he okay?"

After my father's fall in September, which further injured his bum hip, I was constantly worrying about him. I had even offered to move back into his farmhouse to care for him. He refused. He liked being on his own just as much as I did. Now, eight weeks later, he was much improved and resigned to the fact that he had to use a walker at all times for fear of falling again. The image in my mind of him lying on his kitchen floor hurt on Thanksgiving almost took my breath away.

Quinn cocked his head. "He's not here? He called this morning and said that he had another ride. Didn't he tell you?"

"He didn't." I wrinkled my brow. Another ride? Everyone my father would ever consider calling for a ride or help was already at Chesney's house. I hoped this wasn't his way of getting out of Thanksgiving. My dad wasn't much for social situations, not even with close family and friends.

"I'd better call him," I said.

"I don't think you have to do that," Milan said as a sedan in a color that could only be described as "wet sand" came down the long gravel driveway. There was a friendly tap on the horn by the driver, and the car stopped in the middle of the driveway, blocking anyone on the lawn from easily escaping the gathering.

The driver side door opened, and a woman in her seventies stepped out. She wore a long denim skirt, a chunky purple sweater that made her appear much larger than she actually was, and brown loafers. Her silver hair was short and styled in a wave from a bygone time, and a pair of reading glasses hung from a beaded chain from her neck.

"Connie Baskins?" I yelped.

Milan elbowed me in the side.

Connie walked over to the passenger side of the car. The passenger door opened, and my father poked his head out. Dad grabbed onto the top of the doorframe in an attempt to lift himself out of the seat.

"Sullivan, let me help you," Connie said.

Dad waved her away. "I'm a grown man, I don't need help out of a car from a woman." However, the expression on his face told me that he was enjoying the attention.

Connie looked at us and threw up her hands. "Men," she said.

I was still in a state of shock that she was there. Huckleberry was under my feet. By the way his eyes bugged out of his head, it seemed Huckleberry was just as shocked by this latest turn of events as I was.

Milan put his hand on my back and nudged me forward.

It was just enough for me to come out of my stupor and stumble toward Connie's car. "Dad, I'm so glad that you're here. I didn't know that you were bringing a guest." I swallowed. "Connie, it's nice to see you."

She smiled and held onto my father's arm. "I'm happy to be here. When Sullivan invited me, I was just thrilled. I haven't had a family Thanksgiving in decades, so this is a real treat."

I winced and immediately regretted my upset that she was there. Everyone deserved a nice Thanksgiving. I plastered a smile on my face. "In that case, you came to the right place. We are having a makeshift family Thanksgiving of sorts."

She beamed. "That sounds like just the ticket to me."

I told myself to get a grip. Connie was my father's guest, and the more the merrier during the holidays. Even so, I had my reasons for being surprised that my dad invited her. Connie was the receptionist for the town municipal building, which held the fire station, the police station, and the city offices. She had a very outspoken crush on my father, but Dad made it clear he was not interested. In the past, he had always ignored her at best and been outright rude to her at worst.

I cleared my throat. "You are welcome to go inside. There are appetizers and drinks while you wait for the main meal."

Connie cocked her head. "What kind of appetizers? I'm very particular as to what I eat."

"Oh, well," I stuttered. "There are vegetables and dip, and a cheese board, and pastries."

"My daughter makes the absolute best pastries. You will love them," Dad said to Connie.

"I'll try them. No cheese for me, thank you. I will be the size of a balloon the moment one piece hits my stomach."

I grimaced at the visual.

"I have had your pastries before. Quinn has brought your delicious treats into the municipal building more than once. I am lucky that I got one small piece of them. The police officers and firefighters gobbled them up."

I smiled. "I did make some puff pastries, rolls, and desserts, but really the credit for today goes to Jessa. She has done most of the cooking. I would have never pulled it off without her."

Connie stiffened. "Jessa is here?" She looked at my father. "You didn't tell me that she was here. You said it was a family Thanksgiving."

My father's bushy eyebrows knit together in confusion. "It is a family Thanksgiving. Jessa is as much a part of our family as anyone else."

She pressed her lips together. "I would have liked to have a bit of warning before seeing *her*."

"Is there something wrong?" I asked.

She tucked a stray silver lock behind her ear. "No, nothing is wrong. Sullivan, let's go inside. I would like to see where I will be sitting and move my place card if need be."

What I didn't tell her was she didn't have a place card because I hadn't known she was coming. Thankfully, I hadn't thought to put place cards out at all.

I gestured to Connie and Dad to go into the house first. Quinn and Hazel followed them. I held back, and Huckleberry and Milan stayed with me.

Milan cocked his head. "So, I take it that Connie's arrival was a surprise."

"A surprise? It was a shock. Dad doesn't like Connie Baskins, or at least he never did before. She's been pursuing him for years. It's gotten to the point that he won't go anywhere close to the municipal building, where she works, and if he has any issue with the town that he wants discussed, he sends me there to file his grievances for him so he doesn't have to see her. Dad makes a lot of complaints, as you must have guessed. I go there at least once or twice every week." I paused. "That's when I turn the grievances in. I will admit some of the more outlandish ones never make it all the way to Michigan Street."

"Maybe she just finally ground him down, and he wasn't up to saying no anymore." Milan picked a fallen leaf from his shoulder and let it float to the ground.

I made a face. "That's what every woman wants to hear, that she ground down her love interest to the point he agreed to date her. Please don't ever say that about our relationship."

"I mean you keep showing up in my investigations. There had to be a reason for that." He winked.

"Are you trying to make me laugh?" I smiled.

"Maybe. Is it working?"

I chuckled. "A little."

I caught up with Dad and Connie in the house. They stood in the living room, and it was clear to me that they both were scoping the place out: Dad for changes, Connie for Jessa. I had never heard before that Connie had a problem with Jessa. As far as I knew no one in Cherry Glen had an issue with Jessa.

"We're so glad that you're here. We are just waiting for a few more people." I glanced at the table to see where I could squeeze in another chair and place setting. It was going to be tight.

Connie chuckled at something Dad said. "Oh, Sullivan."

What was this Sullivan stuff? No one called my dad that. He was Sully to everyone he met.

"How long have the two of you been spending time together?" I asked, pretending to be casual.

"For the last several weeks. We have loved getting to know each other on a deeper level, haven't we, Sullivan?" Connie asked.

Dad nodded. "Turns out, Connie is quite knowledgeable about Michigan's part in the American Civil War. I haven't met too many people, including Michiganders, who know anything about it at all." He looked at me. "I tried to teach you when you were younger, but your eyes just glazed over when I brought it up."

"Dad, I was a teenager. Few teenagers would be interested in the topic."

"I was," Connie chimed in. "I have been fascinated by history since I was small. That's another thing that we have in common." She patted his hand that held on to his walker.

Another thing? What was the first thing that they had in common? Did I miss it in my daze? I shook my head and told myself to get it together.

I wasn't completely surprised that I didn't know about my father's budding friendship with Connie. Dad and I didn't have the kind of relationship where we would share those types of details with each other. However, I was nervous because Dad was frail, and the very last thing I wanted was for him to get hurt.

I gave myself a mental kick in the pants. Connie had always been sweet and friendly with me. There was no reason to believe she would upset my dad. I wasn't being fair to her. I chalked it up to the fact that I was surprised, knowing Dad's history with Connie.

It wasn't that I didn't want Dad to have friends outside my circle. In fact, I loved it that he had become so involved in Stacey's theater. It kept him active and out of the house, but since his fall he had been more reclusive than ever. He had been so disheartened and spent three weeks at a rehab center. He had been utterly miserable there, and ever since, chased every person he could away from the farm, as if he was determined to become the most notorious curmudgeon in Cherry Glen.

"I hope you have one more seat at the table," Dad said with a grin.

"We have plenty of food," I said. "You know that Jessa always makes more than enough. Let me find a spot to put an extra chair. I'm sure that we can manage it."

When we all walked into the house together, Kristy, who was sitting on the floor playing with her girls, made eye contact with me and mouthed, "What is she doing here?"

At least I had one person in the house who could understand my position. I could always count on my best friend for that.

Chesney came down the stairs.

"Ches, Connie is going to be joining us for the meal. Would you mind setting another place at the table?"

There were tears in her eyes.

"What's wrong?" I asked.

"Whit just texted me and said that she's not going to come back for dinner. We don't have to worry about adding a seat." She looked at the floor.

"I'm so sorry. I know you wanted her to be here."

"She's an adult and can do what she wants now, but I'm worried about her. I can't help it. She's my baby sister. I just don't know what is going on with her. We have always been close, and now she won't even talk to me. I'm afraid she's in some kind of trouble."

I touched her arm. "Has it been that way for a while?"

"Just the last couple of months." She wiped her eyes with the sleeve of her sweater. "She might have been pulling away before that, but I have been so preoccupied with moving and the farm. Maybe I missed something. Some sister I am."

"It's not your fault. We have all been under a lot of stress." I patted her arm.

She smiled. "I don't want you to think that I regret moving here. You were very generous to let Whit and me live here for so little rent when you could have taken this house for yourself."

"And give up my cottage in the woods? Never," I said with a smile, hoping that I might be able to make her laugh.

She didn't laugh, but one corner of her mouth turned up in a small smile. That was the best that I was going to get under the circumstances.

"Whit will come around," I said. "When she's ready to tell you what is going on, she will."

She nodded. "I just hope she does before it's too late."

I wanted to ask her, "Too late for what?" but Jessa popped her head out of the kitchen and said the turkey was ready.

Chapter Four

My father sat at the head of the table with Miss Charity on one side and Connie on the other. At first I thought this was a great idea. The three of them could reminisce about the old days and Thanksgivings past, but I quickly realized that wasn't the case. Every time that Miss Charity said so much as a word to my father, Connie's eyes narrowed, and she looked like she wanted to jump across the table and throttle the other woman. Why, I didn't know. Miss Charity wasn't exactly flirting with my father. She was just asking a lot of questions about his Michigan history collection, which was his very favorite subject of all.

I bit my lower lip and whispered to Milan, "Connie doesn't seem to like your mom."

He squeezed my hand under the table. "Really? Maybe she's tired, or maybe she's heard all these stories your dad is telling before. Mom is fresh blood for him, and she honestly enjoys history. Whatever he's talking about will be right up her alley."

I smiled at him. "I'm so paranoid. I wanted this day to go perfectly, and I'm being so uptight I can't even enjoy it. I'm just sitting here waiting for disaster to strike."

"You can't think like that, Shiloh. Disaster doesn't always strike, and that is coming from a sheriff who sees all kinds of terrible things on a daily basis."

I knew that he spoke the truth.

He squeezed my hand again. I looked up, and across the table Quinn was watching us. He looked about as happy looking at us as Connie. I wondered when it would appropriate to bring the pies out so we could wrap this holiday up.

Hazel sat on Quinn's left side, and Chesney sat on his right side. Chesney just picked at her food. I knew she was upset over Whit's absence.

I made a mental note to casually ask Stacey if she knew anything about what Whit had been up to the last couple of months, but I certainly wasn't going to bring Rhett into it. My cousin can be a bit reactionary at times, and I didn't want her to fire Whit without knowing the whole story.

At the opposite end of the table, Stacey and Rhett laughed together. Stacey looked happier than I had ever seen her. Despite our decades of arguments, I wanted her to be happy. If Rhett turned out to be as rotten as I thought he might be, he would have to answer to me for breaking her heart.

"Here's the bird!" Jessa announced as she came out of the kitchen carrying the turkey platter. She set the platter in front of my father. "If you would do the honors, Sully?"

My father stood up on wobbly legs. Jessa made a move to support him, but Connie stood and pushed her aside. "I will help Sullivan."

Jessa held up her hands and backed away. She sat in the last empty seat, next to me.

I raised my eyebrows at her, and she simply shook her head. There was a story there to be sure, and I wanted to get to the bottom of it. I just hoped it didn't boil over at the meal.

Connie stayed at my father's elbow in case he needed any help.

Dad held on to the arms of his chair. "Before we say grace and eat, I just want to take this moment to say how proud I am of my daughter, Shiloh."

I gasped. My father never said he was proud of me—not when I graduated from college or got a promotion or even when I came back to Michigan to save the farm.

Milan placed his hand on my knee.

"Two years ago, when Shiloh said that she was coming back to Bellamy Farm, I didn't believe it. I also didn't believe her when she said she could save the farm. But she has. Not only that, but she was also able to buy back the land that was sold. Bellamy Farm is whole again. I know that I made a lot of mistakes in my life. I was selfish and thoughtless at times. The only thing I know I did right was Shiloh. Of course, I know my mother, Emma Kay Bellamy, had a big role to play in that. While I was hiding behind my history books, she raised Shiloh from start to finish. She did a far better job at it than I ever could have on my own. My mother filled the empty spots that Shiloh's own mother left behind. Shiloh is living proof of that."

Tears gathered in my eyes. I had never in my life heard my father speak so highly of anyone, much less me. "Thank you, Dad." I choked on the words.

Milan glanced at me. He knew how important my father's words were to me.

Dad waved away my thanks. "I should be thanking you for being such a loyal daughter when I wasn't always the most attentive father."

I opened my mouth to protest, but Dad continued to speak. "Now, let's pray so we can eat. Jessa has made us quite a spread here this afternoon. I, for one, am excited to dig in. She is the absolute best cook in Cherry Glen, if not the entire Mitten State."

Connie made a face when he said this. I had a feeling that she didn't like Jessa getting any words of praise from my father. I had to ask Jessa about what that all meant.

"Thank you, Sully," Jessa said. "You are certainly in a cheerful mood this holiday.

Dad patted Connie's hand. "I have every reason to be cheerful. The farm is safely in my daughter's hands, and I have someone to spend my twilight years with. Now is a good enough time as any to tell them, right, my love?"

Connie smiled at him. "You share it, honey. I will start crying if I have to speak."

Dad beamed. "Connie and I are engaged."

I started coughing.

"To be married?" Jessa asked.

I was glad that she had the wherewithal to ask the question as I was choking.

Milan patted my back.

"Are you okay?" he asked.

"I'm fine," I croaked. "It just went down the wrong pipe."

"She's fine," Stacey said. "If she was really choking, she wouldn't be able to talk."

Across the table, Connie had her eyes narrowed at me. I supposed choking wasn't the reaction she wanted from her future stepdaughter when her engagement to my father was announced. But I couldn't help it. This relationship, engagement, the whole thing came out of nowhere. Dad was over eighty. Was it really wise to marry again at this stage in life? I shook the thought away. Of course, I believed that my father had the right to whatever it was he wished to be happy, but still I was in shock.

Kristy broke the silence. "Congratulations to both of you."

Others sitting at the table followed suit. I noted that Jessa didn't add her congratulations to the mix, nor did I as I guzzled down a full glass of water.

"When is the big day?" Quinn asked.

"We haven't decided yet," Connie said. "He only asked me last week."

"Do you have a ring?" Kristy asked. "Can we see it?"

"It's at the jewelers. I proposed with my mother's old engagement ring, and it had to be resized for Connie's delicate hand."

"We should be getting it back by the end of next week. I can't wait. When I put it on, I will never take it off. Not even to sleep." Connie smiled at my dad.

"I wouldn't want you to." He smiled at her.

There was a pang in my chest when he said that. I glanced across the table, and Stacey's face was stone-cold. I was certain that she was as unhappy as I was that Dad had given our grandmother's engagement ring to Connie.

"As for when the wedding will be, the sooner the better is

our plan. We know we aren't a couple of kids who will have decades together. There's not a moment to waste," Connie said. "I might just be a Christmas bride."

Christmas bride?

Gradually the conversation shifted to other topics, but I said little. The meal was delicious. I was a decent cook and a much better baker, but I had made the right decision in asking Jessa to take on the Thanksgiving meal. I was gratified that everyone seemed to enjoy my organic puff pastries and rolls. Even Kristy's twins were licking their tiny fingers, and each grabbed a third roll. Kristy pretended she didn't see it.

"They are going to be in a coma for the rest the day," she said with a laugh.

Huckleberry and Esmeralda had the time of their lives as the twins continued to drop morsels on the floor for the cat and dog to clean up. The cat was particularly fond of the turkey, and Huckleberry could not get enough of Jessa's mac and cheese. There was an exceptionally good chance my "kids," Huckleberry and Esmeralda, would be in a food coma that afternoon too.

Licking cheese off of his lips, Huckleberry walked to the front door, which I could see from the dining room, and began to whimper. Chesney started to get up as if she were going to take the dog out.

"Chesney, stay in your seat," I said. "I'll take Huckleberry out." This was just the moment I needed to escape the meal and process the news about my father's engagement.

"Are you sure?" Chesney asked.

I nodded. "Diva is out there, and I need to make sure the two of them stay away from each other."

"That chicken is a menace," Dad said, and I agreed with him on that point. But I saved a great deal money by gathering her organic eggs each morning. Eggs, especially organic ones, weren't as cheap as they used to be. Ultimately, my goal was to raise or grow ninety percent of the ingredients in my baking. I couldn't reach one hundred percent as there were certain spices and ingredients that could not be grown in Michigan. Coconut, pineapple, and cardamon were just a few.

I grabbed my barn coat from the closet and went outside with Huckleberry at my feet. I shivered. The temperature had dropped a good ten degrees since the morning. The scent of snow was in the air. I stamped my feet to fight off the cold. It was time to get out the "big coat," as us Midwesterners called it. This was the giant coat that could swallow a person whole and withstand below-zero temperatures. I had been putting off pulling mine out of storage as long as I could. It was also time to get out Huckleberry's winter jacket and booties. He didn't mind the jacket. The booties he hated with a passion.

Thankfully, Huckleberry was a California pup at heart and hated the cold, so he got right down to business when we stepped outside. We were both eager to return to the cozy house as soon as possible.

Even with the windows and doors closed behind me, I could hear that laughter floating through the wall to the outside. It would have put a smile on my face if I wasn't so preoccupied with my father's big announcement.

What was wrong with me? Didn't I want my father to be happy? He was smiling and laughing with Connie. When had I ever seen him do that with another person? It was his life. How would I feel if he told me that he didn't want me to be with Milan? I made myself a promise to keep my mouth shut. Just like I didn't want my father to comment on my life, I wouldn't comment on his. Fair was fair.

I pushed the concerns out of my head. Thanksgiving had been lovely. Everything had gone better than I would have ever dreamed possible. No one was arguing and the food was delicious. I felt at peace for the first time all day.

The door opened behind me, and Quinn came out. My moment of peace vanished.

Chapter Five

I smiled at him. "It's turned out to be a beautiful Thanksgiving. It's cold, but at least the snow has held off for another day or two. It will be here soon enough."

Quinn walked over to me with his hands in his jeans pockets. He had thick blond hair and clear dark eyes. Hazel had the same coloring, but while her face was delicate and small featured, his was manly with a strong chin and deep-set eyes.

I had always thought he was handsome, even when we were teenagers, but back then, I only had eyes for my late fiancé, Logan. Even all this time later, it was difficult for me to look at Quinn and not think of Logan. Growing up, the two of them were always together. I thought that Logan spent more time with Quinn than he ever did with me. They were more like brothers than friends.

I knew that Quinn still thought of him often too. Logan died in a car accident when he was just twenty-three, and Quinn had been as devastated as I was.

"I read that it was supposed to snow tonight. It's about time. Hazel has been chomping at the bit to go sledding," he said.

I nodded. "She said that she was going to make me go sledding with her this year."

His face softened. "That is a terrific idea. We can all go together. I have a toboggan that fits four people."

I could just imagine what Milan would say if I told him that I was heading out on a toboggan ride with Quinn.

"I might be too old for sledding," I said.

"You're being ridiculous," he said with a smile the made the dimple in his left cheek appear. "There is no age limit on sledding."

"Really, so you think my father should go?"

"If we could wrap him in bubble wrap, sure."

I shook my head.

"But you know as well as I do that's not something that your father would be interested in, even as a young man. The only winter sport he will get behind is ice fishing."

How well I knew, as that had been a problem last winter.

"It's going to be another long winter," Quinn said. "We won't be able to see the ground until March if we are lucky, but I look forward to it. I'm a Michigan guy through and through." He met my eyes. "Do you miss the snow-free days in California?"

I turned away and looked straight ahead in the direction of the cherry orchard. I could see Teddy Bear and the other members of our flock in the trees. Teddy Bear was the only ram, and he was keeping a close eye on his ewes. I think he would have been taken a bit more seriously if he weren't so small.

The breed of sheep that I had on my farm was Babydoll Southdown sheep. They were one of the oldest British breeds, and certainly the smallest. The girls were about sixteen to twenty inches to the shoulder, and Teddy Bear was only two feet tall himself.

Teddy Bear and his flock stared at us. They seemed ultra-alert, which was unusual for the sheep. Afternoon was their nap time. They lifted their noses as if they smelled something in the breeze. I made a mental note to check on them before going back into the house. They seemed to be on edge.

Perhaps they sensed the change in the weather. It would be one of the last days that they would be able to forage for some time. In the worst of winter, there would be days, if not weeks, when they wouldn't leave the barn at all. I wasn't looking forward to that time. Just like the sheep, I didn't like to be cooped up.

"Yes and no. I missed the seasons, but I think everyone says that when they move away."

He nodded and cleared his throat. "You and Penbrook seem to be going strong." He tried to make the statement sound casual, but it did not come off casually.

I didn't say anything. I waited because I knew that he had more to say. I wasn't sure that I wanted to hear it, but I would let him have it out. Maybe when he said his piece, the weirdness between us would go away. It was wishful thinking, but I was willing to try it.

"Sheriff Penbrook is a great guy, but you seemed to jump into that relationship without much thought. You haven't known him that long." The disapproval in his voice was evident.

I instantly bristled. "You mean I haven't known him my whole life like, say, you?" I asked.

He shifted back and forth on his feet. "Yeah. History means something, but you disregarded it when you started dating him."

"I don't know what you're talking about. I didn't disregard anything."

"You disregarded me," Quinn said.

"I disregarded you?" I asked in disbelief. "What did you have to do with my decision to date Milan?"

"You didn't ask me how I felt about it." His voice was terse. "You didn't give me a chance to tell you how I felt. If you had, I know that you would have made a different choice."

That was certainly overconfident on his part and disrespectful to Milan too. Milan was a good man. No one had or ever would have said otherwise.

"And how do you feel?" I asked because I wanted him to say it. I wanted to hear the words aloud. I had waited nearly two years to hear it before I allowed myself to move on.

"I care about you," Quinn said. "I want us to give it a shot. You, me, and Hazel. We could be a family. Hazel would love it. I would love it. It's what we need. The three of us against the world. Together."

"Care" and "love" were not synonyms, but I did not blame him for not going all the way in and proclaiming his love to me. He had to protect himself, just like I had to protect myself.

"I needed to tell you this because something that your dad said really struck me. He said that he and Connie couldn't afford to waste time."

"Because of their age," I said.

"Yes, but we can't afford it either because of Hazel's age. She's thirteen. In a few short years, she will be out of the house. We don't have much time to be a family all together."

He knew that he could pull on my heartstrings by mentioning Hazel. He knew how much I adored her. He knew that I had thought about us being a family unit together for months and months. He knew that, but he pushed me away. This was too little, too late.

There was another factor too. Quinn's parents hated me.

Despite Dad's kind speech at the start of the Thanksgiving meal, I already had a tumultuous relationship with my own father and cousin. I didn't need to add more family angst to my life.

"Please say something." Quinn took a step toward me, but he didn't go as far as to reach out and touch me.

"I don't know what to say. I was single for months, Quinn, months. Anytime during that period, you could have said these things to me, and I would have run into your arms."

He started to smile. He misunderstood my intention.

"But," I added quickly. "I'm not single anymore. Milan is a good man who is loving, kind, and thoughtful. He grounds me. I need that. I don't know if you could do that for me, Quinn. We're too much alike. I think that's why we were the closest to Logan. We both were the opposite of him. He was the grounding one. Neither of us were."

Quinn took a step back from me. "You're not willing to try."

I dug the toe of my boot into the gravel driveway. "I can't. I care too much about Milan to do that." I looked up at him. "And I care too much about Hazel. Just think how it would affect her if we didn't work out. She'd be heartbroken. We can't put her through that."

"Why do you think we would fail?"

"There are factors. Your mother—"

"Leave my mother out of this," he said through gritted teeth.

"I wish that I could, but I can't ignore how your parents feel about me. I don't want to make you choose between them and me. It's not fair to you. It would be hard on Hazel too. It's even difficult now with how much time she spends with me, but if you and I were together, it would be worse. Hazel needs her grandparents. I'm not going to take them away from her."

"So, you've made your decision." He dropped his arms to his sides.

I nodded. "Yes, I have. Milan and I are a good match. You were right when you said all those months ago that you and I wouldn't work in a romantic relationship. It would end horribly and impact everyone we loved and cared about."

He leaned forward as if he was going to kiss me. I jumped back and looked at the house to make sure no one was peeking out the window.

"What do you think you're doing?" I snapped.

"I was proving something to you."

"All you proved to me is that you can invade my space."

"What do you want me to do, ask if I can kiss you?"

"Yes. And I would have told you no." My stomach churned. I never for a moment thought that he would be so bold as to try to kiss me.

"Penbrook kissed you right in front of me."

I glared at him. "We didn't know you were there."

He narrowed his eyes. "He knew I was there."

I was going to tell him what I really thought of him when Huckleberry leaned his head back and howled for all he was worth. The next thing I knew, Huckleberry's eyes bugged out of his head, and then he ran straight at the chickens.

"Huckleberry!" I cried.

For the first time, Diva and the chickens scattered when Huckleberry came at them. It seemed that they realized that the little pug was at his breaking point. The flock broke off in all directions, but Huckleberry only had eyes for Diva. He was determined to catch her.

I knew he wouldn't hurt her, but if cornered, she could certainly do a number on the little pug. Diva wasn't the kind of hen to be messed with. I took off after them.

Diva flew over the fence around the cherry orchard with a battle cry that startled Teddy Bear and the other sheep. The little ram ushered his ewes into a circle in one corner of the orchard.

Huckleberry wasn't giving up. He wriggled his barrel-shaped body under the gate. The chicken turned around, ready to strike.

I threw open the gate and ran inside, catching up with them a half acre away. I was panting just as hard as Huckleberry. I thought the backbreaking farm work was keeping me in shape, but I wasn't running like I used to in LA. I needed to get back into the habit.

The pug had Diva cornered on the far side of the orchard where the ground was overturned. Talon marks were all over the ground and deep in the dirt. Huckleberry had something in his mouth.

On the mound of dirt that I assumed Diva and the other chickens had made, Diva flapped her wings and tried to make herself look four times her normal size. She walked toward Huckleberry, and her beady eyes focused on the object in Huckleberry's mouth.

Did he pick it up from the ground? Did she think he stole it from her?

I clapped my hands. "Huckleberry, come."

He turned around, and I saw a bone in his mouth, and not just any bone, a very long one. That could only belong to a large animal. Maybe a deer or coyote bone.

"What do you have there?" I asked.

He dropped the bone at my feet and looked up at me with pride on his face.

"Good boy," I murmured, but my stomach turned. That was no deer or coyote bone.

I couldn't bring myself to pick it up.

Quinn caught up with me. "Shiloh, I had no idea you could run so fast." He pulled up short when he saw what I was looking at Huckleberry's feet. "What is that?"

"A bone," I said.

"It just isn't any bone. It's a human bone. I think your dog just dug up a dead body."

"For the record, it was the chickens who dug it up." I pointed at the patch of scratched dirt that Diva continued to guard as if her life depended on it. If there were more bones under the ground, I wished the person well who tried to unearth them under Diva's watchful eye.

Chapter Six

Nothing shuts down a party like finding human remains. Quinn stayed with the bone while I ran back to the house to get Milan. He would know what to do. As soon as he saw my face, he knew something was wrong.

Quinn and I had been outside so long that most of the guests were helping themselves to pie and cake. How I envied them. I knew it would be a very long time before I would be having dessert.

"What's wrong? Did Quinn say something that upset you? I saw that he went outside right after you did." He rubbed the back of his neck. "I was just about to come out and look for you. You were gone a very long time."

Quinn had said something that upset me, but that was a conversation I could have with Milan at another time. There was a far more pressing issue at hand: the human remains that I found in the orchard.

"The chickens dug up a bone in the orchard. It looks like it's human," I said.

Milan's eyes were wide. "Are you sure?"

I nodded. "Quinn saw it too and thought the same thing.

Being a paramedic, he would know better than I would. He's in the orchard watching over the spot."

Milan didn't argue with me then. As much as he and Quinn were at odds, they respected each other. Quinn was a firefighter and an EMT; he would know what a human bone looked like.

Milan grabbed his cell phone off the table. "Show me."

"What's going on?" Dad wanted to know. "What's with the hush-hush conversation between you two?"

Everyone in the room looked at us at that point.

"Where's my dad?" Hazel asked from where she was playing with the twins on the floor.

I glanced at Milan, and he gave a slight nod as if he were saying it was all right.

"The chickens dug up a bone in the cherry orchard. It looks like it's human. I left Quinn with the remains while I got Milan."

A gasped filled the room.

"Someone was killed?" Mrs. Penbrook cried, a hand to her chest.

"I really don't think there is any danger. The bone looked as if it had been there an extraordinarily long time, but obviously if it is human, the authorities will have to be called."

My words hung in the air as everyone digested what I had said.

"Good heavens, Shi. You find dead people even on major holidays?" Kristy asked. "When will you take a break?"

"Knowing our luck, it will be James Ripley," my father muttered.

My chest tightened. James Ripley was part of our family lore. He disappeared before I was born, but the aftereffects of his life and disappearance on my family could not be ignored. I knew very little about the story, but I did know it had been off-limits when my grandmother was alive.

A memory came back to me like a slap to the face. I had been about Hazel's age when I came across the name James Ripley somehow. While shelling green beans on the farmhouse's front porch, I'd asked my grandmother who he was. She'd snapped at me, "I don't want to hear you ever say that name again, do you hear me?"

She'd never spoken to me so harshly before. I had nodded and kept my word. I never said the name James Ripley again, and in fact had never even heard it again—until now.

"Don't say that, Uncle Sully," Stacey said. "No one is interested in what happened to James Ripley any longer."

"I'm still curious about him," Connie Baskins spoke up. "It was quite a to-do at the municipal building when he went missing."

"Who's James Ripley?" Mrs. Penbrook asked.

My father cleared his throat. "Terrible man. No one was sad when he disappeared, least of all my mother."

"I'm sure this has nothing to do with Ripley," I said, but now that my father had put the thought in my head, I couldn't shake it. I had not thought of James Ripley in years, if not decades. However, hearing about his disappearance had contributed to my interest in true crime and had been why I'd concentrated on that genre in film and television production.

"You all enjoy some pie while Milan and I go check this out," I said as cheerfully as I could.

"Like we can eat pie at time like this," Mrs. Penbrook said.

"Speak for yourself," Jessa interjected. "I can always eat pie." She cut a big piece of pecan pie and slid it onto a plate.

As Milan and I walked back to the orchard, I told him second by second what happened up until I saw the bone. Well, not exactly. I told him that Quinn and I had been talking in the yard when Huckleberry took off after Diva. I didn't tell him what we were talking about, and I was grateful that he didn't ask. Yet. I knew that he would ask soon enough.

We found Quinn crouched by the site where the chickens had been digging. He reached out as if he was going to touch something on the ground.

Diva stood a few feet away, but to my surprise she didn't seem to be angry that Quinn was close to her treasure. Maybe it was just me and Huckleberry she had beef with.

"Don't touch anything," Milan said.

Quinn looked up. "I wasn't going to." He didn't even bother to hide the defensiveness in his voice. "You're not needed here, Penbrook. I already called my dad, and he will be here any second. This is his jurisdiction."

Quinn's dad, Randy Killian, was the Cherry Glen police chief, but everyone just called him Chief Randy. He had been the police chief for as long as I could remember. He was quick to make up his mind about a case, which could be good and bad, and he liked me just about as much as Quinn's mother, Doreen, did—which was not at all.

"Quinn," I said. "What is wrong with Milan offering his expertise?"

Quinn frowned. "My father won't appreciate it. He doesn't like to work with other departments on his cases."

How well I knew that. Milan did too, due to his own past experience working or, more accurately, trying to work with Chief Randy on a homicide that impacted both of their jurisdictions.

The roar of an engine broke through the stillness of the late fall afternoon. Chief Randy rode his motorcycle up the driveway and over the grassy path that led to the orchard. Tufts of turf kicked up behind his back wheel. I bit down hard on the inside of my cheek to keep myself from saying something about that. He didn't care if he tore up the yard.

He parked the bike just shy of the orchard gate and set the kickstand. By the way he acted, you would think he was a bigwig in a biker gang. However, with his potbelly, tufts of hair sticking out of the sides of his head under his department ball cap, and glasses, he looked more like an accountant on a casual Friday.

With his thumbs looped over his belt, he sauntered over to us. The chief was never in a hurry to go anywhere. He got there when he got there, and everyone else could wait, which was why I was surprised that he made it to the farm so quickly.

The sheep watched Chief Randy as if he were an alien who'd just beamed down from the mother ship. That was saying something, too, because my sheep had seen me do a lot of crazy things since moving to Bellamy Farm.

Teddy Bear stood guard in front of his girls. He might

have thought that he looked ready to strike, but in reality, the best he could do was snuggle you to death.

The police chief stopped a few feet from us and folded his arms. "Snow is coming. This might be the last day to ride my old hog until the spring. It pains me to put her away. There's nothing like coming up beside someone speeding through town on a Harley." He wiggled his bushy eyebrows at me. "Isn't that right, Shiloh?"

I grimaced. My first reintroduction to Cherry Glen was being caught in a speed trap by Chief Randy. It wasn't a warm welcome by any stretch. I deserved the ticket, but not Chief Randy's animosity ever since.

"Time's running short on daylight, so you're going to have to show me what you found. Quinn said you had human remains." He raised his eyebrows at me again. "You just can't catch a break, can you, Shiloh?"

"It's over here," Quinn said and led the way through the orchard with Milan and me trailing behind.

As we walked, Milan reached out and gave my hand the briefest of squeezes.

The police chief hiked up his pants when we reached the chicken-scratch mound. The bone that Huckleberry had found lay in the dirt next to the mound. "Yep, that's a human bone all right." He looked over his shoulder at me. "Did your dog dig it up?"

"No, the chickens did."

He eyed me. "What, you have cadaver chickens now?" He laughed. "Now I have heard everything."

I ignored his joke. "We just recently moved the chickens

to this side of the farm because they weren't getting along with the barn cats. The chickens are free to roam during the day, and they love spending time in the orchard. It's good for the farm too. They eat ticks and other insects that aren't good for the trees or us."

He bent over the site where the chickens had been digging. "Could just be the one bone brought from another spot or it could be a shallow grave here. In either case, we will have to dig this all up to take a better look." He nodded at the bone. "Whoever that belonged to is long gone now. The bone has been picked clean. It will be up to the coroner to determine how old it is, and his team will have to dig up this area to see if there are any other remains."

"I understand." I could not believe this was happening. Part of me hoped that the single bone would be all that was found. If that were the case, it could have come from anywhere. There were all sorts of wild animals that lived near or moved through the farm, from raccoons to foxes to bobcats, and even the occasional black bear. Any one of those animals could have carried the bone from somewhere else.

"I'll have to call the coroner, and he won't be too happy to be pulled away from his turkey. That's the nature of the job, as I well know." He nodded at Milan. "Speaking of which, what are you doing here, Penbrook? We aren't in your county."

"I'm just here for the food and company."

"Hmm," the police chief mused and then looked at his son. "I wasn't aware this was the company that you were keeping." He seemed to note how close Milan and I were standing together. "Interesting."

Quinn glared at the ground.

"Assuming this is a human bone, as we all suspect, who could it be?" Milan asked. "I do understand that it could be a body that was dumped from just about any corner of the state, but it wouldn't hurt to start with the missing persons from Cherry Glen and the surrounding area. Are there any unsolved missing person cases in Cherry Glen?"

Chief Randy rocked back on his heels. "The only missing person I know of is James Ripley, but he's been gone for a good forty years. He was never officially declared missing, but he did disappear from Cherry Glen. There were a lot of rumors about him." He eyed me. "If it's him, it is very interesting that he was found after all this time on Bellamy Farm."

"Why's that?" Milan asked.

I grimaced. Milan was asking questions because that was what he was trained to do, but he didn't know anything about the backstory involving James Ripley and my family. I didn't even know the whole story. I just knew that it was volatile.

Chief Randy's eyes slid in my direction again. "We will discuss that if we confirm it's him. It could just as easily be an outsider or someone who was passing through. You know hikers come through this area all the time since we are so close to Sleeping Bear Dunes."

I didn't buy Chief Randy's idea that the bone had come from a vagabond who was wandering around the countryside. If there was a dead body lying around the farm, someone would have stumbled upon it. If there was more than just a bone there, it was purposely hidden so that it would never be found. And hiding a body screamed *murder*.

"It could have been anyone," I said, just as much to convince myself as well as the men standing with me.

"It could be, but do we really believe it is?" Chief Randy sauntered away to make his phone call to the coroner.

I had met the coroner several times in similar situations, and I knew that Chief Randy was right that the coroner would not be pleased to be pulled away from his Thanksgiving dinner and football game. Not that I blamed him. Standing in the cold looking for human remains was a terrible way to spend a holiday; it was a terrible way to spend any day.

Milan stared at the bone with a determined look on his face. I couldn't begin to guess what he was thinking, but I wished so much that he was the sheriff of my county so he could be involved in the investigation. If he were, I would feel much more confident that this case would be taken seriously. I knew Chief Randy would never invite Milan to assist on the case. To say the police chief was territorial about his cases was an understatement.

There was also the issue that I didn't trust Chief Randy. He viewed being the chief of police as a security job. He would much rather pull someone over for speeding than spend time on a more serious crime. Any case that had the potential to be time-consuming, he tried to solve as quickly as possible, even if that meant coming to the wrong conclusion. He didn't want problems, and what bigger problem was there than murder?

That thought led me to the next question, which was, was it murder? If the coroner and his team found more than one bone in the same place, I would have to assume it was. No one could bury themselves.

Quinn stood a few feet away from Milan and me and stared at the ground. I could feel his discomfort.

Quinn cleared his throat. "Could it be the person just died in an accident and fell here?"

"And not be noticed for decades?" I asked. "This orchard has been in constant use for years and years; someone would notice a fallen person in the corner. Besides, it appears the victim was buried. That can only mean one thing," I said.

"What?" Quinn asked.

"Murder," I said.

The chief rejoined our little group around the bone. "Did I hear someone say something about murder?"

"It's a possibility," I said.

"Any time you find human remains, it's a possibility. But I would be very surprised if that proved true."

"You will check dental records, right?" I asked. Perhaps it was a condescending question to ask a seasoned officer like Chief Randy, but that just showed how little I trusted him.

He scowled at me. "Please let me do my job."

Milan set a hand on my shoulder, and I sighed. I was being too hard on Chief Randy about the investigation. I need to put the brakes on my questions before I alienated the police chief completely. It wasn't like we were the best of friends to begin with.

To my surprise, Chief Randy said, "Assuming that the skull and teeth are under the ground, we will be able to check dental records."

"What about DNA?" I asked. I couldn't help myself.

"We can run it through." He gave me a look. "But we

would have to have a match in the system, and that's not as easy as it looks on TV."

Could the bone really belong to James Ripley? It was hard for me to imagine that this missing man, who had been gone for so long, was buried under the cherry orchard. If it were him, I knew that it would come back to my grandmother because one thing was for sure: Grandma Bellamy hated James Ripley, and everyone in town knew it.

Chapter Seven

The coroner and two more officers arrived, and soon, the orchard became crowded with crime scene techs, EMTs, and other emergency personnel. It was Thanksgiving Day, but everyone was there ready to work. It wasn't often a human bone was found lying around Cherry Glen.

I shuffled to the middle of the trees, and Teddy Bear and his ewes gathered around me. I didn't know if they did that to protect themselves or me, but I was grateful the flock trusted me.

Thankfully, Chesney had been able to corral Diva and her gang of chickens back into the coop. Diva wasn't happy going to the coop so early, and there would certainly be repercussions for upsetting her schedule, but everyone was a lot safer with the chickens tucked away.

From where I stood, I couldn't see what they were digging up, but I could hear them. I bit the inside of my cheek, praying the single bone was a fluke and they wouldn't find anything else.

Milan and Quinn stood near the excavation site, where the crime scene techs worked. I suppose they were given the professional courtesy to watch. The same wasn't extended to me. Chief Randy shooed me away and told me to go bake something inside. It took all my willpower not to snap back at him. From past experience, I had learned that it was never a good idea to aggravate the police when a dead body was found on your farm. This wasn't Bellamy Farm's first dead body. Unfortunately.

"We got something!" one of men cried.

My heart sank. They hadn't been digging for very long, and they had already found something. That couldn't be a good sign at all.

I stepped out of the cherry trees, hoping to catch a glimpse of whatever it was they had found, but Teddy Bear wasn't having it. He headbutted me in the knees, trying to herd me back into the trees.

I stumbled. "Teddy Bear, I need to know what's going on."

He headbutted me again. It was time to lead the sheep back to the barn.

It was beginning to grow dark, and the crime scene techs set up portable high-powered lights, which abruptly put everything in the orchard into high relief. The sheep blinked in confusion.

Esmeralda jumped down from one of the cherry trees and pranced in the light as if she was walking the runway. All the while, the men standing around the patch of dirt the chickens had dug up didn't notice a thing.

Although I couldn't see what they were all looking at, I could still hear the conversation, and the tech spoke again. "It's a rib cage. A human rib cage."

My heart sank to my feet.

"All right," the coroner said. "My guess is that the whole thing is there unless some critter dragged it away. If that were the case, I think someone would have noticed it earlier."

"Not if the whole family was dead set on keeping whoever was buried here a secret." That was Chief Randy's voice.

"We shouldn't jump to any conclusions just yet," the coroner said. I was grateful that he was discouraging Chief Randy from settling on one story without evidence, but I also knew it was far too late. The moment the chief heard that a possible human bone had been found at Bellamy Farm, he would assume that I was behind it. And if not me, someone in my family.

He had been waiting to arrest me for some time.

I knew I didn't bury those bones in the orchard, and I could not for the life of me believe that anyone else in my family did.

A memory came back to me from when I was a kid playing in the orchard. I had been going through a potion-making stage as a child, so I would walk around the farm and collect ingredients for my potions, from leaves to straw from the barn to soil samples from different parts of the farm.

One time I was in the orchard with my grandmother. I had my little spade in my hand to collect samples. My grandmother had said to me when I walked to the corner of the orchard, "Don't dig in that part of the orchard, Shiloh. It's too dry there. It's not good for trees. Or anything. Promise me that you will never plant a tree there."

I blinked at her. "I promise, Grandma."

And I had kept my promise to this day. While I was living in California, Dad had kept that promise too, but that had more to do with neglect of the orchard than anything else; when I took over the farm a couple of years back, it was in horrible shape and half the trees were dead.

I felt ill. Did my grandmother really say that because she believed it wasn't good for the tree, or did she say that so I wouldn't find the body? And if she knew there was a body there, did she have something to do with it?

I pushed the thoughts from my head. My grandmother didn't know a body was in the orchard. It might not have even been there when she was alive.

But doubt still lingered in the back of my mind.

The coroner stepped out of the circle with Chief Randy just a few paces behind him. "This is going to take some time." He sighed. "I hope the wife saves a piece of pie for me."

Chief Randy clapped the coroner on the back. "I'm sure she will."

"I don't know. If my grandson asked for it, she would gladly hand it over. She does everything for that boy. Spoils him horribly," he said grumpily.

"Spoiling your grandchild is the best part of getting old," the police chief said.

My heart softened to him just a little because I knew how much he loved Hazel. Doreen was the same. Perhaps I should cut them a little bit of slack. They were protective of Quinn and Hazel because of what they had been through. Quinn had been working as a firefighter in Detroit when his wife died. He brought his young daughter back to Cherry

Glen to be closer to family. His parents picked up the pieces for both Quinn and Hazel. That could not be ignored.

Milan, who had been in the circle, walked over to me. He nodded at Teddy Bear, who stood on my foot. The ram was keeping a close eye on me like I was one of his ewes.

"I should go back to the house and tell everyone what's happening," I said.

"I'll walk with you to the gate," Milan said. "If your sheep will let me."

I patted Teddy Bear on the head. "It's okay. I'm with Milan now and safe."

He eyed Milan and slowly removed his hoof from my shoe.

"I don't think he likes me," Milan said.

"It's not you. He just doesn't like competition."

I called Huckleberry to join us, and the little pug yipped before galloping toward us. He grinned from ear to ear, and his tongue hung out of his mouth as he ran. It was clear that he was quite pleased with his findings. He was turning into something of a cadaver dog, I supposed.

Huckleberry ran through the gate and looked back toward Milan and me as if to ask us what was taking so long.

Milan stopped just before the gate. "I'm going to hang back here to keep an eye on things. I think we both have a healthy distrust of Chief Randy, and I want to make sure everything is done on the up and up."

I glanced over his shoulder at the crime scene. "You don't think Chief Randy will do a good job?"

He grimaced. "Chief Randy is a good cop when he wants

to be. The issue is he only wants to keep the peace. I get that, but sweeping things under the rug to retain calm is not always on the side of justice."

I nodded. That was my assessment of Chief Randy too. If he had his way, he would be sitting just outside of town on his Harley waiting for speeders to fly by. The man reveled in handing out speeding tickets.

"A cold case, which this is likely to be," Milan said, "will dig up old wounds in Cherry Glen. That's the last thing he wants." He studied my face. "Who is this James Ripley person that everyone is talking about, and how is your grandmother connected?"

"I don't know everything. It was a name that I heard whispered from time to time when I was a child. Whenever his name would come up around Grandma Bellamy, she was livid. Overall, she was stoic woman, so practical and no-nonsense that I thought nothing would get a rise out of her, but any mention of Ripley would send her over the edge. I started to ask her about him once, but she shut me down. Another time, I asked Stacey, who told me to never say his name in front of Grandma if I knew what was good for me."

"So Stacey knows more about him?"

"I don't know. Ripley disappeared before I was born, but Stacey would have been alive, even if she was just a very young child. I'm not sure if she knows more about him or if she just knows that Ripley wasn't someone we talked about in front of our grandmother."

He nodded. "The most likely person to know anything would be your father."

I nodded.

"I'm sure Chief Randy will want to talk to him if this turns out to be Ripley. But we have to keep in mind that it might not be him. We don't know the age or gender yet. Sadly, thousands of people go missing every year. These bones could belong to a whole host of people."

I nodded. I knew this from my previous work in true crime. However, I didn't say that to Milan because I knew there was a great distance between being a true crime television producer and being a police officer investigating a cold case.

He looked behind him for a second. No one was looking at us, and he leaned forward and planted a brief kiss on my cheek. He pulled back. "I'll make sure that Chief Randy gives this case the attention it deserves."

I smiled up at him. "Good luck with that."

"I'm going to need it."

I turned to walk to the house.

"Shiloh?"

I turned again to look at him.

"What were you and Quinn talking about?"

My stomach turned. This wasn't the time for that conversation, especially when he was going to be standing next Quinn and his father during the investigation.

"It was nothing to worry about."

Milan furrowed his brow.

"I promise," I reassured him.

He nodded and walked back to the group of men standing around the bones.

Chapter Eight

When I approached the house, Kristy was waiting by the back door. "Tell me everything."

I sighed and gave her a quick rundown before we went into the house.

"It couldn't possibly be James Ripley, could it?" She asked the question that would be at the top a lot of peoples' minds for anyone of a certain age in Cherry Glen.

"Chief Randy seems pretty convinced that it's him," I said. "But they won't know for sure until they check dental records. We don't know if it was even a man or a woman. We don't know how the person died."

She sighed. "I wish I could stay and watch it all unfold, but we have to head to Kent's parents' house for our third Thanksgiving of the day. I never thought I would ever say this, but if I see one more piece of pumpkin pie, I might be sick. You will give me all the updates." It wasn't a question; it was a statement.

I would expect nothing less from Kristy. "I will."

"Good. Kent and the girls are already in the car ready to go. Call me if you need anything. I can always leave Kent and the girls and come back here if you need me."

I hugged her, then stepped into the house. Milan's mother was waiting for me.

"Shiloh," Miss Charity said. "Where has my son been all this time? He didn't even finish his meal. And I'm ready to go home. I'd like him to come back to take me home." She was already wearing her coat and had her purse in hand.

"I don't know when he will be available to take you home," I said. "He is helping with the investigation."

"That boy. This isn't even his county. He certainly can take his mother home. You tell him that."

"Do you live out by Torch Lake, Miss Charity?" Stacey asked.

She turned to look at my cousin. "I do. How did you know that?"

"The sheriff mentioned it during the meal because that's where Rhett lives. We're headed there now. We could take you home."

Miss Charity smiled. "That would be lovely. I will need to tell my son before we go. I think he will be relieved. He hates to leave in the middle of a case. He always gets called away at the worst times. His ex-wife hated that." She looked at me. "I suppose it is something you will have to get used to if the two of you marry."

Marry. Who said anything about getting married? Milan and I had only been dating for a few months, and we were both so busy that most of our interactions had been via text message. I didn't believe that was the best foundation for a marriage.

"I'm ready to go home myself," Dad said. "Connie, are you ready to leave?"

Connie looked out the window. "I'm not sure I should leave just yet, Sullivan. What if the chief needs me in my official capacity?"

"Then he can call you. I'm not going to stay here all day and night while Chief Randy is in the orchard picking at some bones."

"I really think I should stay," Connie said. "I have my official duties."

Jessa came into the living room, wiping her hands on a tea towel. "If you need to stay, Connie, I can take Sully home. It's on my way back to town."

Connie glared at her. "No, I will be the one to take Sullivan home. Are you ready to go, Sullivan?"

If Dad was surprised by Connie's sudden change of tune about staying at Chesney's house, he didn't show it.

After everyone left, I was alone in the house with Chesney. I fell into one the folding chairs and let out a great sigh.

Chesney stood at the living room window. "This holiday was a bust. Not only did Whit miss the whole meal, but now there's another murder."

"We don't know that it's a murder," I said.

She looked over her shoulder at me. "Do you really believe that?"

I wrinkled my nose. "No, but I really want to."

Chapter Nine

The next morning was Black Friday. I was up before dawn, but it wasn't because I was hitting the sales at the Traverse City mall. I rose early every morning because that was the life of a farmer.

Even on the edge of winter, there was much to be done. All the fields had to be cut down and closed up before the snow flew, last crops needed to be harvested, canning had to be done, herbs needed to be dried, and there were always animals to feed and stalls to clean. The work never stopped.

I knew that Chesney would be up on her side of the farm too, collecting eggs from Diva and her gang, and letting the chickens out for the day. In the dead of winter, there would be times that the chickens would be stuck in the coop for weeks, so right now they needed to be outside as much as possible. Diva was cranky when she wasn't allowed out of the coop, even if it was for her own good.

Huckleberry and I walked the sheep to the orchard that morning, while Esmeralda was happy to stay snuggled on my bed back at the cottage.

As we walked by the coop, Diva flapped her wings and

came down the ramp like a boxer ready to enter the ring. She was always ready for a fight.

Teddy Bear stopped in front of me when he saw the hen. Few things could strike fear into the heart of our sheep as Diva and her band of chickens. Teddy Bear began to turn around as if he was ready to go straight back to the barn.

"Come on, Teddy Bear. You're a sheep. You're covered in wool. Diva can't even get to you."

He pointed his little black face up at me and stared at me with soulful brown eyes as if to ask me if I was serious. Yesterday's events had frightened the little ram, and me too, if I was being honest. I'd hardly slept last night, as I had been so preoccupied with the bones found in the orchard and worry over the fact that they might be those of James Ripley.

The ewes didn't seem to be bothered in the least and headbutted me on the back of the leg as if to ask why we had stopped. The female flock knew Teddy Bear would protect them at all costs, so why should they have to worry? It was a lot of pressure on his wooly shoulders.

"Come on, Teddy Bear. Diva will leave you alone, I promise."

As ridiculous as I sounded, I would do just about anything to get Teddy Bear to move. The quicker I completed the morning chores, the sooner Chesney and I could prepare for our big Small Business Saturday tomorrow. We would be selling handmade soap and cherry jams at a local church as part of the first indoor Farmers Market and Artisan Fair. It was Kristy's brainchild, and I knew that she was hoping that it would be a hit. If it was successful, her plan was to have the farmers market host more indoor events during the winter months. It helped the market and, of course, helped the farmers too.

Teddy Bear stared at me for a long moment and then, putting one hoof in front of another, marched through the gate. The ewes followed him in like this had been the plan all the time. The sheep and the chickens seemed to have the same government structure. There was one dominant animal who told the rest of them what to do, but while Teddy Bear nudged his ladies with gentle headbutts and sweet baas, Diva ruled her chickens with talons and fear.

Maybe Dad was right, and I should get rid of the chickens. I just couldn't bring myself to abandon any creature I took in, no matter how rotten they could be. Having an animal was a commitment, and to me, it was a lifetime commitment. Sadly, not everyone felt the same way.

Chesney stood outside of the orchard fence. "Are you sure the sheep are allowed in there with the dead-guy situation and all?"

"The dead-guy situation? Is that what we're calling it?" I pulled my stocking cap down over my ears. It would most certainly snow sometime that day. I just hoped the weather forecaster was right, and it wouldn't be more than a dusting, as a blizzard would certainly negate any chance of a successful Farmers Market and Artisan Fair.

"Do you have a better name for it?" Chesney pushed her glasses up her nose. She was dressed for the cold weather too. She wore a university hoodie with a thick down vest on top and a winter hat with a bright red pompom.

I shook my head. "I don't. Chief Randy said they got everything that they needed, so we are free to use the orchard again. I would hate to keep Teddy Bear and the girls from it now. With the shift in the weather, the sheep don't have much time left to graze. Snow is predicted for this weekend, so I would like to put fresh straw down in the barn to get it ready for them just in case the weather gets bad. After we do that, we can start getting prepared for tomorrow."

"Can you tell me what exactly is happening tomorrow? I know it's part of the farmers market, but you were sparse with details."

"I'm sorry about that. I was so focused on making Thanksgiving perfect, I couldn't think of much else. It's going to be inside the Community Church. Kristy has been planning it for months. I think we'll have a good turnout. There'll be a lot of people there buying holiday gifts for friends and family, so I think we should focus on gift baskets of jams, jellies, and syrups, and the soaps too."

She nodded. "It's not like we have fresh cherries to sell them." She sighed "What's our setup going to be? There is no way our booth will fit inside of the church's door."

We had a gorgeous cherry basket booth that we used for outdoor events. We had debuted the booth that summer at the National Cherry Festival in Traverse City and had used it at every outdoor event since. The Traverse City paper did a write-up about the booth, which brought more attention to the farm. It had been a huge investment, but it had more than paid off. But Chesney was right; the booth wouldn't even fit through the door to make it into the church basement.

"We will just have to go back to where we started, with folding tables, tablecloths, and decorative signs. We can make it look special, and as far as I know, we will be the only ones there selling cherry products. That might help us too. Everyone who comes to this part of the state wants something cherry, no matter the time of the year."

Teddy Bear seemed to sense that something was off in the far corner of the orchard, so he kept his girls in the front. He was a very smart little ram.

Chesney nodded at them. "He seems nervous. I can't believe that they found a fully intact skeleton. I was convinced that it was just one bone that a coyote or some other animal had dug up. Did you hear about the bear?"

"Bear? What bear?"

"You must have been outside with the police when Jessa brought it up, but a juvenile black bear was spotted in town right outside of the brewery. He was in their dumpster. By the time animal control got there, he had moved on."

"Yikes."

Black bears lived in the area, and their population was growing. Even so, they tended to keep to themselves and stay out of the center of town. It wasn't often that one was spotted so close to people.

"Yeah, it was very early Thanksgiving morning, from what Jessa said, so nobody was around. The bear wanted a Thanksgiving meal too." She shrugged.

"Let's hope that he's left the town and is not headed this way. The last thing we need to contend with right now is a bear."

"If I was a bear, I wouldn't come anywhere near Bellamy Farm with Diva on the prowl."

She had a point.

Chesney pulled her beanie down over her ears. She was twenty-eight, but standing there in her vest and beanie, she looked no more than fourteen. "I'm sure the bear will keep Chief Randy occupied if he's still around," she said. "Is he going to give much attention at all to the bones?"

"He doesn't have a choice. One bone or a whole skeleton, it wouldn't matter. The police would still have to investigate who it all belonged to. Having the whole skeleton will make it easier to identify the person, assuming a missing person's report was filed."

"Wow, Shi, you are really in the know with this murder investigation stuff, aren't you? It must be from dating a cop." She wiggled her eyebrows.

I rolled my eyes. "It's from my old job as a producer. True crime thrives on cold cases. You would be surprised how little Milan and I talk about his work. He likes it that way."

"But you will talk about this case. It happened here on the farm."

"We don't know the murder happened on the farm, and it's likely it didn't. The body was probably hidden on the farm. That's a big difference."

She shrugged as if she wasn't so sure about that.

"Besides, I don't know how much Milan will even be able to learn. This isn't his case; it's Chief Randy's."

"That's unfortunate. It'd be better if it was Milan on the

case. Chief Randy hates you. He would love to blame you for something."

"If you're trying to make me feel better about the situation, it's not working."

"I wasn't. I was only being factual."

I made a face.

"I'm kind of surprised that he still dislikes you so much," Chesney went on. "I thought he would get over it when it became clear that you and Quinn didn't have a future together."

I agreed with Chesney that Quinn and I didn't have a future together. The issue was I was no longer sure that Quinn believed that. I didn't say a word to my farm manager about the conversation I had with Quinn yesterday. My hope was that I wouldn't have to say a word about it to anyone. I did plan to tell Milan out of respect for our relationship, but my goal was to avoid going into details. That might be tricky. He was a cop, after all, and he would have questions. I knew he trusted me, but maybe he didn't trust Quinn.

"I'm glad that we will be cleaning out the sheep stalls today. I could use the physical activity." She patted her perfectly flat stomach. "I think I'm getting a little soft around the middle. I'm pushing thirty, you know."

"Please," I muttered.

"I also need to clear my head." She glanced back at her farmhouse. Just the edge of the roofline could be seen in the distance through the trees.

"Because of Whit?" I asked, feeling bad that I hadn't asked her about it before. I had been too preoccupied with my own problems. Not that a dead body on the farm was a small issue, but I knew how upset Chesney had been when Whit didn't come to the Thanksgiving meal.

She nodded. "I was up until one in the morning listening for her to come home. She finally did just as I was drifting off."

"Did you talk to her?" I asked.

She shook her head. "What was I going to say? She's an adult. She can come and go as she pleases. If I had gotten up and confronted her, we would have just gotten into a huge fight."

"And this morning?"

She chuckled. "She's still sleeping. We will be lucky if she's up by noon. It's Thanksgiving break. She doesn't have any classes to hurry off to, and play practice is this afternoon."

"Maybe that's for the best. The two of you will have time to cool off." Again, I thought about Jessa saying she saw Whit at the diner with Rhett, Stacey's boyfriend. Maybe they had been talking about the theater, but that didn't ring true to me. I tried not to worry, and I didn't say anything to Chesney because I didn't want to worry her either. Also, there was a good chance that Chesney already knew. Cherry Glen was a gossipy little town. I would not be surprised if one of the busybodies who had lunch at Jessa's Place every day had already called Chesney and spilled the tea about Whit's lunch meetings. If that was true, why hadn't Chesney reacted when she saw Rhett at Thanksgiving? Did that mean she didn't know, or did she believe it was completely innocent?

I decided that I would learn more about Rhett before I

broached the topic with Chesney. She had enough worries when it came to her sister.

I whistled for Huckleberry, and he came barreling from the orchard. The little pug was small enough to crawl under the fence. The three of us made our way to the barn in silence.

Chapter Ten

"Everything looks absolutely gorgeous. Doreen, you have outdone yourself," a woman who was selling crocheted scarves and hats said. Most of the items were in the colors of red, green, and white. It seemed that my fellow vendor at the Farmers Market and Artisan Fair was betting on a lot of people wearing Christmas colors all winter long. She had a long multicolored crocheted scarf around her neck and a matching beret on her head.

Doreen Killian, Chief Randy's wife, adjusted the strap of her leather purse on her shoulder. "Thank you. It's nice to be appreciated." She shot a glance at me.

I pretended to busy myself by straightening brochures about my organic baking business, which I was doing my best to get off the ground. I had not gotten a custom order yet, but I was hopeful that Small Business Saturday would go a long way toward breaking that streak.

I hadn't expected to see Doreen there, but I should have. This was Doreen's church, and since Doreen seemed to need to have her hand in everything, she would most certainly be there. I wished that Kristy had reminded me that it was

Doreen's church, but I had a feeling that she had left out that little bit of information on purpose.

The warning would have been nice, but either way, I had to be there. This was the biggest event that the farmers market would have for months. I could not afford to miss it.

Chesney nudged my shoulder. "Man, she really doesn't like you. That look on her face is cold."

Doreen stopped in front of our booth, and Chesney took a big step back. Huckleberry cowered under the table. Neither one of them was any help at all.

Doreen cleared her throat. "I hope you like your spot. I chose where all the vendors were and picked the placement on where I thought it was most fitting for them."

Right behind the booth, a toilet flushed and the hand dryer in the bathroom came on with a vengeance. I didn't doubt for a second that Doreen had chosen this spot just for me. She was thoughtful like that.

"It's certainly convenient to the restrooms," I said. "Everyone has to go there eventually, right? We should get a lot of traffic."

Doreen frowned as if she hadn't thought of that. Perhaps she was even rethinking where I should go. I was certain out by the church's dumpster came to her mind.

"Well, my granddaughter will be here later. I trust that you won't try to recruit her to work for you." She gave me a beady look.

Before I could answer, she moved on to torment the next vendor.

The toilet flushed on the other side of the wall again, and Chesney gave me a look.

Kristy walked over to our booth. "Before you say anything, I didn't have a say in where all the vendors would be placed. The church wanted to be in charge of that because they knew the layout of the room better."

I cocked my head. "Don't worry. We aren't blaming you. Doreen already stopped by and told us that she picked this spot especially for Bellamy Farm."

Kristy grimaced. "I suppose that I should be happy she came clean about it."

I shrugged. "Maybe. She enjoyed telling me."

Kristy winced.

"Don't worry. I can manage Doreen, and I'm glad we are here. Chesney and I wouldn't miss it."

Kristy's shoulders relaxed; she brushed a lock of her thick black hair over her shoulder. "This is a bigger event than the normal market because I opened it up to local artisans and artists in addition to my farmers and growers. It would be a big help to me if you could walk around when you have free time and let me know what you think and if we should expand the summer market to include more artisans in the area."

"You don't want it to turn into a craft fair," Chesney said. "The farms have to come first."

"I agree," Kristy replied. "But we have to change to garner new business. More and more farmers markets are adding crafters, and you saw how many were at the National Cherry Festival this summer. It got me thinking that this might be the direction to go to keep us viable. Anyway, I have to check in with a few more vendors before we open. I want a full report from you both at the end of the day." She waved at us and walked away.

"I wish I had her energy," Chesney said.

"Please, no. I could not handle two of you."

She laughed, and we finished setting up the booth. As planned, we were selling soap, jams, jellies, syrups, and our newest offering: candles. I had always wanted to get into candle making, so I had a pilot batch of cherry chocolate and cherry vanilla candles that I was trying. If they did well, I would make more. In the name of being sustainable, all the candles were made in interesting teacups, mason jars, and glasses that I bought at yard sales and thrift stores. I had gotten a little carried away on the yard sale circuit that summer collecting teacups and jars. If the candles did well, I would have more than enough containers to sustain me all year round. It seemed that I had a little bit of my father's collecting tendencies buried deep inside of me.

I also had my baked goods. As there were no fresh cherries from Bellamy Farm in season, I used cherries that we had dried and canned earlier in the fall. Our table had a lot to offer, and I was looking forward to hearing the reception—if I could hear anything over the flushing toilet just behind the wall.

After we were all set up, Chesney's eyes darted back and forth through the large room.

The number of artists and artisans there was impressive. There had to be fifty. There were wood-carvers knitters, textile artists, painters, and more. I looked down at my homemade organic candles, which I had been so proud of, and wondered how I measured up in the arts and crafts department. Maybe I should stick to cherries.

Chesney walked around our table and looked up the aisle.

When she came back, I said, "Okay, what's going on?"

"What?" Her eyes were wide behind her glasses.

"Something is up. You're as scared as a squirrel that comes face-to-face with Diva."

"For the record, you don't have to be a squirrel to be afraid of Diva. She's terrifying to every living creature, including people."

"So?" I raised my brow.

She lowered her voice. "The guy Whit has been hanging out with is here."

"Oh? Is she seeing someone?" I asked.

"All I know is she's been spending time with him."

"Who is it?"

"Stacey's boyfriend, Rhett."

"Oh, you know about that?"

She cocked her head. "Know about what?"

I wrinkled my nose. "Jessa mentioned at Thanksgiving that Whit has been meeting Rhett at the diner over the last several months."

"Yeah, a couple of people have told me that too." She frowned. "It's weird Jessa didn't say anything to me about it."

"She knows that you have a lot going on."

Chesney frowned as if she wasn't buying that excuse, and I didn't blame her.

"Where is Rhett?" I asked.

Chesney peeked over the table. "At the other end of the aisle. He's sitting down."

"He has a table?"

"Looks like it, but I can't see what he's selling from this angle. I wish I knew more about him and what he is doing with my sister."

"Why didn't you ask him at Thanksgiving?" I asked.

"There were too many people around, and I don't know if Stacey knows they have been spotted around town together. I didn't want her to have one of her huge blowups and ruin the meal."

My cousin did have a temper, so that was the right call.

"The market is about to open, but I can handle any sales. If you want to go talk to him now, that's fine with me."

She pushed her glasses up the bridge of her nose. "Are you sure?"

"Of course I am. We're going to have to take turns stepping away from the booth all day as it is or be driven mad by the sound of toilets flushing."

As if on cue, two toilets flushed in tandem behind the wall.

She made a face. "That's the truth. Thank you, Shi." She hurried away.

Chapter Eleven

The decibel level in the church hall rose considerably when the doors opened and shoppers flooded into the building. I wasn't the least bit surprised at the healthy attendance. Kristy had been working double time promoting this event, not only to Cherry Glen, but to the whole region. I was happy to see a good turnout for my sake, but mostly for hers. She had great plans to expand the market that would benefit everyone involved. Kristy was right: to survive, the market had to adapt.

It took a few minutes, but shoppers started coming to my booth after stopping at the ones much closer to the front door.

A woman picked up one of my teacup candles and inhaled deeply. "These smells just like summer, and the teacup is adorable. What a clever idea. Why did they put you so far in the back? You should have been at the front. I know a lot of people won't make it back this far, and they will be missing out."

It was a loaded question, and one it was best not to answer truthfully. I simply shrugged. "I'm just so happy to have a spot at the market. Everyone has been lovely." The last part was a bit of a white lie, at least as far as Doreen Killian was concerned.

"I'm so happy that every candle is unique. They will make great Christmas gifts for my granddaughters. I would like to get five."

"Wonderful," I said with a smile. "Please pick out the five you want, and I will wrap them up for you."

I was just wrapping up the woman's purchases when another person sauntered up to the table, but he wasn't there for candles.

Chief Randy picked up one of the cherry chocolate soap bars and sniffed it. "It smells like candy. I don't like soap that smells like food. I find it confusing. Am I supposed to smell it or eat it?"

My shopper wrinkled her nose at him. "Some people have no taste." She collected her purchase and hurried away from the table.

Even knowing that the police chief wasn't there to shop, I put on my best salesperson's face. "We have a variety of items for sale if you don't care for the chocolate cherry soap. There is something for everyone."

He looked up and down at my table as if he wasn't so sure of that. "I'm here on official police business." He straightened his shoulders and looked me in the eye as if he were trying to drive the words home.

"And what is that?" I asked as pleasantly as I could.

He hiked up his pants. "I wanted to be the first one to let you know. The dental records matched. The bones that were found in your orchard match those of James Ripley."

I gasped. I couldn't help it. Ripley had been gone for forty years. The odds of his remains turning up now just seemed to be too far-fetched, but here Chief Randy was telling me that his bones were in my orchard.

The police chief smiled as if he was pleased with my shocked reaction. "I knew it would be like this from the start. I didn't even have to pull any missing persons files. I knew it was Ripley in my gut. Of course, where the bones were found was a huge giveaway. We all know your family's history with Ripley."

We didn't *all* know it. I didn't know it.

What did it mean that Ripley's remains had been found all these years later? What did it mean for the farm since the bones were discovered in the orchard?

"The Cherry Glen Police Department has determined that your late grandmother, Emma Kay Bellamy, is behind the murder, but we can't ask her since she's been gone a good many years. It seems like the only right thing to do it close the case and move on."

My mouth dropped open. "That's it? You're going to assume that my grandmother is behind Ripley's death with no investigation or evidence? What proof do you have?"

He shrugged. "I can't help it that all the players are dead. We don't always have a clear answer about what happened to a person when they died. In my fifty-five years of police service, I have come to terms with that and accept it as part of the job."

"That doesn't mean I have to accept it. You need to investigate. A man is dead and deserves justice."

He rubbed the back of his neck. "Really? Does he? He wasn't a good guy when he was alive. Your grandmother had her issues with him, and so did other people in the community. No one was crying or gnashing their teeth when he disappeared."

"I don't want my grandmother's reputation to be ruined. People will talk and assume the worst. Whatever you might think about my family, I can promise you that my grandmother didn't do this. To make a statement that she is guilty with no evidence whatsoever can be very damaging."

He scowled. Some of his glee at surprising me had seemed to have fallen away. "It's not like this will be talked about. No one had seen or heard from Ripley in decades. And what does it matter? You grandmother isn't here any longer."

I stiffened and had to close my eyes for a brief moment to keep myself from snapping at him. "It matters to me. It matters to my family. She's not here to defend herself, so I will defend her."

He glowered at me. "I'm telling you this is an open-and-shut case."

"You can't do that. You have no proof. You can't ruin my grandmother's reputation on a theory." I was so angry that I began to shake.

I knew our heated argument was chasing away potential buyers for my candles, soaps, and food items, but I didn't even care.

He eyed me. "Who said it was a theory? I have Emma Kay Bellamy's signed confession in my evidence room."

Chapter Twelve

I felt lightheaded. This couldn't be real. My grandmother would not confess to a murder because she would not commit murder. I knew this. I knew her. Until her death, she was the person I was closest to in the world. She raised me. She understood me. She encouraged me to go into true crime production. Why would she have done that if she had committed a decades-old crime? It just didn't make any sense.

"I want to see that letter," I said.

"Not a chance."

"Then I'll sue you to see it. If it truly was my grandmother's legal document, it now is mine as her descendent." I glared at him.

"Not going to happen. Just let it go, Shiloh. Your family has made enough problems for Cherry Glen over the years. Don't add to them. It seems that you all were a lot worse than we thought. A lot of people wanted James Ripley dead, but Emma Kay Bellamy was the only one with the nerve to do it."

"What do you mean? Who else wanted him dead? If you have more suspects for the crime, you have to talk to them. You can't close the case so quickly."

"Sure I can when I have a signed confession, and that's what I have." He set his ball cap on his head and tipped it at me before he walked away.

I wanted to run after him and demand that the letter be given to me, but I had let Chesney leave the booth. That meant that the only person who could mind the booth at the moment was me. The worst part was I didn't even know when Chesney was coming back.

On autopilot, I helped customers. I smiled at them and told them about everything that we had for sale. I was kind and charming, but on the inside, I was seething.

My grandmother wasn't a murderer, and even if she was—which she wasn't—she was way too smart to write a confession down and sign it. I had serious doubts this alleged document was even written in her hand. I had to see it. She had very distinctive penmanship, and I would be able to recognize it. I was certain Chief Randy could not.

Could Chief Randy be making this all up just to close the case, or was he just closing the case to upset me? It was likely that both reasons were in play.

Chesney came back to the booth out of breath. "I'm so sorry I was gone so long. Have you been busy?"

"It's been steady," I said.

Her eyes widened behind her glasses. "What's wrong?"

"Chief Randy was just here." I closed my eyes for a moment.

She wrinkled her nose. "That's a reason to put a frown on anyone's face. What did he want?"

I looked around to make sure that we didn't have any

customers coming our way. "They identified the bones as James Ripley's."

"Whoa. But that is what everyone expected from the start, right? His disappearance is the most notorious in Cherry Glen. I would say it would almost come as a relief."

"I wouldn't say it's a relief. I can't believe that he has been buried in that orchard all these years." Again, the memory of my grandmother telling me not to dig in the back corner of the orchard came to mind. Was that because she knew what was under the dirt? She must have known, right? But that didn't mean that she killed him. It didn't mean that she put him there, and I refused to believe it.

"Now the police can focus their investigation and speak to the people who might have known Ripley." Chesney frowned. "But it was a long time ago, like forty years. If he were alive, he would at least be in his eighties. It seems to me that anyone who really knew him would be old or also gone."

"That's exactly what Chief Randy was thinking."

"So then, how does he investigate the case?"

"He claims he already solved it."

She blinked at me. "How?"

"Apparently with a signed confession from my grandmother."

"No way."

I nodded. "That was exactly what I said. No way, and I'm going to do everything in my power to prove him wrong."

Chesney and I weren't able to continue our conversation, as business at the booth began to pick up. When there was a small lull in customers, Chesney shooed me away from the booth. "You gave me a break to deal with my stuff. You most definitely have your own issues to handle."

She couldn't have been more right about that. "Are you sure?" I asked. "Will you be okay if I run over to the theater to talk to Stacey?"

"Yes, yes, go."

I thanked her and clipped Huckleberry's leash onto his harness. I promised to only be gone for an hour or two. It wasn't until I walked way that I realized that I hadn't asked her what she had learned from Rhett about her sister. That would have to wait. I had to find out more about my grandmother's relationship with James Ripley.

I couldn't get out of there fast enough. I felt like I was suffocating in the church basement, and when Huckleberry and I walked out the church doors, I was surprised to find a thin layer of snow on the ground and even more snow falling from the sky in huge flakes.

I licked my lips. The very first snow of the season. It was always a special time. When I was a little girl, my grandmother would pull me outside for the first snow even if it was in the middle of the night. It didn't matter what time the snow came; she always knew and made me appreciate it.

On that day, it felt like a sign from my grandmother and a bit of encouragement. I couldn't understand why she had never told me what happened with James Ripley. Why did she hate him so much? And why weren't we even allowed to speak his name?

I knew that my father most likely would have the answer, and he and Stacey were both at the theater that afternoon, practicing for the winter performance of *A Christmas Carol*. The first performance was set to be the following weekend, and the show would run every weekend until Christmas. My father was beside himself because he was able to play his dream role of Jacob Marley. He claimed it was the role he was born to play.

Stacey hated it when anyone interrupted practice, but that was no matter. Both of them needed to know what was going on and what Chief Randy was up to.

Michigan Street Theater was a short walk from the church, and Huckleberry appeared to be as happy as I was to escape the church basement and stretch his legs. I hadn't thought to pack his snow boots, so every time he stepped into snow, he kicked his paw out in front of himself as if to flick the offending flakes from his toes.

You can take the pup out of California, but you can't take California out of the pup. He was a fussy little pug, and he didn't care for wet paws at any time. The cold didn't help either.

As we walked, I said, "I guess it's time to break out your boots and winter coat."

Huckleberry shivered at the very idea. He hated being cold, but he hated his boots and coat even more. He wasn't one of those dogs that tolerated being dressed up.

I marveled at the theater when it came into view. It was the largest building in Cherry Glen, even larger than the brewery down the street, and for most of my life it had been an abandoned eyesore.

The theater had fallen into disrepair before I was born

and was set for demolition until Stacey scrounged up the money to buy it and refurbish it.

I thought that I had spent a fortune on saving Bellamy Farm, but I couldn't even begin to guess what kind of money Stacey had spent to save the one-hundred-year-old theater. As far as I knew, the theater was successful. Every time there was any kind of performance, the place was packed, and going to Michigan Street Theater in Cherry Glen had become a major local pastime.

She not only used the theater for the musicals and plays that she produced herself, but she showed movies there and rented the space for events. The lobby was huge and a great gathering space for any kind of party. If I remembered correctly, the town officials had held their holiday party there last year.

Stacey had diversified to keep the theater doors open, and I couldn't fault her for that as I felt the same way when it came to the farm.

I walked up to the front double doors of the theater and grabbed the handle. I was fully expecting the doors to be locked.

To my relief, the door opened, and I went inside.

I walked past the ticket booth and into the lobby, which was quiet as a tomb. The only sound was the clicking of Huckleberry's toenails on the marble floor.

Before I headed into the theater proper, I peeked into the concessions area on the off chance Whit was there restocking snacks and candy. When I first met Chesney's sister, it had been in this very spot. She had just started working for

Stacey selling candy, and now, she was the stage manager. It was a lot for her to be proud of in a short amount of time, and it made me all the more concerned that she would risk her position by meeting with Stacey's boyfriend, Rhett. There had to be more to the story.

The ceiling above my head was blue and white like the spring sky, and there were elaborately carved floating cherubs in each corner of the ceiling. It was an over-the-top place from a bygone era.

The three sets of double doors leading into the theater were made of elaborately carved dark wood. I had to use both of my hands to pull one open. It didn't help that Huckleberry was trying to tug me in the opposite direction while I opened the door.

The stage was in the process of being changed into a nineteenth-century English village, and actors in tracksuits walked about the large room muttering lines to themselves.

An actor wearing jeans, a sweater, and a top hat stood in the middle of the stage, looking at the others, and sneered. "If I could work my will, every idiot who goes about with 'Merry Christmas' on his lips should be boiled with his own pudding and buried with a stake of holly through his heart. He should!"

"Cut!" Stacey called from the front row of seats. She stood up. "Murrey, I know that you have your lines down, but you need to say that with more feeling."

This surprised me; I thought he delivered the line well.

"Can we take a break?" one of the other cast members asked. "We've been practicing for two hours straight."

"Fine," Stacey said, making it clear that she didn't think that her actors deserved a break. "But while you are on a break, I want every one of you to be looking over your lines. This is the first time Michigan Street Theater has shown *A Christmas Carol*, and we already sold out on our first two weekends. We can't mess this up."

The actors fled the stage like my sheep when Diva and her chickens showed up. Now that I thought about it, Diva the hen and Stacey had a lot in common.

Connie Baskins stood up from the first row of seats and clapped. "I think that was lovely."

What was she doing here?

Huckleberry bolted forward, catching me off guard, and his leash slipped from my hand. He ran full tilt to the stage. He loved the theater because he was quite certain he was a star. I thought so too, but I still didn't want him to be running up on Stacey unannounced. That wouldn't be good for either one of us.

Huckleberry lifted his head and howled as he skidded into the middle of the stage. His audition had begun.

Chapter Thirteen

"What in the heavens?" Connie clutched at her glasses chain. "Is it the bear? Is the bear in the theater?"

"Does it look like a bear?" Stacey asked. "It's my cousin's pug."

As if he had been announced like he was receiving some type of award, Huckleberry galloped a few steps and leaned his head back to howl again.

I felt my cheeks flame red from embarrassment. Huckleberry was known to howl now and again, but recently it seemed to be becoming a habit. Not to mention I didn't know what role he could possibly be trying out for in *The Christmas Carol*. I didn't remember any howling dogs.

I hurried down the aisle. "Stacey, I'm so sorry. He was so excited to be here, he just took off without me.

Stacey arched on brow at me. "Why is he here?"

"I wanted to talk to you and Dad. It seems like you're on break. Do you have a minute?" I gave her my most winning smile, the one I had paid for, since I had all my teeth capped in California. It was expected in Hollywood.

The smile did not dazzle Stacey. I should have known better, as it had never had much success with her before.

"This had better be important," my cousin snapped. "I'm not ever on a break. I am the director and the producer. I don't have time for chitchat. I have to keep the show going at all times."

"Stacey." Dad hobbled onto the stage with his walker from the wings. "Everyone could use a break now and again. Even you."

Connie hurried up the stage steps and helped my father to the park bench in the middle of the stage. She sat down next to him and held his hand.

Stacey folded her arms. "Fine. What is it?"

I glanced at Connie, then back at Stacey. "I wanted to talk to you and Dad alone. It's family stuff."

"Anything that you have to say to me, you can say in front of Connie. She is practically family. We are engaged, after all." Dad smiled.

I had been trying to forget that.

To be honest, I didn't know why I was being a curmudgeon about my father's engagement. I suspected it had something to do with the fact that the farm was finally stable and making a little bit of money. I didn't want a new person to come in with differing opinions and upset the applecart—or cherry cart, in my case—and I had a feeling that Connie had a lot of opinions about just about everything.

"I didn't expect Connie to be here," I said.

Connie sniffed. "The government offices are closed today. Shouldn't I be able to support your father in the play when I can? I work so much that I don't have much time to spend with him. I can assure you the mayor would not be able to run Cherry Glen without me. I know more about the goings-on here than anyone else." She narrowed her eyes, and that last comment seemed to be pointed at me in some way. How, I didn't know. I wanted no part of Cherry Glen government and went to the municipal building as seldom as possible.

Connie wrapped her arms more tightly around my father's arm. She wasn't going anywhere.

"Okay," I said. "I know you all need to get back to practice, and I need to return to the church for the farmers market too. I left Chesney there alone."

"Then out with it," Stacey said as she made a note on her clipboard.

I licked my lips. "Chief Randy stopped by my booth today and told me the bones found in the orchard are those of James Ripley."

Stacey looked up from her clipboard, and Dad paled. Connie squeezed my father's arm even tighter. If she wasn't careful, she was going to give him a bruise.

Dad cleared his throat. "It was what we all expected, but it doesn't make it any easier to hear. Ripley was a crooked man. When he disappeared, I always thought he came to a bad end."

"But a bad end in the farm's cherry orchard?" Stacey asked. "No one expected that."

"No, that is a surprise," Dad said.

I noted that my father was staring down at his hands and not looking at anyone. Was that intentional? Was he just tired from shuffling around on his walker during play practice?

Connie nodded. "James Ripley was always a topic of conversation at the municipal building. He must have been in there once a month for one arrest after another. I, for one, was glad when he disappeared. He was always so rude when he was brought into the station. Had he been smaller, I would have taken him by the ear and cleaned his mouth out with soap."

"You're not the only one," Dad said. "My mother practically threw a party when he disappeared. She was so happy when he was gone. She hated James Ripley with a passion. Mother was loving and kind, but she was a woman not to be crossed. No one had ever crossed her as badly as Ripley."

I swallowed. "How did he cross her? No one has ever told me the story."

Dad pursed his lips together. "Now is not the time to speak of it."

"I think it's a very good time to speak about it, because Chief Randy decided that Grandma killed Ripley. In fact, he's so convinced, there will be no other investigation."

My father bolted out of his seat and would have fallen if Connie had not been there to catch him. "How dare he?" Dad sputtered. "He can't do that. It's outrageous."

"Sullivan, Sullivan, dear, sit down." Connie grabbed his arm. "You're going to give yourself a fit." She eased my father back onto the park bench.

"How can he do that?" Stacey asked. "Doesn't he have to at least try to find out what happened? How does he even know Ripley was murdered? How did he die?"

I wrinkled my nose. "He didn't tell me, and I didn't ask. I

was just in such a shock over what he said about Grandma. I'll ask Milan to find out. He knows the coroner. Maybe he can get some insight from him."

"I don't care where he gets this insight from," Stacey said. "Grandma hated Ripley. We all know that, but she would not kill someone."

Dad nodded. His face was dangerously red. "Chief Randy has been an annoyance to me for decades, but now he has gone too far. I plan to tell him just what I think about him too." Dad turned to Connie. "How can you work for a man like that?"

Connie dropped her hands from his arm. "I don't work for Chief Randy. I work for the town of Cherry Glen. I might help out with the police, answering calls and that sort of thing, but I do not report to Chief Randy and I never have. I report to the mayor."

"Even so…"

"Sullivan, how can you say something like that?" Connie asked. "I have worked for the town of Cherry Glen for over sixty years. I am very good at my job."

"Yes, I know." Dad reached out to her, but she stayed out of reach. His hand fell to the bench seat. "I'm sorry. I'm upset by this news. You have to understand what a shock this is to me."

She let out a breath. "I understand that, and I plan to talk to the chief and tell him just what I think of his decision. It's one thing to not try to solve the case because the trail is cold, but it is quite another to not investigate and blame someone with no evidence at all. It's even worse when that person can't defend herself."

No evidence at all. I knew that Chief Randy had evidence, or claimed he had evidence, in the signed confession. I had to see that piece of paper to know if it was truly written by my grandmother. Dad was right that Grandma Bellamy hated James Ripley, but that didn't mean that she hated him enough to kill.

I did not mention the confession. I thought it was best to hold on to that information until I knew more.

"What are you going to do about this, Shiloh?" Stacey asked.

I looked my cousin in the eye. "I think there is only one answer. I have no choice but to find the real killer to clear Grandma Bellamy's name."

Chapter Fourteen

Connie pursed her lips together. "That is a terrible idea. You shouldn't get involved in a police investigation."

"It's not like it's the first time," Stacey said. "Shiloh is an expert in poking her nose where it doesn't belong."

I bit my lip. If I hadn't poked my nose into where it didn't belong last summer, Stacey might be in prison now, as she had been wrongly accused of committing a crime. I stopped myself from saying it. Stacey would spin the story in such a way to blame me for the trouble she had found herself in. She was an expert at that.

I ignored both of them and said to my father, "If I'm going to find out what really happened, I need to know the real story about why Grandma hated Ripley. Everyone keeps dancing around the reason."

Stacey flipped her hair over her shoulder. "I'm surprised she didn't tell you herself. She told me." She cocked her head. "Maybe Grandma Bellamy and I were closer than the two of you were."

Leave it to Stacey to get in an unnecessary dig.

"She never told me," I said.

Dad looked down at his wrinkled hands on his lap. "I hate to even speak of it because it makes her case look worse, but I suppose this was Chief Randy's main reason to blame her."

"What was it?" I asked.

He looked up at me. "James Ripley killed my sister, Edna Lee, and Mom would tell anyone who listened that was exactly what happened."

My father's answer took my breath away. I didn't know what I had expected him to say, but it most certainly wasn't that.

My aunt died years before I was born, and I remembered my grandmother speaking of her fondly. She adored her daughter. She would do anything for her, just as she would for all the people she cared about.

I hadn't known that Edna Lee had been murdered.

"I thought she fell through the ice at Herchel Pond."

Dad nodded. "That's true, but Mother always thought Ripley was involved somehow."

"Why?"

"He was there and spotted running away from the pond by an ice fisherman. He claimed that he was out for a walk and didn't see a thing."

"Grandma Bellamy didn't believe him?"

"No." Dad shook his head.

"Was he questioned by the police?"

"I can answer that," Connie said. "He was, but Chief Randy had to let him go. There was no proof he had anything to do with it."

"How long was this before he disappeared?" I asked.

Dad cocked his head. "I can't remember exactly."

"Almost nine months to the day," Connie interjected.

We all stared at her. "I work in the municipal building, and Edna Lee's death and James Ripley's possible involvement were the main topics of conversation that year. They became even more so when Ripley went missing."

"Did he push her in?" I asked. "Why did Grandma Bellamy think he was responsible?"

"Don't know," Dad said. "But she was convinced."

"Didn't she ever talk about it?" I asked.

"Not to me," Dad said.

"Did you ask?"

"My mother and I didn't speak about such things."

I turned to Stacey. "But she told you?" I couldn't keep the doubt out of my voice.

Stacey had a smug smile on her face. "She did because I reminded her of her daughter. She wanted to be an actress just like I did."

I raised my brow and realized how little I knew about my aunt. Was that my fault for not asking the questions when I was a child?

"Edna Lee always wanted to go to Broadway," Stacey said. "And when I told Grandma Bellamy that I had the same dream, she told me to go. She said Edna Lee never went, and she blamed herself for that."

The other actors walked back on the stage. They might not be one hundred percent refreshed, but they did appear to be less stressed than they had been when they stumbled off a few minutes ago.

"Places, people. Connie, Shiloh, I need you off the stage," Stacey said.

I scooped up Huckleberry and tucked him under my arm. Connie helped my father back onto his mark and then made her way down the stairs. The whole time, she kept looking over her shoulder as if to make sure that he was okay. She really did care for him.

Before I went down the steps, I asked Stacey, "Is Whit here?"

She shook her head. "Whit took the day off. I can't say I was happy about it since we have so much to do, but since she hadn't asked for a day off in over a year, I let her have it."

"Did she tell you why?"

"No, and I didn't ask." Stacey clapped her hands. "Enough of this murder talk. The stage waits for no one, and we have to get back to work. Shiloh, get off my stage."

I sighed. It seemed the conversation I wanted to have with Whit about Rhett wasn't going to happen today. Perhaps that was for the best. It might not be the conversation to have with Stacey in such close proximity.

I started to walk down the center aisle to the exit. I heard footsteps behind me.

"You're leaving, Connie?" Dad shouted from the stage.

"I should go home and start that roast that I promised you, Sullivan," Connie said.

Dad smiled at her. "It's been such a long time since anyone has cooked for me."

That wasn't true. I cooked for my father all the time. He just hated my low-calorie organic recipes. Connie's roast was more up his alley. No wonder he wanted to marry her if she was going to cook food like that for him on a Saturday night.

I held the theater door open for Connie.

She smiled at me. "Thank you kindly, Shiloh. I wanted to speak to you for a moment if you don't mind."

I didn't like the sound of that. I let the theater door close and set Huckleberry on the plush red carpet at our feet, wrapping his leash around my hand two times. He wasn't getting away from me this time.

"What about?" I asked.

"I know it must be odd for you to see your father in a serious relationship, and I just want to tell you that you have nothing to worry about. I have every intention of taking care of your father in his twilight years."

I frowned. "That is a lot to take on. Why would you want to do that?"

"There is only one reason that would make sense for me to do this, and that it is because I love him. Sullivan is such a special man. I feel so lucky that he cares for me."

She sounded sincere, but in the back of my brain I still had doubts, and I couldn't quite pinpoint why. My dad certainly deserved to have someone who loved him as much as Connie claimed to.

"I am happy to hear that," I said.

"Good. Good." She reached out and grabbed my hand. "I'm glad. You are Sullivan's only child, so your opinion matters to him."

I almost laughed, but I was able to control myself. My

opinion had never mattered to my father; I doubted that would change for his romantic relationship.

"Thank you for that," I said. "I need to get back the market."

I turned to go, but she still had my hand. She squeezed it tightly in both of hers. "Stay out of the James Ripley stuff. You'll just make life harder for Quinn if you don't."

"How?" I asked.

"I'm sure he will tell you if you are willing to listen." She walked away with her chin up and the strap of her purse high on her shoulder.

Chapter Fifteen

I felt like I had been away from the Farmers Market and Artisan Fair for hours, but when I got back, I realized only an hour had passed. Verbally sparring with Stacey always exhausted me, and now I had Connie to contend with too.

I started down the long aisle to Bellamy Farm's table with my eyes out for Doreen Killian. I knew she'd have a thing or two to say if she saw I had left the church.

"Shiloh? It is Shiloh, right?" a man said.

I looked around and spotted Rhett sitting at a table lined with paperback books. All the covers had his name on it.

"Oh, hi," I said. "I heard you were here today." I stopped in front of his table. "These are all your books?"

He nodded. "I'm not one to talk about my work much, but I do have several books out." It looked like a lot more than several to me. The covers were dark and foreboding.

"What do you write?"

"Strictly true crime."

That explained the covers. "That takes a lot of research."

He smiled. "I understand that you would know, as you worked in the genre."

"For television," I said.

"Still, I'm sure there were some cases you were attached to. It seems that your professional background has helped you in Cherry Glen with all the murders you have solved."

I raised my brow. It was very possible Stacey would have told him all of this about me. He was her boyfriend. But then again, I never got the impression that Stacey thought of me much at all, even when I was right in front of her. It was unlikely that she had spoken about me on their date nights.

"I imagine," he went on, "that you will be looking into the death of James Ripley. It was quite advantageous for me that I was there the day the bones were discovered. I never thought I would get that lucky."

"Why is that lucky?" I asked.

He smiled. "Because I write true crime. It's good to see the police in action whenever I can."

I wrinkled my brow. I didn't believe that was the whole story. "And where does Whit fall into all of this?"

"Whit?" he asked, as if he had never heard the name.

"Stacey's stage manager."

"I don't have an answer for that."

"You were spotted with her at Jessa's Place a few times over the last few weeks."

He laughed. "The rumors are true that a small town is downright nosey. I know of the young girl you mean." He waved his hand as if it were nothing at all to worry about. "As you said, she works for Stacey, which is why I was seen with her." He leaned over his table. "Tell me what people are saying. Is it some kind of scandal?" His eyes danced with amusement.

"I need to get back to my own table. Good luck selling your books," I said.

He sat back in his seat with a knowing smile. "They have done very well here. Crime always pays."

I walked away from his table with the knowledge that if I really wanted to know what was going on between Whit and Rhett, I was going to have to get that answer from Whit herself.

Chapter Sixteen

It was after five o'clock when I got back to the farm that night, and it was already dark. Chesney left at three-thirty so she could get back to the farm and perform all the nightly chores, which this time of year mostly consisted of putting the sheep back in the barn, the chickens in the coop, and feeding all the animals on either side of the farm. Chesney was a pro at it all, and she'd have all the tasks completed within an hour's time.

Instead of going straight to my little cabin in the woods when I got home, I went to my father's farmhouse. I found Dad sitting at the kitchen table with the pieces of a Civil War pistol strewn out in front of him. He was cleaning every piece before he put the firearm back together. Once a year when the weather turned cold, he polished every piece in his collection. He was meticulous about it; it took him months.

When I lived with my father for the first few months after I moved back, the collection had been a bone of contention between us. He was up at all hours of the night researching pieces and looking online for new ones. It took up all of his time, not to mention his money. It always had for as long as

I remembered. The collection that was so important to my father represented something painful for me. It was a constant reminder that he cared more about old things than he did his own daughter. He had his mother raise me because my mother died when I was young. He was so crushed by my mother's death, he poured all of his energy into the collection. He ignored me and he ignored the farm, which led Bellamy Farm into disrepair and crushing debt. The fact that in two years I had been able to bring the farm back from the brink of foreclosure was the greatest accomplishment of my life.

My regret was I had never been able to reach my father like Stacey had. Through the theater, she had been able to pull him out of his shell and away from the collection. I needed to thank her for that. I had never properly thanked her for taking such good care of him all those years I was away.

Dad wore magnifying eyeglasses on the tip of his nose. "Shiloh, I didn't expect you to stop by after seeing you at the theater. Seeing me once a day seems to be your limit."

"Dad, that's not true."

He used a cotton swab to clean out the barrel of the revolver. "You stop by in the morning when you let the sheep out most days, and that's the last time I see you."

"I've been busy." I hated how defensive I sounded.

"I'm busy too, Shiloh. Don't I look busy now? And then I have the play too, and a wedding to plan. You are not the only one with many tasks in front of you."

I bit the inside of my lip to keep myself from saying

anything that I might not be able to take back. I told myself that I had made peace with my father and his collection a long time ago, even if that didn't seem to be the truth at times.

"Where's my boy?" Dad asked.

On cue, Huckleberry wandered into the room and went straight for my father.

Dad leaned down to scratch the dog between the ears and praise him for being the smartest pug. I knew Huckleberry was bright, but I wouldn't call him the smartest of all pugs. He had his goofy pug moments like every other pug did.

He shook his head and removed his glasses. With slow, measured movements, he folded the arms of the glasses and placed them in his eyeglass case. Dad never did anything too quickly. That was another thing that we didn't have in common. I moved fast and tended to think of the repercussions later. I supposed there were still some lessons that I could learn from him.

Maybe my way wasn't the best way to do it, but Dad's hesitation wasn't great either. There were times when I thought that was how he lost control of the farm's finances in the first place. When he didn't know what to do, he shoved all his financial problems to the back of his mind and concentrated on his collection.

I pulled out the chair across the table from him and was stunned to find a crocheted pillow on the seat. I held up the pillow. "Where did this come from?"

Dad smiled. "Connie. She made one for every chair at the table. I was telling her how sore I get from sitting for hours working on my collection. The next time I saw her she had made these pillows for me."

The pillow was pink. It wasn't the first color I associated with my father. In fact, the only pink thing in all the farmhouse was my own bedroom, which stood like a time capsule on the second floor.

I flipped the pillow over, and there was a white tag from a store on the back of it. She said she made it? Didn't look like it to me. Why would she lie to my father about that, and what else did she lie to him about?

"How long have you and Connie been spending time together?"

He looked into the barrel of the gun and then up at me. "You mean *dating*. You want to know how long we have been dating."

"Sure," I said. For some reason I could not bring myself to say the word. On his next birthday, my father would be eighty. It was hard for me to imagine that after all this time he finally decided to date again, especially someone he had tried for so long to avoid.

And what was Connie thinking? She had to be at least fifteen years younger than my father. She was in good health too, and my dad had more medical issues than I could count. What did she see in him?

I shook the thoughts from my head. Connie Baskins was a perfectly nice woman. If my father wanted to date her and she wanted to date him, it wasn't my place to say a word about it.

I sat in the chair across from him at the kitchen table.

There was velvet cloth with a line of freshly polished Civil War–era knives in front of me. I kept my hands on my lap for fear of cutting myself. My father's romantic relationship wasn't the reason I was there. I had much bigger problems… like my late grandmother being accused of murder.

"Why did Grandma Bellamy blame James Ripley for Edna Lee's death?"

Dad picked up his glasses case again, removed his magnifying reading glasses from the case, and put them on the tip of his nose. "I told you he was there and seen running away from the scene."

"There has to be more to it than that," I said.

"It is in the past, and everyone involved is long gone. Mother didn't want to talk to you about it, and I don't know if I should talk about it now."

"Why?" I asked.

He sighed. "She had her reasons."

"I need to know," I said in a pleading voice. "Chief Randy blames Grandma Bellamy for Ripley's death. I need to know how to clear her name."

Dad snapped the barrel into the revolver he was polishing and set the gun on a piece of velvet next to the half dozen others that he had already cleaned. "I never cared much for Chief Randy," he said with a sniff. "He was good for nothing as a young man, and he's good for nothing now. He fell into the job of police chief in this town because no one else wanted it. I've never said how I feel about him for Quinn and Hazel's sakes. He might seem lazy now, but when Ripley disappeared, he was relentless with your grandmother. He thought then, just like he does now, that she was behind it. He was convinced that Ripley was dead too. It's strange how the world works. All these years later, he was proven right." Dad picked up a bayonet that needed to be polished. He set it on the piece of muslin in front of him, put on his rubber gloves, and dipped his cotton cloth into a small container of polish.

"Proven right? You think Grandma Bellamy killed him?" I asked.

"No, but maybe Connie is right and none of it matters all these years later. I don't want to go backward."

"That's an odd thing for a person who loves history as much as you do to say."

He looked down at the revolver in his hand. "Maybe it is."

"Then just tell me about your sister."

He began polishing again. "I can try."

Chapter Seventeen

Edna Lee was Mother's favorite, and my brother and I knew that. She was fifteen years younger than me. Mother always called her her surprise baby. She was the star of the family and was always putting on performances and singing and dancing."

"How old was she when she died?" I asked.

"I was almost forty, so she must have been twenty-three or twenty-four."

I might not have been born yet when my aunt passed away, but Stacey would have been close to ten years old when Edna Lee drowned. She would remember our aunt.

"Stacey said that she wanted to go to Broadway," I said.

He nodded. "She did. It was all she ever wanted."

"Why didn't she do it?" I asked.

"Our parents were against it. Back then, I think it was more difficult to defy your parents than it is now. People held family and loyalty in higher esteem when I was a young man."

I wasn't certain that was true, but I wasn't going to argue with my father about it, especially when he was finally opening up to me about his sister.

"What did she do instead?"

"I'm surprised Jessa has never mentioned it to you, but she was a waitress at Jessa's Place. Jessa's father was running the diner at the time, and Jessa and Edna Lee worked together there. They were like two peas in a pod."

I blinked. Even though she was quite a bit older than me, I considered Jessa to be one of my best friends in town. Why had she never told me that she and my aunt were close? I thought it would have come up in the last year or two I had been home.

"Mother always thought Edna Lee met Ripley at the diner. My mother found out that the two of them were seeing each other, and she told Edna Lee to break it off. Ripley had a horrible reputation in town for getting into trouble. He was a handsome man, and he had a long string of broken hearts in his wake."

"And did Edna Lee break it off?"

"I don't know. I did my very best to stay out of my sister's drama. The less questions that I asked about it, the less I had to hear about it."

"How long after Grandma Bellamy asked her to break it off did Edna Lee fall through the ice?" I asked.

Dad shook his head. "I can't remember that sort of thing."

"What was she doing at Herchel Pond that day?" I asked.

He looked up at me. "Now, how would I know that?"

I frowned. Edna Lee had to have gone to the pond for a reason. It wasn't on the way to get anywhere else. Herchel Pond was right outside of town and one of many smaller bodies of water that led the way to Torch Lake in Antrim County, where Milan was sheriff, and eventually to Grand Traverse Bay and Lake Michigan.

In any other state, the pond would have been considered a lake in its own right, but in Western Michigan, its twenty-foot depth and quarter-mile length wasn't at all impressive.

"Were they ice skating?" I asked.

Herchel Pond was a popular ice-skating location, especially for teenagers. I had gone there a few times growing up even though I don't ice skate. I never felt confident enough with my balance to attempt it. When we went, I would sit on the snowbank with my girlfriends and watch Logan, Quinn, and the other boys from school play ice hockey.

I never lasted very long before I was bored and cold, and would leave while the other girlfriends would stay until the bitter end with their boyfriends. Something that I liked most about Logan was he wasn't offended when I left. He knew that I wasn't interested in sports, and he didn't care. He liked me for me.

Since the terrible accident that took Logan's life, Milan was the first man who had that same attitude about me. It was refreshing and familiar all at the same time.

Dad shook his head. "I don't know why they were there, but I suppose ice skating was as good a guess as any. It would have been a bad time to try it. It was the end of March. Temperatures were getting warmer, and breakup was happening in all of the lakes and ponds."

I nodded. Breakup was when, after the long winter, the ice began to break and thaw. It was the most dangerous time to be on the ice. I had to believe that Edna Lee would have known that as a Michigan native.

"All I know is Ripley was out on the ice with Edna Lee that

day. She fell through the ice, and instead of helping her, he left. He didn't tell anyone what happened, but someone saw him running away from the pond. Hours later, my mother was supposed to meet Edna Lee in town at the general store. When Edna Lee didn't show up, my mother went looking for her. She knew that Edna Lee was going to Herchel Pond. By the time my mother reached the pond, Edna Lee was dead."

I shivered. "What did Grandma say about that day?"

"I never asked." Dad wouldn't meet my eyes. "Maybe I should have, but I knew it pained her to talk about it. Your grandmother wanted to forget about that terrible time in her life. If she could never speak of it again, she would. The only reminder was Ripley. He never left town. Every time Mother saw him, it would set her off in a black mood. The day he disappeared was the first time I had ever seen her genuinely happy since my sister died."

I frowned. I was born after Ripley disappeared, so the only grandmother that I remembered or that I had known was the practical yet happy one. The reputation of my family and my grandmother's memory was on the line.

Dad worked on cleaning another bayonet next. He hummed under his breath.

"What do you think about all this?"

He looked up at me like he had forgotten I was there. "What do you mean?"

"What do you think about Chief Randy dropping the case and using Grandma as a scapegoat?"

"I don't like it, but I don't know what can be done about it. We will have to leave it be."

"Leave it be? Don't you want to clear Grandma Bellamy's name? Everyone in town will assume that she is a killer. We don't even know how James was murdered."

"Weren't you going to ask your boyfriend about that?"

I pressed my lips together. "Yes, but I haven't spoken with him yet. What if Ripley died of natural causes? We need more information." My voice shook.

Dad went back to polishing his bayonet. "Do you think he buried himself in the orchard?"

"No, but the cause of death should at least be settled. There are steps that have to be taken in any investigation."

"You know I don't like Chief Randy either, but he has to have a very good reason not to investigate," Dad said.

Again, I stopped myself from telling my father about the signed confession that Chief Randy claimed he had from my grandmother. I couldn't bring myself to believe that Chief Randy was outright lying about the confession, but I also couldn't imagine where the confession had come from.

Had it been discovered with the bones? If so, how? Wouldn't a piece of paper have decomposed in forty years or at least be illegible? It just didn't make any sense. If Chief Randy had had the confession the whole time, why was Ripley's disappearance still considered unsolved?

At the same time, it wasn't unheard of for my grandmother to leave hidden messages to be discovered later. She had left a note for me after she died, leading me to her collection of stocks that had allowed me to save the farm. My grandmother had had her secrets. I knew that.

"There is always the possibility that Chief Randy is just

doing this to get back at you. He's not happy with how close you have become with Quinn and Hazel."

"I am just friends with them. Hazel is like a little sister or niece to me. That's all it is. Quinn and I have known each other all our lives. We have Logan in common; his parents know that."

Dad set the bayonet down by the other pieces on the table and wiped his hands on a cloth. "Quinn cares about you. I can see it. His parents can see it. Maybe they worry you will see it too." He stretched his arms. "That is enough polishing for the night. It's time for my nightcap and to go to bed."

It was just six in the evening.

"I can't let Chief Randy get away with this," I said. "I can't stand the idea of people having the wrong impression of Grandma Bellamy. She was a pillar in this community for so long. Her reputation will be tarnished by the police chief's laziness."

He looked me directly in the eye. "Your grandmother is dead, Shiloh. It makes no difference to her now. If you go down this path, I am telling you that you will find trouble and bring trouble onto the farm. Do you think your grandmother would want you to do that?" He took hold of the arms of his walker and slowly pushed himself to his feet. When he was standing, he paused for a moment to gather his bearings. "My advice is to just let it go."

I bit the inside of my lip. I could see his point, but I didn't agree. Grandma Bellamy deserved better than that, and James Ripley, regardless of his involvement in Edna Lee's death, deserved better than that too. Shouldn't justice be served?

I most certainly wasn't going to just let this go. Not by a long shot.

Chapter Eighteen

That night, Milan and I had plans to meet for dinner in Traverse City. Part of me didn't want to go. I would have much rather snuggled under the covers in my bed in my little cottage and hide. Dad had gone to bed at six, and that didn't seem like a bad idea at all. It was cold and dark outside. Honestly, the early bedtime was appealing.

Despite my urge to be a hermit, I made myself go because there weren't many nights that Milan was off duty and I was also free. I didn't want to disappoint him. Besides, I had a particularly important favor to ask of him.

Downtown Traverse City was buzzing with holiday shoppers, and Christmas lights shone all around the small city. The main shopping district, with its bright twinkling lights, cheerful holiday banners, and dusting of snow, made the charming brick-lined streets appear storybook perfect. The small city just on the edge of Lake Michigan looked like it was the set for a Christmas romantic comedy, but one that was so perfect no one would actually believe the place existed.

I had always believed that Traverse City was a hidden

gem in the Midwest. Chicago, Detroit, and Milwaukee got all the attention from investors and people who made the lists of best places, but Traverse City had culture and events too, and it should not be forgotten that it was the home of the National Cherry Festival, the largest of its kind in the United States. I was so grateful that Bellamy Farm had been permitted to have a booth there last summer. It catapulted our business to the next level and attracted more attention than we had ever had before.

I parked in the lot across from the city park on the shores of Grand Traverse Bay and walked up the hill to the main shopping district. I knew that Milan was already in town because he had texted me not that long ago.

I reached the top of the hill to find Milan waiting for me. His face broke into a wide smile when he saw me. Over the last several months, he had grown a beard, and it gave him a distinguished look that complimented his glasses. Walking down the brick-covered streets of Traverse City, he looked more like a college professor from the local university than a country sheriff.

"You should have texted me when you arrived," Milan said. "I would have walked down and met you."

I smiled. "That's sweet of you, but there is no reason for both of us to trek up the hill, and the little walk gave me time to gather my thoughts."

He raised his brow. "Oh, that sounds dangerous. Should I be concerned?"

"It has nothing to do with us, but everything to do with my family. I learned a lot today, and I'm still processing it all."

I gave him a hug. "I am so glad to see you. It's been a very long day."

He wrapped his arm around my shoulder. "How was the farmers market?"

"Interesting."

"You're talking in riddles again."

I looked up at him. "It's a long story. I thought it would be better if I started over dinner."

"Sounds serious."

"I'm surprised you're not in uniform," I said, changing the subject. "You're not on call?"

"I'm always on call. I'm just not the first one in line tonight. I don't expect to hear from any of my deputies tonight unless things really go south. Our main concern this time of year is ice anglers who are out on the lakes before they should be." He shook his head. "It seems like that happens every year. They get so eager to fish and set up their shanties, they just can't wait for the lake to freeze over well enough. I have so many extra deputies out by the lakes in the county."

I shivered. My father had entered an ice-fishing contest last winter that had ended with my discovery of a dead body. I had no interest in going on the ice for a very long time, but I might not be able to avoid that if I really wanted to get to the truth of Edna Lee's death. I thought if I understood how and why Edna Lee died, I might also be able to understand James Ripley's death too.

"There's a new Cajun restaurant that I want to try. From what I have heard, the fare is as good as you can find in New Orleans," Milan said.

"Sounds perfect."

The restaurant was bright and festive. Jazz music played in the background, and the interior looked like it was decorated for Mardi Gras. The place was packed—people in Traverse City loved trying something new. Milan and I opted to sit at one of the high-top tables in the bar.

The server took our drink orders, and Milan looked around. "This isn't exactly how the restaurants in New Orleans look. The owner leaned into how he thought people in Michigan imagine the Big Easy looks."

"You've been to New Orleans?" I asked.

"Twice. It's one of my favorite cities in the world. It's so unique, and you can walk just about anywhere. You would love it. The food is the best. I'm sure this meal will be good, but it will be hard pressed to be as good as you can find way down south."

This was something new I was learning about Milan. "Do you travel a lot?"

"I used to more when I was younger, but yes, I try to get away at least twice a year, even if it's just to Canada or a neighboring state. Now that I'm sheriff, it's not as easy to leave as it once was, but I am able to make it work, even if it's just a few days. I think that it's essential to reset my mind. You must have traveled a lot when you lived in LA."

I shook my head. "I worked all the time. I only traveled to come back to Michigan to check on Dad, or for work. The higher up in the production company I got, the less I would have to go on the shoots. I could stay home while the younger producers went out in the field. There were times I missed the excitement of being in the field or on location."

"I just would have thought you would have been all over the world living in LA."

I shook my head. "The more projects I had on my plate, the more money I would make and be able to send back home to Dad and the farm. I knew he needed help. Until I decided to come back to Michigan for good, I didn't know how far into debt he really was."

The waiter appeared with our drinks and took our food orders. It was a cold night, and we both opted for gumbo. The waiter assured us it was just as good as we would find on Queen Street in New Orleans. Milan made a skeptical face.

When the waiter left, Milan reached across the table. "We'll have to plan a trip to make up for lost time. I think a visit to the Big Easy would be a good place to start. February would be a nice time to go."

"Do you really think you could leave for a vacation?"

"Everyone is entitled to time off, even a sheriff."

"I would say that you deserve it more than most." I blinked away unexpected tears.

"What's wrong?" he asked.

I didn't meet his eyes. "I haven't made plans like this with someone I was seeing for a very long time."

His brow furrowed in concern. "Is that bad?"

I waved away his concern. "No, no, not at all. It's wonderful. Just noteworthy, I guess."

"We could go somewhere you like more."

I shook my head, reached across the table, and touched

his hand. "No, New Orleans is perfect. I have always wanted to see it, and I truly can't imagine going with anyone else."

"Then it's a plan."

I smiled. "It's a plan."

I was so happy just having a nice meal and chatting with Milan about the future that I almost hated to bring up murder, but I knew it had to be said.

"Is there any way you can get the autopsy report for James Ripley?" I asked.

He paused with a look of regret on his face.

I nodded. "I don't know if an autopsy was performed, but I would like to know the findings."

"The discovery was only bones and a few scraps of cloth, so it wouldn't be a traditional autopsy. There's nothing to open up."

I grimaced at the image that came to mind. I was grateful our food hadn't come out yet.

"But the bones would be examined," he said. "A forensic anthropologist would be asked to look at them. There is just one who works with the counties in this region of Michigan; I could give him a call. Should I ask why you're making the request?"

"I need to know the cause of death." I went on to tell him what Chief Randy had told me when he stopped by my table at the church.

"I wish I could say that I was surprised Chief Randy doesn't want to bother with this case, but I'm not," Milan said. "I'll talk to the anthropologist." He removed his phone from his pocket and began scrolling through his contacts.

"You're going to call him now?" I asked.

"Sure. Why not? You want to know how Ripley died, don't you?"

"I do. Of course I do, but it's Saturday night on a holiday weekend. Do you really think he will answer?"

He gave me a look. "People in my line of work always answer."

He held the phone to his ear. "Cuppler, it's Penbrook. No, I don't have a new case you need to look at. I'm calling about the Ripley case." There was a pause. "I know that, but I was the first officer on the scene and am following up. What's the cause of death?"

Milan was silent for a little while, and I twisted my cloth napkin in my lap. Whatever the forensic anthropologist was telling Milan would have a major impact on my grandmother's memory. Maybe Dad was right, and I should let it go. I couldn't do that though, because I knew if roles were reversed, my grandmother would stop at nothing to prove my innocence.

"Thank you. That's all I needed to know. Do me a favor and don't mention my call to Randy Killian." He laughed. "I owe you one."

He ended the call and set his phone on the table. He sipped his drink. I felt like I was watching him move underwater.

"And? What did he say?" I asked.

He set the glass down and looked around the bar area, as if to check that no one was listening to our conversation. "The coroner believes James Ripley was murdered just like the police chief told you."

"But how? Chief Randy never told me how." I was on the edge of my seat, and I had twisted the cloth napkin into a tiny ball.

"He was shot." He paused. "In the chest. The bullet was recovered from his spine."

I gasped.

Chapter Nineteen

Our gumbo arrived, and my stomach turned as I looked into the bowl. I didn't know what I had expected him to say was the cause of death, but a gunshot wound had never crossed my mind.

Milan thanked the server and waited until he left before he spoke again. "Did you see the bullet at the scene?"

"No, I didn't see any of the bones other than the one Huckleberry showed me. Was he shot in the orchard?"

"Not necessarily." Milan blew on his gumbo. "He could have been shot anywhere and the body moved to that spot to be buried."

"This makes it even less likely my grandmother was the one who killed him. She was a strong woman, but she couldn't move and bury a full-grown man all by herself. I don't even know if I would have the strength to do that."

"Or the devil's advocate could say that she had help."

"Help from who? I can't think of anyone in Cherry Glen who would agree to help my grandmother bury a body in the orchard, and if they did, it's even harder for me to believe that this secret has been kept all these years."

"What about your father?"

"My disabled father?"

"Was he disabled forty years ago?" Milan asked.

I shook my head. Yes, my father would have been in much better health all those years ago, but that didn't change the fact that I didn't believe he or my grandmother had anything to do with Ripley's death.

"Okay, let's just say that someone shot Ripley and buried him in your family's orchard with the hope of framing your grandmother or another member of the family. What motivation would they have to do that? Why would they bury him there?"

"Because my grandmother hated James Ripley." I went on to tell him about Edna Lee's death.

He nodded. "That fits with what Cuppler said. Cuppler told me that Chief Randy made up his mind who was behind this almost right away."

"He told Cuppler it was my grandmother?" I shivered at the very idea.

The more people who knew Chief Randy's suspicions, the less I would be able to save my grandmother's reputation.

He nodded. "You know Chief Randy doesn't keep his suspicions to himself."

The server came back to the table and noticed that I hadn't touched my food. "Miss, is there something wrong with your gumbo? Can I get you something else?"

"No, I'm just not very hungry," I said, wondering how I could possibly eat with so much going on. "Can I have a to-go box?"

"Of course." He disappeared from the table.

"What did your father say about all this?"

"That I should drop it. He said Grandma Bellamy is dead, and what people think about her now doesn't really matter."

Milan nodded. "He's not wrong about that, but I won't tell you to drop it, because I know you won't, nor would I expect you to."

Milan was speaking from experience.

"I would much rather that you tell me what you are up to," he said. "It's the best way for me to protect you."

"Protect me from what?" I asked.

"If you're right and your grandmother is innocent of this crime, the killer might very well still be alive. They've been able to keep this secret for forty years. They won't want that to change."

When Milan and I left the restaurant, he said, "Let's walk along the lakeshore. I'm a little reluctant to go home. I want to take advantage of as much time with you as I can. I'm a little surprised I haven't gotten a call yet, but I'm not going to question it, even if it feels like it's the quiet before the storm."

"That's a glass-half-empty view of things," I said.

"Just experience talking."

The edge of the lake was frozen, and the waves crashing against the ice were angry, like they were lamenting the fact that they couldn't quite make it to the shore. An osprey perched high on the bare tree, looking out into the water. He seemed to sneer at the waves as if their roughness was disrupting the view of the fish just below.

Milan took my hand in his as we walked, and it felt right.

For the first time that day, I wasn't thinking about Ripley, my grandmother, or the bones in the orchard.

Milan interrupted that peacefulness when he asked, "Do you want to tell me about your conversation with Quinn?"

"Quinn?" I blinked at him. I had completely forgotten about that uncomfortable situation. When your beloved grandmother is accused of murder, everything else tends to fly out of your mind.

"Yes, at Thanksgiving, right before you discovered the bones."

"I remember," I said and searched for the right words to say. Tensions between Milan and Quinn were already high, but I would like them to get along. Milan was my boyfriend and Quinn was an old friend with a young daughter I was close to. I would be devastated if I didn't get to spend time with Hazel any longer because of this entanglement.

At the same time, I didn't want Milan to think I was keeping anything from him. Honesty really was the best policy.

"He told me that he had feelings for me. It seemed to be something he had to get off his chest, but I told him I was with you now. That was the end of it."

"I expected it was something like that." He kicked at a rock along that path, and it went skittering into the grass.

I squeezed his arm. "You don't have anything to worry about. I'm happy with you."

He smiled down at me. "And not just because I can get you autopsy reports?"

"No, but that's a bonus."

We walked a few feet.

"I actually have another report I would like to see too," I said.

"Oh boy. Is your grandmother being blamed for another murder?"

"No," I said. "I want to see Edna Lee's autopsy report or find out if she even had one."

He arched his brow. "A forty-year-old autopsy report? That might be a lot more difficult to scare up, but I'll try."

I nodded and stared out onto the lake. "My grandmother was a good woman. She wouldn't have committed murder, but she was relentless too. If Ripley hung around Cherry Glen for all those months after her daughter died, she would have gone out of her way to make his life difficult. That's why it is so easy to blame her for Ripley's death. She would have told everyone who would listen how she felt about him. I would like to know more about Edna Lee's death and find out why my grandmother blamed Ripley for it. If she really thought he was guilty, she wouldn't give up until he was held accountable."

He cocked his head to the side. "Sounds like someone I know. You can be pretty relentless yourself."

"I'll take that as a compliment."

"It can be half the time."

I lightly shoved him. "Hey."

He chuckled, then took my hand in his again and resumed walking.

"In the meantime, I'm going to do some research of my own. Winter is almost here. I have the time," I said.

He shook his head. "I don't like the sound of that at all."

I made a face.

"I want you to be careful. Just because it's a cold case doesn't mean it's not a dangerous case. We don't know who is behind this."

His phone buzzed in his pocket, and he looked at the screen. "Looks like I have to cut our walk short."

"You have to go?" I said.

"I'm sorry. An ice fisherman fell into the lake." He shook his head. "They think if they do it at night, they won't get caught putting up their shanty, but at the same time that's when the most accidents can happen."

"I hope the fisherman is okay," I said.

"They already got him out, but they need backup. He's being belligerent and won't go to the hospital. We have to send him when there are any signs of hypothermia. It's a good thing that we drove here separately since I have to head to Torch Lake." He shook his head. "I wish I was going back to the farm with you."

"I think we'll have to drive separately to places for the rest of our lives." I looked up at him. "But it is worth it to be with you."

He smiled and kissed my cheek.

Chapter Twenty

The next day, as soon as I finished my chores, I headed into town. It was Sunday morning, and most of the businesses on Michigan Street wouldn't open until afternoon, if they opened all. Cherry Glen was still very much a small town that stayed closed during church hours.

One establishment that was always open on Sunday mornings was Jessa's Place.

I parked my pickup in the small lot to the left of the diner along with at least a dozen more trucks just like it. Cherry Glen was a farm town through and through.

I climbed out of the cabin and clapped my hands to wake up Huckleberry, who had taken a little snooze in the passenger seat. He opened one eye and lifted his nose in the air. He could smell the scent of bacon coming from the diner.

He jumped up on the seat and leaped out of the truck.

I grabbed him before he could dash across the gravel parking lot. "Not so fast!" I clipped the leash onto his harness. "I know you are looking forward to whatever fatty food Jessa plans to sneak to you, but you can't run around loose and risk getting hit by a car."

He looked up at me with those soulful brown eyes and sighed.

He tugged on the leash to lead me into the diner. The bell over the door rang when we went inside, and Huckleberry immediately went to his little spot by the revolving pie display to the left of the door. I unclipped his leash and tucked it in my pocket as he sweetly folded his paws in front of him and waited for his treats.

Jessa carried a full tray of pancakes, eggs, and sausage by us as she laughed. "We have the little pooch well trained. Let me drop this off, and I'll meet you at the counter in the back."

Huckleberry whimpered.

Jessa chuckled. "I didn't forget about you, you silly pug. I have cheese and bacon coming up."

I walked to the back of the diner, passing eight men at a table. They wore camouflage, but they weren't hunters; instead of shotguns, they were holding cameras with giant lenses. I wondered if they were birders. I had run into my fair share of intense birders in Cherry Glen.

I took my usual seat on one of the vinyl stools at the counter. At the far end sat an old farmer in a sweat-stained trucker hat and overalls with a giant hole in the right knee. He had his head down and was digging into his bowl of grits.

I knew better than to say hello to him. If he wanted to speak to me when he came up for air that was fine, but I knew you never distracted a tired farmer from his breakfast. My father taught me that lesson long ago.

I lightly tapped my fingers on the counter. I was nervous

about bringing up Edna Lee to Jessa. There had to be a reason she'd never spoken about her to me.

Jessa slid back behind the counter.

I jumped.

"Steady there," Jessa said. "You're wound tighter than a yo-yo."

"Sorry. It's been a weird few days."

"I can see that," she said with a nod.

I glanced over to the men with the camera. "Birders?"

She laughed. "No. They are bear hunters, or at least that's what they are calling themselves."

"Bear hunters?"

"You know a black bear has been spotted in town, and they are all hoping to get a good snap of him. They have been here since six waiting for the next sighting report." She shook her head. "I heard the indoor farmers market was a huge success. So many people came in here afterward and said how much they enjoyed it. I wish I could have stopped by, but the diner was packed all day. There were a lot of out-of-towners here for Christmas shopping."

"Business was good," I said.

She cocked her head and slid a white coffee mug toward me, then picked up the coffeepot and filled it to the brim. She didn't leave any room in the mug, because she knew I liked my coffee black.

I supposed that wasn't completely true. I didn't like my coffee black; my waistline liked it black. I wrapped my hands around the mug and inhaled. Jessa made the best coffee I had ever tasted, and I have been to some of the best coffee shops in LA. None of them compared to hers. I don't know how she did it. Maybe the appeal to me was it reminded me of home. Jessa claimed it was the clean Michigan water.

"If business was so good at the market," Jessa said, "why the long face?"

"The farm did really well. I just got some bad news."

She propped her elbows on the counter. "I am all ears."

I gave her the short version of what Chief Randy told me, and I left out the part about Milan calling the forensic anthropologist for the cause of death.

She clicked her tongue. "Isn't that just Chief Randy? I knew when the first bone was found that it was going to be James Ripley. I think all of us were thinking that. His was the only open missing person case in Cherry Glen." She sighed. "I had hoped for your sake that we were all wrong. Not that I wanted another person to be the victim, but I knew this would come back on your family."

"Why didn't you ever mention you were close friends with my aunt Edna Lee?"

Jessa's face paled.

When she didn't say anything, I went on in a low voice. "My father said Edna Lee's death is the reason Chief Randy blames Grandma Bellamy for Ripley's murder."

"Jessa!" one of the men at the front of the diner called. "I need a warm-up."

She waved that she heard him. "I need to get back at it. Can I get you anything other than coffee?"

I knit my brow together.

"I know that we need to talk about this, but this isn't the

place with all these prying ears around." She lifted a glass dome that had been covering a platter of apple cider donuts. She put one of the donuts on a saucer and slid it across the counter. It came to rest right next to my coffee mug.

I raised my eyebrow. "You might want to take up the sport of curling with those kinds of skills."

"I just might," she said and picked up her coffeepot. "We will talk about all this, I promise." She walked away.

Doing my best to ignore the donut, although I knew it was futile attempt, I pulled a notepad out of my purse and tried to make sense of what I knew. In the middle of the piece of paper, I wrote, "James Ripley," and circled his name. From that circle, I made lines jutting out from it like a child's drawing of the sun.

"Family?" went in one circle as I realized I knew nothing about Ripley's family. I didn't know who they were or if they still lived in the area. It surprised me that Chief Randy hadn't mentioned next of kin. Then again, he was trying to shock me with his announcement about Granddad Bellamy. He had certainly succeeded.

Next, I wrote, "Edna Lee," my aunt. I knew that Edna Lee was innocent, as she died before Ripley did, but I wrote my grandmother's name next to her since Edna Lee's death was presumed to be Grandma Bellamy's motive. I didn't believe my grandmother was involved, but I couldn't rule out that Ripley's death wasn't tied to Edna Lee's in some way.

At that point, I ran out of names to put around Ripley's. My shoulders sagged. No wonder Chief Randy was ready to blame my grandmother and be done with it. There was next to nothing else to go on.

"Shi," Jessa said in a stage whisper. "Shi."

I looked up from my notebook. "What's wrong? Did Huckleberry eat something that he shouldn't have?" That was always a concern when I was at Jessa's Place. There was just too much temptation there for the little pug.

She set her coffeepot back on its warmer behind the counter. "No," she hissed. "Rhett is here." Her eyes were wide. "He just sat down at the booth to the left of the front door."

The bell over the door rang. Jessa reached across the counter and grabbed my hand. "Whit is here now too and sitting across from him!"

I started to turn my head, and she gripped my hand like it was in a vise. "Don't do that; she will see you."

I did as I was told, but I said, "Whit and I live on the same farm. We see each other almost every day. She will know what I look like even from behind."

"Maybe you're right, but she's not looking over here, and I don't want you to attract her attention. It will ruin everything."

"What's everything? What will it ruin?" I asked.

"She'll think that I told you."

"You did tell me," I said. "And you're sure Stacey doesn't know about their meetings? I feel like she has to know." I was dying to turn my head so I could see what was going on.

"Maybe she knows, but you have to admit it's odd they are spending so much time together, and he always pays their bill," she said, as if this was a kind of crushing blow of evidence.

Maybe he always paid her bill because Whit was a poor

college student, not because they were in a romantic relationship right under Stacey's nose.

I frowned. "It doesn't make sense. If they wanted to keep their relationship a secret, why they would come here? Whit knows people in town talk."

She wrung her hands. "She asked me not to tell you. Usually, I am a vault with these sorts of things. You would not believe what I know from overhearing conversations here at the diner. What I can tell you for sure is every person in Cherry Glen has secrets. As for Whit, I'm worried about her. Her private meetings with Stacey's guy are worrisome. Even if nothing at all is happening, you know how Stacey can be. Whit is putting her job at risk."

I knew exactly how Stacey could be, and after the disaster of her last relationship, I have a feeling she would be even more likely to react first and ask questions later.

Jessa looked over my head. "They are engrossed in their conversation." She came around the counter and tugged on my arm. "What I need you to do is go out the back through the kitchen, and then come through the front door like you just got here." She pulled me out of my seat.

The farmer at the end of the counter grunted into his coffee to make his displeasure at our conversation known.

"Why can't I just walk over there from here?"

"Because you don't want it to look like we were waiting to see them, do you?" She tugged on my arm."

Why would they think that?" I asked.

She pulled on my arm again. "Because you're nosey. Everyone knows it!"

"I'm up," I whispered and dislodged my arm from her grasp. "Wouldn't she have seen my truck in the parking lot?"

She shook her head. "I don't believe she would have come in here if she had. Now, go. This is the best way you can find out what's going on without involving me."

I grabbed the apple cider donut from the plate. I had a feeling that I was going to need it.

Jessa pushed me into the kitchen. The line cook stopped chopping potatoes and stared at us.

"Get back to work, Jay," Jessa said and shuffled me through the crates of carrots and onions to the back door. She opened it and pushed me out. "See you up front." She closed the door in my face just as I realized that Huckleberry was still inside by the revolving pie display. Wasn't that a dead giveaway I was there?

I tried to open the door, but it was locked.

It seemed that I had no choice but to walk around the front and do this Jessa's way.

Chapter Twenty-One

Before I made the short walk around the diner, I stood on the back stoop and ate my donut. After being thrown out the back of Jessa's Place, it seemed like the right thing to do.

There was a rattle coming from one of the two giant dumpsters behind me, and I spun around in time to see just a bit of black fur disappear into the dumpster.

I finished my donut quickly and skirted away from the dumpster. It must have been a raccoon. There wasn't much time for the raccoons in Cherry Glen to fatten up for the winter. Raccoons don't hibernate, but they slow down in the winter months and go in and out of torpor depending on the low temperatures.

I could see the appeal. I would love to get a little fluffy and then burn off the weight as I slept, only to come outside when it was warm.

The dumpster shook and I hurried to the other side of the building. It sure was a loud raccoon, and a big one too. I didn't want to meet face-to-face. I didn't have my attack chicken with me for protection.

I walked around the diner and opened the door. As soon as I stepped into the building, Huckleberry jumped to his feet and stared at me as if he didn't understand where I had come from. I bent over to scratch his head. "Don't worry, buddy; I'm confused by all this too."

Jessa carried a tray of French toast and omelets to one of the waiting tables, and she winked at me as if we were on some kind of undercover mission. Maybe in her mind, we were.

Whit and Rhett sat on the same side of the booth and had their heads tilted together in a very serious-looking conversation. It was the first time I actually thought they might have a romantic connection. The idea made my chest ache. Whit could find herself in a real mess if she wasn't careful.

"I have followed every avenue I can," Rhett said. "We've run into a dead end. You may just have to accept that."

"I can't accept that." Whit scooted away from him. "There has to be a way to find out more."

"When cases like this are sealed, there is only so much we can do. I did this to pay back a favor, which I feel like I have more than done. You have to keep up your side of the bargain."

I wrinkled my brow. This was sounding less like a romance and more like an illegal deal of some sort.

"Hey, Whit," I said in my most cheerful voice. "Mind if I join the two of you?"

Before either one of them could answer, I slid into the opposite side of the booth.

There were two coffees on the table, but nothing else.

Whit jumped in her seat. "Shiloh! What are you doing here?"

"I just dropped in for a coffee." I smiled. "Looks like that's what the two of you are doing too. I didn't expect to see you here. Nice to see you again, Rhett. How is my cousin?"

He narrowed his eyes as if he was well aware of how pointed my question was.

Whit slid out of the booth and stood over me. "What do you want, Shiloh?"

"I just want to know if there is something going on between the two of you."

Whit started laughing. "Rhett is helping me out with research for a project. Research is his expertise."

"Is it for school?" I asked.

"It started that way, but then I branched out on my own."

"What is it about?" I asked.

She folded her arms. "I'm not telling anyone until it's done."

I turned to Rhett. "That's very nice of you to help her."

He folded his hands over the legal pad in front of him, probably so I couldn't read whatever was written on the paper. I would be lying if I said that I wasn't trying to read the words upside down.

"As an author, I find it gratifying when anyone is willing to delve into research. This is especially true with someone as young as Whit." He looked at his watch. "Look at the time. I should be on my way." He stood up from the booth. "Whit, it was a pleasure to chat with you again. I'm sure we will see each other at the theater soon." He nodded at me. "Shiloh, given your background in true crime, I would love to meet with you and pick your brain about my current book if you have time."

"What is the book about?"

"We can discuss that at the meeting." He said with no expression on his face. "I'll be in touch." He walked out of the diner.

Across the room, I spotted Jessa watching us as she tugged at her multicolor braid.

"Whit? What's going on?" I asked.

She pointed out the window. "Is that the police chief going a mile a minute?"

Chapter Twenty-Two

I looked out the window just in time to see Chief Randy fly by on his motorcycle. He was in quite a hurry. Maybe he was looking for the bear. I knew it wasn't because he was on the trail of a murderer. If it was a bear, I wondered if that giant raccoon that I had heard in Jessa's dumpster out back might have in fact been the black bear in question.

I shivered at the thought.

The front door slammed open, and the group of diners who had put themselves into the position of bear hunters trooped back into Jessa's Place with their heads held low.

"My guess is that you didn't see him," Jessa said.

"He ran behind Michigan Street Theater," one man said in a disappointed voice. "I was really hoping to snap a picture of him for the newspaper. Nothing much has been happening in Cherry Glen as of late, and it's hard to find stories to put in the community paper."

"What do you mean nothing is happening?" his companion asked. "I would say the police chief solving James Ripley's murder after all this time is a very big deal indeed."

The would-be reporter shrugged. "Is it?" he asked. "I think we all knew that Emma Kay Bellamy was behind it."

I stood up, nearly knocking into Whit in the process. "You should be careful about what you say. It's not right to accuse someone who can't defend herself."

The reporter's face turned a deep shade of red. "You wouldn't know, Shiloh Bellamy. You weren't even born yet when he died."

I seethed.

"I caught sight of the bear," one of the other diners spoke up. "Looks like he was a juvenile to me. Definitely not a cub. He stood over five feet."

"He was probably just looking for a place to stake his territory," Jessa said. "That's what young male bears do when they leave their mother's protection. The park rangers will catch him in due time and take him to Sleeping Bear Dunes. He will do very well there."

"How are they going to catch him? He's a fast runner. I tried to chase him down the street, but he was far too fast."

"You're an idiot to try to chase a bear," Jessa said, not mincing words. "You're lucky he didn't turn around and maul you."

The man paled as if he hadn't thought of that before. I found it alarming that it hadn't crossed his mind that chasing a bear was a mistake until Jessa pointed it out.

While I was occupied by the bear conversation, Whit was tiptoeing toward the door. She wasn't going to get away that easily.

I jumped out of my seat and scooped up Huckleberry

before I stepped foot outside. With a bear loose in the town, I was taking no chances with my pug. He wriggled a bit as the fresh air hit us, because he couldn't understand why I wouldn't let him walk.

"Where are you going?" I asked Whit.

Whit spun around on her heels. "Why are you following me?"

"You never answered my question. Why are you avoiding me?"

She zipped up her puffer coat. The temperature had dropped considerably since I had first arrived at the diner that morning. With my free hand, I fished my stocking cap out of my coat pocket and pulled it down on my head.

"Are you sure we should be talking out here with a bear on the loose?"

I knew she was stalling.

"Chief Randy chased the poor thing out of town by now. I know *I* would run if I saw him coming at me on his motorcycle."

"It does give Wicked Witch of the West vibes."

I agreed. "So, tell me what is going on."

She sighed. "I was doing some research on our ancestry, Chesney's and mine. I had to do a project for one of classes and just go into it. I learned that my mother was adopted. Chesney and I never knew that."

"How did you find that out?"

"There are all these boxes of old papers from our grandmother that we have moved from place to place. They were left to us when she died. Chesney and I never bothered to look at them, but when I had this project about ancestry,

I thought there might be something in there I could use. I never expected to find so much. My grandparents saved all the paperwork from when they adopted my mother."

"When was she adopted?" I asked.

"Like forty-something years ago from the foster system. She was ten or eleven." She shook her head. "If she were that old, she would've remembered she was adopted. I don't know why she never told Ches and me about it. There are pages and pages and pages about the adoption."

"And your mother's birth parents?" I asked.

"That's what I'm trying to find out. It was a closed adoption, but I thought since my grandparents are gone, I might be able to find out."

"How is Rhett involved in all of this?" I asked.

She twisted her mouth. "He does a lot of research for his books. He talks about them all the time and all the research that he has to do. I thought he might be able to help me."

"What's in it for him?"

"What do you mean?"

"When I first got to your table he said something like you owed him now."

Whit kicked at the fallen leaves at our feet. Half a dozen leaves rose from the ground in a puff of air from her motion and floated back down to where they had come from.

"Someone like Rhett doesn't do anything for free."

The way she said that turned my stomach. "Did he threaten you?"

"He only threatened to tell my sister before I was ready for her know what I was working on."

"Why haven't you told Chesney about this?" I asked.

She looked down at the tips of her combat boots. "Because I know she would tell me to stop and that it was a waste of time. She would say there was a reason Mom never told us about her adoption, and I should respect her wishes." She looked up at me again. "But I just can't do that. If I have family out there, I have to find them. Mom could have had brothers and sisters that she didn't know about, and that would mean I could have cousins."

"How old was your mother when she died?"

"She was forty-four."

"And how old were you?"

"Ten." She rubbed the back of her neck. "I just thought that if I could find out where we came from, we could maybe find more family." Tears came to her eyes. "Chesney is the only family I have, and I love my sister more than anything or anyone." She wouldn't look at me. "But I just wish my family was bigger, you know? I wish there were more people to lean on."

I came from a small family too and could see why she felt that way. All I had were my father and Stacey. Neither of them was particularly supportive of me, nor did they support my choices for the farm. However, we had made inroads in our relationship since I moved back to Michigan. If I needed her, I knew Stacey would come to my rescue. She would complain about it, but she'd show up. The showing up was important.

"Please don't tell Chesney." Whit met my eyes. "It would be better if I had all the information before I told her about it. If I don't, she will just be able to rip it all apart. She's so logical that she can talk just about anyone into anything."

I had noticed that about Chesney too. She was always suggesting the next big project we could do for the farm. It could be exhausting at times because I felt like we never took the time to celebrate our wins. We finished a major project, and she was waiting in the wings with ten more that needed to be done.

For the farm, Chesney kept me on task, so the way that she operated helped. However, I could see how it would hurt a sister who just wants to talk about what used to be, especially when it came to their parents.

At the same time, I think Chesney would hear Whit out if Whit gave her a chance.

"Is this why you were behaving so strangely at Thanksgiving?"

She nodded. "I had just learned something big about our history, and I couldn't sit there and pretend I was enjoying the food."

"What did you learn?"

"I can't tell you before I tell my sister."

"Okay, where did you go on Thanksgiving then?"

"I went to the theater. I knew Stacey wouldn't be there." She looked up the street in the direction of the theater. "It's the place where I feel most like myself. I love drama because nine times out of ten there is a happy ending. It doesn't seem like that happens all that much in real life." There were tears in her eyes.

"And from what you know, does your research lead to a happy ending?" I asked.

She looked up the street again. "That's yet to be determined."

I nodded. "I would like to tell her that you're okay. She has been worried."

"Please don't."

"Why not?"

"Because she'll grill you for more information. She got her interrogation tactics from you. She won't let up." She flipped her black and orange hair over her shoulder.

"She's worried about you. I have to say something. She's losing sleep over this. If I can't say anything, you have to. You don't know how hard she is taking this. She feels like she is losing her sister."

"That's not it at all," Whit said. "I'm trying to bring us closer together."

"She needs to know that, and she needs to hear it from you."

Whit kicked at the leaves again. "Give me twenty-four hours. Please. I promise to tell her everything. I just want to confirm a few more things first. I know Chesney will have a thousand questions, and I want to be ready to answer all of them."

I shifted Huckleberry in my arms and scanned the parking lot just to make sure the bear wasn't anywhere nearby. Contrary to popular belief, bears can run fast, even up to thirty-five miles per hour at a sprint. He could have circled back to the diner by now.

I sighed. "I don't like lying to Chesney."

"You're not lying to her. You're just not telling her everything." She looked up at me with her big blue eyes. Despite the orange and black hair and heavy black eyeliner, she looked like an innocent Disney princess.

"All right," I agreed. "I'll give you twenty-four hours. I can't promise any longer than that."

She wrapped her arms around me and gave me and Huckleberry a hug. "Thank you so much, Shi. I promise it will be worth it to all of us in the end."

All of us? What did she mean by that? Why would I be counted in that number?

"I have to get back to the theater. Stacey will be fuming that I've been gone this long." She looked both ways and then dashed across Michigan Street in the direction of the theater.

"Keep your eye out for the bear!" I called after her.

She waved her arm in the air to tell me she heard me.

I sighed. I hoped that I wouldn't regret not telling Chesney what I knew about her sister.

I turned back to the diner and noticed Jessa watching me through the window.

Chapter Twenty-Three

I went back inside the diner to find the place half-full of discouraged bear trappers.

"He's just so darn fast," Carter Johnson, who worked as a bartender at the brewery down the road, said. "I don't know how the park rangers will have any luck in catching him."

"They will have to use a tranquilizer on him," another man said. "It's the only way."

"That seems cruel."

"Not at all. He will go to sleep and wake up in the woods at Sleeping Bear Dunes. I can't think of a better place for a bear to be."

"Still," Johnson said.

"Well, they have to do something a little more drastic. Chasing him through the streets of Cherry Glen sure isn't working."

Jessa walked over to the group of men, which spanned three tables, and passed out waters and coffees. "If you all think that you're going to have any luck catching a bear, you're going to need some breakfast. Eggs and bacon all around?"

The men heartily agreed.

"Pancakes too, Jessa," Johnson said. "Your pancakes will be a big help."

"They always are," she agreed. Jessa glanced at me, and a pained expression crossed her face. She had never looked at me that way before, even when the whole town was against me when Logan died. Jessa had always been on my side. What had changed? Was it because I asked her about Edna Lee?

Jessa turned back toward the kitchen.

I settled Huckleberry down in the spot by the revolving pie display and followed her into the kitchen.

"I think two dozen eggs, fourteen pancakes, and thirty pieces of bacon will work for the bear hunters," she told her line cook. "If they need more after that, go ahead and make it."

He nodded without a word.

The reason why she and her line cook worked so well together was Jessa liked to give him orders and he barely said a word.

Jessa turned around as if she was going to go back into the dining room and pulled up short when she saw me. "Shiloh!"

"Can we talk?" I paused. "About Edna Lee?"

She pressed her lips together. "Yes, yes, I want to, but now isn't a good time. It's the breakfast rush, and the after-church crowd will be pouring into the diner in about an hour or so."

"I really need to know what's going on," I said. Unexpected tears came to my eyes. "I can't let Chief Randy frame Grandma Bellamy."

She rushed forward and gave me a hug. "Oh, honey, don't cry. I know how difficult this is for you. You adored your grandmother, and the feeling was mutual. We can talk, I promise." She stepped back and held on to my upper arms as she looked up at me. "I should have a lull between three and four. Can you come back then?"

"Jessa!" one of the men from the bear search committee called. "We need more creamer for the coffee."

Jessa made a face and released me. "This is a conversation that I want to have with you. It really is, but we will need time."

I sighed. "All right." It wasn't like I had any other choice.

After Jessa went back to the bear search committee to deliver creamers and refresh their coffees, I collected Huckleberry and left the diner. I wished that I could get answers from Jessa right then and there, but I knew that we needed time for the conversation, and the after-church rush at Jessa's Place was extreme.

I had two options: I could go home, or I could keep looking for answers. In reality, looking for answers was the only choice.

I hadn't felt completely satisfied by my brief conversation with Rhett. My best guess was he was at the theater with Stacey. I knew how my cousin would feel if I showed up at the theater uninvited for the second day in a row, but that couldn't be helped. It might be true that Rhett and Whit weren't a couple, but I still worried that Rhett was taking advantage of Whit in some way. And if he was taking advantage of Whit, could he be taking advantage of Stacey too?

Because the bear was still out there wandering the streets of Cherry Glen, I carried Huckleberry from the diner to the theater. As I suspected they might be, the front doors of the theater were locked. That meant I needed to go around to the entrance in the back of theater. I paused and wondered how smart that would be. Didn't someone say at the diner that the bear ran behind the theater?

At the same time, I really needed to find out what Rhett was up to. There was something about him that didn't sit well with me, and it wasn't just the fact that Stacey had poor taste in men. He was up to something.

Before I could make up my mind, the theater door opened, and Stacey stood in front of me with a scowl on her face. "I thought you were those bear people again," she said.

"Bear people?" I asked.

"They have been lurking around the theater all morning because someone claimed they saw a black bear out by my dumpster. I have been in and out of the theater multiple times, and I can assure you that I have not seen a bear. They are a bunch of alarmists if you ask me, and they are driving me insane."

"I think the bear sightings are true. More than one person has seen a juvenile black bear in town."

Stacey snorted as if she couldn't believe it. "What do you want? And don't tell me you are looking for the bear too."

Leave it to my cousin to get right to the point.

"Is Rhett here?" I asked.

"Rhett? What do you want from my boyfriend?"

"I saw him at the diner, and I just wanted to finish our conversation. We were interrupted."

"He was at the diner? He told me that he was on his way to Traverse City to research his next book. But I suppose he could have stopped at the diner for a coffee before he left." She said this last part with uncertainty. It was clear to me she didn't know what her boyfriend was doing.

It was on the tip of my tongue to tell her that he was there with Whit, but I was afraid of how she would react. Stacey could be explosive, and Whit would have to deal with the brunt of her boss's displeasure.

"He's on Orchard Street!" someone on the road cried.

I looked over my shoulder and watched as a half dozen bear search and rescuers ran down the street.

Stacey shook her head. "You might as well come inside in case there is a bear out there somewhere. I don't want Huckleberry to be hurt."

I noted that she didn't say the same thing about me.

She held the door open just wide enough for me and Huckleberry to slip inside. When we were in, she locked it behind us. The bolt made a thudding sound into the doorframe.

"Give it a few minutes, " Stacey said. "The bear people will run up and down Michigan Street for a little while, and then they will give up and go home. If I were a bear, I would stay as far away from Cherry Glen as I could with so many nutcases running through the town."

She began to walk through the lobby, presumedly back to the theater itself.

I set Huckleberry on the floor. He walked beside me while I caught up with her. "Why didn't you tell me the connection between James Ripley and Edna Lee?"

She spun around and looked at me. "I don't want to talk about it."

"But you would have been old enough to remember Edna Lee and when she died. You were ten."

"I was almost ten." Stacey corrected me just because she could. "Who told you about Edna Lee and James?"

"Dad."

She nodded. "What else did he say?"

"Edna Lee was friends with Jessa."

She raised her brow at me. "Then why are you here talking to me about it and not Jessa? I was just a little kid. Jessa would know a lot more about Edna Lee's life than I would. She was just my pretty aunt to me."

"I'm going to," I said.

Stacey gave me a look as if she didn't believe me. "Listen, Shiloh, I didn't say anything about it because I didn't know anything about it. I was just a kid."

"Were you close to Edna Lee?"

Tears came to her eyes.

I blinked. I had only seen Stacey cry one time before, and that was when our grandmother died. I didn't even see her tear up when she lost her parents.

"She was everything that I wanted to be. She was going to be an actress on Broadway. She always said that to anyone who would listen."

"She never left Cherry Glen," I said.

"I know that," Stacey snapped. "She was trying to save up for months so she could leave."

"Did you have money when you left Cherry Glen?"

"Yes."

"How did you have the money to go?" I asked. I was just

a kid myself when Stacey left for Broadway at eighteen, but I don't know how she would have saved up enough to go right after high school.

"Grandma gave it to me." She resumed walking.

"What?" I asked.

"She made me promise not to tell anyone. Uncle Sully doesn't even know."

"Then why are you telling me now?"

"Because I know you, and you are like a pit bull on a bone at times. You will just push and push and push to get what you want. I don't have the patience to listen to you yammer on about wanting to know. Your persistence can be very annoying."

I sighed. Stacey wasn't one to keep her opinions about someone to herself.

"So, she stopped her daughter from going, but she funded her granddaughter. Why?"

"Isn't it obvious? Guilt. Grandma Bellamy was so worried that Edna Lee would find trouble in New York, but what she learned was a person is able to find trouble anywhere. She told me that she learned her lesson. She was never going to stop someone from following their dreams again. Instead, she actively supported me as much as she could."

"Do you remember anything about James Ripley?" I asked.

She started to shake her head, and then she said, "There was one thing. He and Edna Lee took me the general store for an ice cream float just a few days before Edna Lee fell through the ice. She called it a going-away party."

It seemed to me that that was a very important detail to remember.

Chapter Twenty-Four

When I left the theater a few minutes later, I held Huckleberry close to my chest and looked up and down the street for any sign of a bear or the group people chasing the poor creature. I didn't know much about bear psychology, but I was willing to bet that chasing a bear around town wasn't the best way to endear people to him.

Seeing that the coast was clear, I walked back to Jessa's Place, where I had left my car. It was still too early to talk with her.

As I collected my truck and drove back to the farm, I mulled over what I had learned from Stacey. Edna Lee had said that when she and Ripley took Stacey to the general store that final time, it had been a going-away party, but for who? Edna Lee? Ripley? Both of them?

And more importantly, had my grandmother known that they were leaving?

When I pulled into the farm's driveway near my father's farmhouse, there was another pickup parked by the barn, and I recognized it right away as belonging to Quinn.

I parked in the grass to leave him more than enough room

to get out and opened the door to my truck. Huckleberry used my lap as a springboard and leapt out. He galloped toward the pickup. Quinn walked around, held out his arms, and Huckleberry jumped into him.

He could be a traitorous little pug at times.

Quinn scratched Huckleberry under the chin. "Who's a good boy? You are."

The little pug ate up his compliments.

Quinn set Huckleberry on the ground, and the pug danced around his feet. "I walked up to your cottage, but you weren't there."

I frowned. "I went to Jessa's this morning."

He nodded. "I suppose I should have guessed that."

I peeked around him. "Is Hazel here?"

If she was, she would be in the barn with Esmeralda and the other cats. It was her favorite place to be when she came to the farm, and the cats adored her. Esmeralda would keep the clowder of orange cats at bay though. She believed she was the only one worthy of Hazel's affection.

"She's with my mother. The church is having a potluck today. Why they are having a potluck Thanksgiving weekend after everyone is already stuffed to the gills is a mystery to me, but I was glad that Hazel was able to go. She is making more friends at church. It's been a long road for her to make friends since moving back to Cherry Glen. Coming to a new place in the midst of middle school is not ideal."

I couldn't think a single thing about middle school that was ideal. I was just happy to have survived it. "I'm glad."

I waited for him to say something more, but when he

didn't, I said, "You didn't have to wait around for me. You could have just called or sent a text."

"I didn't mind waiting. This is a conversation that I need to have in person."

"Why didn't you go inside and talk to Dad?"

"I did, but he was so engrossed in his collection that I thought I was in the way."

I knew what that felt like.

I folded my arms. "What did you want to discuss?" My stance could not be more closed off to him if I tried.

Quinn ran his hand through his hair. It had been a little while since he had gotten a haircut, and his hair curled around his ears. It made him look younger than he actually was and reminded me of the boy he'd once been.

"I heard about Ripley," he said. "It's hard to believe that he's been buried in the orchard for all this time."

"Very hard to believe," I agreed. I wasn't sure what he was getting at.

"I stopped by because I wanted to let you know that I don't agree with what my dad is doing. I don't think your grandmother killed Ripley. I do think that he should have a full investigation."

I didn't know what I expected him to say, but it wasn't that. "Thank you."

"I've told my dad as much. I can't say it's made much difference. When his mind it made up on a subject, it is very difficult to change it."

How well I knew that. "I do appreciate you telling me," I said.

"My father believes you're trying to solve the case, but I told him that you're far too smart to try to solve a case that's so cold."

I said nothing.

He studied my face. "Don't tell me that he's right."

"It's my grandmother, Quinn. You know how important she was and still is to me. She raised me. She saved the farm by hiding those stocks for me to find. The least that I can do is clear her name. I might never find Ripley's murderer, but I will remove the blame from my grandmother, because she's not able to do it for herself."

He pressed his lips together. "I had a feeling you might say something like that. My dad is not going to take kindly to it, especially if you involve Penbrook too."

"Milan has nothing to do with it."

Quinn made a face as if he didn't quite believe me. "I know that he called the forensic anthropologist for the cause of death. That was overstepping."

I winced. Hadn't the forensic anthropologist promised he wouldn't tell Chief Randy that Milan called?

"He was the first officer on the scene," I said.

Quinn gave me a look. "Just tell him to be careful. His opponent could use that sort of information against him when he comes up for reelection."

"And who is going to tell his opponent?" I asked. "You?"

"I didn't come here to fight."

"I don't want to fight either." I picked up Huckleberry. "Thanks for stopping by."

"I have to tell you one more thing before I go. I know you've made your decision about who you want to be with, and I respect that. I won't get in the way. I won't cause problems."

I studied his face, trying to tell if he was truly sincere. It seemed like a swift change of heart. With how quickly Quinn changed his mind about his feelings for me, I was sure I had made the right decision. I wanted to be in a relationship that I could rely on, not one that could change on a whim.

"Thank you," I said. I didn't need any more complications in my life, nor did I need Milan feeling uneasy when I spent time around Quinn. He was still my neighbor, and in a small town, that meant something. More importantly, he was still Hazel's father, and I loved her like she was family.

I didn't know how it would end for Milan Penbrook and me. We were too new of a couple to know the outcome, but at the same time, I knew that Quinn and I weren't meant to be. It felt good to know that we had both closed the door to that possibility.

"As hard as this is to say, I think you and I are better as friends," Quinn said.

"I agree."

He blushed. "And I'm really sorry that I tried to kiss you the other day. That was a jerk move."

"It was," I said. "But let's start over. Just friends." I held out my free hand, the one that wasn't wrapped around Huckleberry's waist.

He shook my hand. "Friends."

And wasn't it my luck that when Quinn and I were looking at each other, hand in hand, Milan drove up the driveway. I really couldn't win.

Chapter Twenty-Five

As soon as I saw Milan's SUV, I dropped Quinn's hand like I had just received an electric shock. I hoped he hadn't seen our handshake, but by the thunderous look on his face, he had seen it and jumped to the wrong conclusions.

"Milan, what are you doing here?" I asked.

"I heard on the wire that the black bear was still in the Cherry Glen area. I was close by following up on another call, so I wanted to stop by to see if you needed any help getting the animals back in the barn."

"You think the bear is headed this way?"

"According to reports, that's what it looks like."

"I didn't hear these reports," Quinn said.

"I'm surprised your father doesn't tell you every little thing that happens in town."

"I'm not interested in every little thing."

Milan made a face.

I suppressed a sigh. Quinn claimed that he no longer had any romantic interest in me, but he certainly was going out of his way to get under Milan's skin.

"We can bring the sheep in. I don't think the bear would

hurt them, but we don't really know how hungry he might be. I'm not taking any risks with Teddy Bear and his ladies."

"I'll leave you two to it," Quinn said. "Shi, please tell your father I said goodbye. I don't even know if he noticed I was there. He was so engrossed in his collection, and he was whispering his lines from *The Christmas Carol* to himself."

"I'll tell him," I promised.

Quinn looked to Milan. "She's all yours, Penbrook." With that he walked to his truck and drove away.

Milan watched his pickup bump down the gravel driveway. "That was a rude thing to say. You are your own person. You don't belong to anyone."

"I appreciate you saying that."

"And I have my eye on him."

"You have nothing to worry about," I said. "I'm more than done with him, and I have been for a very long time."

Milan smiled. "Why don't we get those sheep?"

"They aren't going to like coming in early since the day is warm enough for them to be outside. At the same time, I think if Teddy Bear saw a real bear, he would faint dead away. He's brave for a Babydoll sheep, but he's still just a lamb in so many ways." I set Huckleberry back on the ground. "Go get the sheep," I told the pug.

He looked at me as if to ask why we were collecting the sheep so early in the day, but then he seemed to shake it off and toddled down the well-worn path to the other side of the farm. Every few steps he would look back at Milan and I as if to check that we were still following him.

"What about the chickens?" Milan asked.

"I'd be more worried for the bear than for Diva and her hens."

"Point taken."

As the orchard came into view, I knew something was wrong. Teddy Bear and his ewes were pressed up against the gate that led out of the orchard.

"Oh no, the bear!" I broke into a run.

"Shiloh, stop; you can't just run at a bear!" Milan called after me.

But I wasn't listening. All I could think about was protecting my sheep. I threw the gate open. "Go! Go! Back to the barn!"

I didn't have to tell Teddy Bear twice as he ushered his girls down the path that Milan and I had just taken. Much to my relief, Huckleberry went with them to make sure none of the sheep turned back. He wasn't a bad herding dog for a pug.

Milan grabbed my hand before I could race into the orchard. My adrenaline was so high I wasn't even thinking.

"Before I call it in that the bear is here, let me confirm we are right." He walked through the gate.

I followed him.

He looked over his shoulder. "What are you doing?"

"If you're going in there, so am I," I said. "You might need help."

He didn't argue with me because he knew darn well it was pointless to try.

"Just stay a few yards behind me, okay?"

"Sure." I knew the trick to surviving a charging bear was to run faster than the person you were with. I was certain Milan could outrun me in any race, so I needed the head start.

There was a snap of a branch and then a yelp that didn't sound like a bear at all.

Milan took off running toward the sound, and I was right behind him. I still left a bit of space between us in case I had to turn around and run in the opposite direction.

Stacey's author boyfriend, Rhett, hung from his trousers off the orchard's back fence. A cherry tree limb lay on the ground nearby. The chain-link fence was tall in this part of the orchard—it stood eight feet high. It appeared that Rhett had climbed the tree in hopes of making it over the fence. Unfortunately, the limb couldn't hold him, which was how he ended up in his present state.

He was lucky that the fence had just ripped his pants and hadn't impaled him.

Rhett twisted his body, trying to reach the bit of fabric that was entangled with the fencing. He flailed his arms. "Will one of you help me out of this?"

Milan folded his arm. "Not until you tell us what you're doing here."

"I'm doing research. It's nothing more than that," Rhett said.

"You're trespassing," I said.

"I'm Stacey's boyfriend. This is her family home. I'm not trespassing."

"It *was* her family home, you mean. I'm the owner of both sides of the farm now, and you are trespassing."

He dug his right heel into the chain link and wriggled

back and forth like a worm on a hook. "What are you going to do? Arrest me because I got stuck on your fence?"

"She can't," Milan said. "But I can. I'm a sheriff."

Rhett paled ever so slightly. I guessed it never occurred to him that I would have an actual police officer with me. I saw no reason to tell him that we were outside of Milan's jurisdiction.

Milan removed a pocketknife from his coat.

Rhett waved his hand. "What are you going to do with that?"

"I'm going to free you from the fence."

"With a knife? Do you know what you're doing, and you can't cut my pants! These trousers cost more than you get paid in a month," Rhett said.

"That sounds like a you problem, not to mention a poor financial choice on your part." Milan closed the pocketknife. "If you don't want me to help, I will happily leave you up there to wave back and forth in the wind."

"Can you take your pants off?" I asked.

Rhett's face turned beet red. "What would Stacey think if she heard you ask me that?"

"I think under the circumstances, she would agree."

"Will you at least turn around?"

I did as he asked. Truth was I really didn't want to see him in his underwear.

"Both of you," Rhett cried.

"Sorry," Milan said. "But I'm going to watch you the entire time to make sure you don't run off. You promised to answer our questions, and I'm going to hold you to that. I'll come around to the other side of the fence and help you down." Milan jogged through the orchard toward the gate.

Rhett groaned while he waited for Milan to run to his rescue, and I watched as Huckleberry came back, barreling through the orchard gate in the opposite direction from Rhett. The little pug must have gotten the sheep settled in the barn and ran back to the orchard to reassure himself that I was okay. He really was a wondrous little creature.

I held out my arms, and he ran full tilt to me and then leaped. I caught him against my chest like he was a basketball.

Behind me there was great tearing sound. I turned around for a peek.

Rhett had one leg halfway out of his trousers, but it was pulling the material away from the fence. As he did this, the trousers ripped open and he fell to the ground in a heap. His pants were all tangled around his thighs.

Milan, who was on the other side of the fence, helped him up. As he did, Rhett's trousers fell to his ankles. And that's when I noticed the solar system underpants. I had not expected that.

With as much dignity as he could muster, he pulled up his ruined trousers and buttoned them. I didn't see how in their current condition they did much to keep him warm as there was a giant hole in his backside.

I could feel laughter bubbling up.

"Don't you dare laugh," Rhett said. "Don't you dare. If you do, you won't get a single answer from me. I promise you that."

"Shiloh, meet us at the gate," Milan said.

I nodded, turned, and took off running as I stifled the laugh Rhett had sensed was coming. I didn't want him to know how much his predicament tickled my funny bone. Also, there was the very real and serious matter of finding out what he was doing in my orchard.

One thing was for certain: I knew it had something to do with Ripley. There was no other reason why Rhett would be in that very spot.

Chapter Twenty-Six

Milan and Rhett came around the side of the fence. Rhett's face was bright red, and he held on to the seat of his pants to close up the massive hole there. His hair stuck up in all directions, and he had dirt on his cheek.

"We have some questions for you," Milan said.

"Can I go home and change first? You can't expect me to stand here in the cold with my rear end sticking out."

Milan and I shared a look. The temperature was dropping, and over our heads the clouds looked like they were heavy with snow. I wouldn't want to be outside in Rhett's position, but I also knew full well that if we let him leave, he wasn't coming back and would do whatever he could to avoid our questions.

"We can go back to my father's farmhouse, and I will find a pair of my father's sweats for you to wear. That will make you more comfortable," I said.

"Your father is all of five-six. His sweatpants will be like a pair of women's capri pants on me."

I shrugged. "Sorry, everyone else living on the farm is a woman, and I don't think you want to wear any of our clothes."

He made a face. "You can't keep me here against my will. My car is parked just down the road. What is keeping me here?"

Milan pulled a car key fob from his pocket. "This."

"How did you get that?"

"It fell out of your pocket when you toppled from the fence. I picked it up so it wouldn't get lost."

Rhett held out his hand. "Give that back to me."

"I will after we talk at the farmhouse," Milan said.

"I can report you."

"You can," Milan said. "But I think it will a lot easier if you just come back to the house and answer a few questions."

Rhett glared at him. "I'm only going because I'm cold. I hate being cold. I wish I'd never moved to Michigan."

"Where are you from?" I asked.

"Arizona originally," he said. "But I live wherever my work takes me."

We started back to the farmhouse. "And your work brought you to Cherry Glen?" I asked.

He sniffed. "I'm not going to answer any more questions until I get new pants."

I nodded. It seemed like a reasonable request to me.

Milan was walking a few feet ahead of us with Huckleberry. His shoulders shook up and down. The sheriff was laughing and doing a poor job of hiding it.

At the farmhouse, I held the back door open and we trooped into the kitchen. Dad was sitting at the kitchen table with his collection. He was still in the middle of cleaning all of his antique guns.

He peered over his reading glasses at us. "You look like you all went three rounds with a hyena." He pointed at Rhett. "The hyena won in your case. What are you all doing here?"

"Rhett was in the orchard and ripped his pants," I said. "I'm going to go grab a pair of your sweats for him."

"You find the bear?" Dad asked Rhett. "Looks to me you found the bear. Maybe that's the tussle you got into. More likely than hyenas in this part of the world."

That was true.

"Bear? What bear?" Rhett asked, looking around as if a black bear might pop out of one the kitchen cupboards right then and there.

"There is a black bear loose in town."

Rhett shook his head. "This just keeps getting worse and worse."

I left the room to collect the sweats for Rhett. When I stepped back into the kitchen, I handed him the clothes. "There is a bathroom down the hallway."

He nodded and left the room.

When Rhett was gone, Dad shook his head. "I don't know how I feel about Stacey dating that guy. She has terrible taste in men."

I wasn't going to argue with him on that, and I might have been mistaken, but Milan looked as if he might start laughing again.

Rhett came into the kitchen wearing a pair of my father's navy sweats. He had been right that the clothes would be too small. The elastic cuffs of the sweatpants dug into his calves.

"You look ridiculous," Dad said.

"Dad," I said.

"What? He looks like a grown man dressed up in children's clothes, and I might add I don't like comparing my size to a child's, but there you have it." He narrowed his eyes at Rhett. "For the record, I used to be taller than even my daughter and she's tall for woman. You shrink when you age. Just wait until it happens to you."

Rhett grimaced.

Milan was already sitting at the kitchen table with my father. "Have a seat," he said to Rhett.

Rhett looked at all the gun parts on the table. "What on earth are you doing? Building an arsenal?"

"This is my collection. I clean every piece this time of year. I didn't know I would have company today or I wouldn't have gotten it out. Actually, I would have, but then not let you inside. Shiloh said this was an emergency, though, so what choice did I have?" Dad picked up a bullet chamber and began to polish it.

Rhett tentatively sat at the table, and I perched on a wooden stool near the back door. Was I trying to keep Rhett from running away? Maybe. Not that I thought he would get very far. My dad's sweats were far too tight on him to allow him to run fast.

"Now, tell us, what were you doing in the orchard?" Milan said.

Rhett ran his hand through his hair. It was still standing up in all directions. The gel that he had used that morning to style it was now working against him. I guessed that he was just as upset over the state of his hair as the clothing. "As I told

Shiloh, I'm a true crime author. I travel the country looking for stories to include in my work. Not all the stories pan out, but the books I have written have been well received. I have even been considered for a few national awards."

"Nice humblebrag," Dad muttered.

I sighed. It would have been easier if I asked my dad to leave for the interview or if we had this conversation with Rhett in another room. However, I knew if I did that, Dad would have never agreed to give him the sweats. Truth be told, my dad was as nosey as I was. I had to get that trait from somewhere.

I put my hands on my hips. "So, the next big true crime story you're working on is about James Ripley?"

Rhett looked at me. "Yes."

I blinked. I was surprised that he came right out and said it.

I scowled. "Did you know that Ripley would be found in the orchard?"

He held up his hands. "I had no idea that you would find Ripley's remains that day. I assure you that I am grateful that you did. As soon as I learned that they belonged to Ripley, I let my publisher know. They are quite enthused about this project."

I bet they were.

"How did you hear about the Ripley case?" Milan asked. "It was long ago and certainly didn't get any national attention."

"I got an anonymous email." Rhett dropped his hand to his lap. For a man that was so fastidious about his appearance, his current state had to be killing him.

"Did you try to track who the email was from?" Milan asked.

"It's complicated. I have a form on my website where folks can send tips about cases in. Most of the time when I get a tip through my website, it's completely bogus. I expect that. A lot of the stuff I get is garbage, but every once in a while, I get a tip that is worth looking into. That's what I thought about the James Ripley tip." He glanced at me. "Cold cases are very popular in the true crime genre."

I nodded. I understood his email tips too. The production company I once worked for had the same thing on their website. They were always looking for the next big case. And he was right; most of the tips went nowhere, but the ones that panned out were completely worth weeding through the rest of them.

Milan sat back in his chair. "It's a bit hard for me to accept that you were writing a book on Ripley's case, started dating the granddaughter of the primary suspect, Emma Kay Bellamy, and just so happened to be at the family's Thanksgiving dinner when Ripley's remains were discovered."

Rhett shrugged. "It was stroke of luck. What can I say?"

"Does Stacey know you are working on this book?" I asked.

He pressed his lips together. "Yes, she does now. I told her after the bones were identified as belonging to James Ripley. It was the right thing to do."

"She didn't know when you started dating?"

"Why would I tell her then? I had just started on the project, and at that point, I didn't know if there would be enough there for a whole book. It was only when I sure that the book would be a go that I told her."

"And how did she take it?" I asked.

"Not well." He looked down at his hands.

I suspected as much. With her sketchy dating history, Stacey would have zero tolerance for a man who lied to her. Rhett might not have lied outright, but he did omit his real reason for being in Cherry Glen. I couldn't help but feel sorry for my cousin. She had had zero luck in the love department.

"I do care about Stacey, and I never meant to hurt her. However, I have a great opportunity with this new book."

Dad set the bullet barrel on a piece of velvet next to another piece of dismantled gun sitting. "And what is your opinion on this case? Do you agree with Chief Randy that my mother killed him?"

"No," Rhett said. "I don't believe that for a second. I know the killer is still out there and have proof."

I stood up. "What kind of proof?"

He looked at me. "I got another email, this time from someone threatening me to get off the case or else."

Chapter Twenty-Seven

"I need to see that email," Milan said.

"I'm not comfortable sharing my source material," Rhett said hotly.

"Have you shared it with Chief Randy? This is something he needs to know," Milan said.

"I interviewed Chief Randy about the case. He was tickled at the idea of being in a book. He told me all about the Bellamy family connection to James Ripley, and he was more than happy to point the blame at Emma Kay."

"He would." Dad snorted.

"I had this interview with him before the bones were discovered. The day after the bones were found, I received the anonymous email."

"What did it say exactly?" I asked.

He looked at me as if he wasn't going to answer the question, but then he said, "It said, 'Drop it, or you will be the next to get buried.'"

I shivered.

Milan folded his arms. "And we are just supposed to take your word for it?"

"It's true," Rhett said and removed his phone from his pocket. The sweatpants were so tight, he had a little trouble getting it out.

When he finally had the phone in his hand, he tapped on the screen and held it out for Milan to see. "See. That's what it says, and you can see it was sent using the form on my website."

Milan reached for the phone, but Rhett pulled his hand back. "Not so fast. I let you see the email. I'm not handing over my phone without a court order."

"Okay, if not my grandmother, who do you think killed Ripley?" I walked across the room and leaned on the kitchen counter.

"That's the problem I'm running into. I don't know. I thought if I came here today and looked over the scene where the body was discovered, that it might jar something in my brain to give me some clarity."

"And did it?" Milan asked.

"No, because I wasn't there long enough before you ran me over the fence."

"You ran him over the fence?" Dad asked.

"He climbed the fence of his own accord," Milan said. "Because he was trying to not get caught."

Dad shook his head and polished the revolver hilt in his hand.

"So, you have zero suspects," I said.

"I didn't say that," Rhett snapped. "I have people of interest on my list who certainly would have the right motive to want Ripley out of the picture."

"Who?" I asked.

"Your friend Jessa, for one," he said, looking me straight into the eye.

I gasped. "Jessa would never hurt anyone," I said. "She is the most well-liked person in town."

Rhett shrugged. "Maybe you don't know her as well as you think you do."

"Why would you think that?" I asked.

He looked me in the eye. "You'll have to ask her. She can better answer that question than I can." He turned to Milan. "I think I have said enough to get my car key back."

I disagreed, but Milan removed the key fob from his pocket and slid it across the table.

Rhett scooped up the fob and stood up.

"You just keep those pants," my father said. "I can never wear them now anyway since you stretched them out."

Rhett gathered up the sad remains of his ripped clothing and walked out the door without saying goodbye.

Dad shook his head. "I hope Stacey dumps him like a bad habit."

It sounded to me like she already had.

I looked Milan. "Why did you let him go?"

Milan stood up. "I have to get back to Antrim County. There will be a lot of ice fishermen out on the lakes today looking for spots. Let's talk outside."

I sighed. I knew his real reason for wanting to discuss it outside: he didn't want to have an argument in front of my father.

Milan said his goodbyes to Dad and went out the door.

I patted my father on the shoulder. "I'll see you later, Dad."

He glanced up at me. "Don't ruin your friendship with Jessa over this. There aren't many people in your life you can one hundred percent rely on, and she is one of them."

His comment came off as a warning.

I whistled for Huckleberry and left the house. I found Milan outside, leaning on the hood of his truck.

"Where's Rhett?" I asked.

"My guess is he is halfway back to Michigan Street by now. He couldn't leave this house fast enough."

I checked the time on my cell phone. "I need to head into town myself. Jessa said I could come back to the diner after the church rush to talk about Edna Lee." I paused. "We have a lot more to talk about now."

He nodded. "I wish I could go with you, but I really do have to get back to the lakes."

I nodded. That was the thing about dating a police officer. Milan tried to make himself as available to me as he could, but there were times when he just couldn't be there. In this case, I was relieved. Jessa was my friend, and I wanted to have this conversation with her alone.

I cleared my throat. "I just don't understand why you let Rhett leave just then. There are so many more questions that I wanted to ask him."

"We don't want to completely alienate Rhett. I could tell it was time to back off in case we ever had more questions for him."

I twisted my mouth. I wasn't in total agreement with Milan on this, but he had far more experience with interviewing witnesses than I did.

He studied my face. "What's wrong?"

I looked up into his dark eyes. "I can't believe that Jessa killed anyone as much as I can't believe that my grandmother did."

We stood in the driveway outside the farmhouse, and I kicked at a tuft of brown grass that grew through the well-worn gravel. It was amazing to me how well some plants survived in poor conditions. At the same time, being a farmer, I knew that many crops were temperamental and needed ideal conditions to thrive. That was especially true on an organic farm like mine, where no chemicals were used to protect the plants from insects or disease. It was water, soil, air, and tender loving care that made my crops grow. If any one of those were out of sync, the harvest would fail that year, and I would have to wait a whole year for a chance to grow the failed crop again.

"It's hard for me to believe too, but Rhett seemed confident that she could be a good suspect. That's not something that we can rule out, even though we might want to."

I knew he was right, but that didn't change the fact that it hurt me to even consider it.

Chapter Twenty-Eight

Huckleberry placed his front paws on the dashboard and wriggled his stubby curl of a tail as I turned the truck into the gravel parking lot next to Jessa's Place. He looked at me with a silly grin on his face. It wasn't often that we went to Jessa's Place more than once on the same day, and for him that meant twice the snacks. You could not find a happier pug.

I shifted the truck into park and cut the engine. "Tomorrow, we are both going to stay off of fatty food. We can't eat like this all the time."

He dropped his paws to the seat and looked at me like I was a traitor. I really needed to stop talking about diet in front of Huckleberry. He just found it to be too triggering.

The parking lot only had a few cars in it, and when Huckleberry and I walked into the diner, there was a group of elderly ladies sitting in the very back laughing and enjoying desserts and coffee. Jessa had been right: this was the best time to stop by and talk.

My stomach churned at the thought of the conversation I needed to have with her, and it was made even worse with the news I had just learned from Rhett, assuming that I could trust it. It was possible Rhett had said Jessa was a suspect in Ripley's murder as means to escape from my father's kitchen.

Jessa sat in one of the booths by the front window, wrapping paper napkins around silverware. She smiled when she saw me, but her smile didn't make it all the way to her eyes, which was unusual when it came to Jessa. She always smiled with her eyes. It was one of her most welcoming characteristics.

I pointed to the revolving pie display to tell Huckleberry to sit there, but Jessa spoke up. "Huckleberry can come over here and sit under the table with us. There aren't enough people in here to make a fuss about it."

I tugged Huckleberry's leash in Jessa's direction, and I didn't have to ask him twice to see his friend.

When we reached Jessa's booth, Huckleberry promptly placed both of his front paws on her knee. She leaned over and gave him a kiss on his forehead. "You're such a good pup. Let me finish these and I will go fix you up some bacon."

His tail wagged so hard that his entire body shook.

I slid into the booth across from her. "I can help you with these."

"You don't have to do that. I can have it done in no time."

"And with my help, you can have it done faster," I said. "I worked as a waitress when I first moved to LA. It was at one of those fancy restaurants in Beverly Hills. I couldn't afford a single item on the menu, not even the water, because it was all imported."

She placed a knife, fork, and spoon on a paper napkin and

rolled them together. She moved with the assurance of someone who had done this a million times before. Jessa had been working at Jessa's Place since she was eleven years old. Her father opened the diner and named it after his only daughter. Jessa always said it was his legacy, which he planned to leave to her, and that's exactly how it happened.

I never knew Jessa's father. He died long before I was born, but the stories I heard told me he was a lot like Jessa—kind and personable and beloved by everyone in Cherry Glen.

I watched her wrap two more sets, and then, seeing the pattern that she wrapped them with, I got to work on it myself. "Tell me about Edna Lee."

She sighed. "She was the best friend that I ever had. I was absolutely crushed when she drowned. There are times that I still think about it and wonder where she would be if she had lived. She was so talented. I have always seen a lot of her in Stacey. Edna Lee would be so proud of Stacey for saving the theater. Before it shut down, she used to be in community productions there when we were kids. She stole the show every time. It closed down right before we entered high school, and she was heartbroken over it, but even with the theater closed, she never lost the acting bug. In fact, she was even more determined to leave Cherry Glen and make a name for herself on Broadway."

"How did the two of you meet?"

"In school. We were in the same grade. But at the same time, everyone knows everyone in Cherry Glen. We had known each other since we were in diapers, but it wasn't until we went to school that we became close. We respected each other. Edna Lee had been dreaming of Broadway, and I knew from a very early age that I would take over the diner from my dad someday."

"What was Edna Lee's relationship with James Ripley?"

She wrinkled her nose. "Edna Lee hated her name, so everyone in school called her Eddie. She liked that better, but not by much. She said that Edna Lee wasn't a good stage name, but she went by that professionally because she claimed Eddie wouldn't get her any respect in the theater."

I rolled another set of silverware.

Jessa rolled two more sets of silverware.

"James was nearly twenty years older than us. He had left Cherry Glen and come back. He claimed that while he was gone, he lived in New York and worked as a showrunner for Broadway." Her voice was heavy with doubt.

"You didn't believe him?" I asked.

"No. It was just too convenient for him to happen to have worked on Broadway. Back then there was no Internet or anything to verify that he was telling the truth. Eddie showed me a few snapshots of him in New York, but as far as I could tell, he could easily have been a tourist in those pictures." She shook her head. "For her, it was enough proof. She so desperately wanted her dream to come true that she blindly believed him."

"Were they a couple?" I asked.

She nodded. "Eddie told me more than once that she was in love with him, but I always thought she was more in love with the idea of what she thought he could do for her."

"She was in her midtwenties, in love with Ripley, and he

had connections in New York. What was keeping her here? Why didn't they just go? Why did they wait?" I put another roll of silverware in the basket at the end of the table.

"Eddie said that James said she had to save up five thousand dollars before they left so that they could make a down payment on an apartment. He claimed that he had gone to New York the first time with no money, and it had been really difficult. He didn't want her to go through that. This time he wanted to do it right."

"Five thousand dollars was a lot of money back then."

"It's still a lot of money in my eyes," Jessa said. "It was taking time for Eddie to save that much too. She worked here at the diner with me. Do you know how many tables you have to wait to make that much money with your hourly rate and with tips, especially forty years ago? We were making maybe two dollars an hour, and the tips weren't much better than that."

"What about Ripley? What was he doing to save up the five thousand dollars?"

"That was just Eddie's half. He said that he was saving up five thousand dollars of his own for that down payment."

I knew apartments in New York had always been expensive, but that sounded like a lot of money for forty years ago. "He wouldn't go to New York until he had ten thousand dollars?"

"That's what Eddie told me."

"How was he earning it?"

"I don't know. I don't know what he did for work, and I don't think Eddie knew either. She wasn't one to ask him a lot of questions. I thought that was because she didn't want to learn anything that might ruin her idea of being a Broadway star."

"What happened to her money after she died?"

She shook her head. "I don't know. I just have to assume that James took it."

"Did you tell this to the police or my grandmother?"

She wouldn't look me in the eye. "I wanted to, but Eddie was already gone. I couldn't see the point of it."

"It could have spurred Chief Randy to investigate her death."

She shook her head. "Nothing was going to make the police chief to do that."

I knew that was mostly true, but I still felt like my grandmother should have known that she had been right to suspect Ripley. From what Jessa was saying, he was scamming her, not only out of her money but also out of her dream.

But maybe my grandmother did know, which was why she was so set on Ripley being responsible for Edna Lee's death. Something that my grandmother said to me when I was in college came to mind: "Shiloh, never trust a man with your money. Make sure you always have your own money. Men are vain creatures and will spend their money on just about anything other than what they should. Women are better at such things."

At the time I thought she had been talking about my father, who at that point was spending a large portion of the farm's funds on his history collection. But maybe she had been thinking of what happened to Edna Lee too.

I looked down at the silverware in front of me. The questions I needed to ask Jessa next were going to be the most difficult. "Milan and I caught Rhett snooping in the orchard today. He said that you had a motive to want Ripley dead."

She wrinkled her brow. "That was rude of him to say. I don't go marching around saying that he is a possible killer."

"Why would he say that?"

"Probably something I said in my interview."

"Your interview?" I asked.

"I'm sure you know by now that he is writing a book on James Ripley's disappearance. I'm sure he's over the moon now that he can call it a murder. From what I understand, murders do better in the true crime genre than missing persons do."

"Usually," I agreed. "How did you find out about the book?"

She didn't look at me. "I knew that he was writing a book on it because he asked to interview me. Somehow, he had found out that Eddie and I were friends. He wanted to better understand James's connection with Eddie. I told him what I just told you."

"When?" I asked.

"A few days before Thanksgiving."

I frowned. "If you knew that he might have anything to do with Ripley, why didn't you say something to me sooner?"

"He's not the killer. He would have been a little kid when both Eddie and Ripley died. I thought it was interesting that he wanted to write a book about it, and maybe I was a little flattered to be interviewed. I didn't know how your family would feel about it, considering the history with Ripley, so that's why I didn't say anything. I didn't want to upset your father."

"What could you have said to him that made him think you might have something to do with Ripley's death?"

She rolled the last set of silverware, tucked it into the basket, and slid the basket in front of her as if she was building some kind of barrier between us. "I said one of the happiest days of my life was the day he disappeared."

"Because of Edna Lee?" I asked.

"In part, but also because he hurt everyone he came across." She paused. "Myself included."

I stared at her. "You loved him too?"

"I never loved him, but after Edna Lee died, we did have a short romance. I think we came together because we were just so distraught over losing her. It only lasted for a few weeks, and I came out of it surer than ever that he wasn't a good guy. I swore off men after that. I'd rather be alone and run this place on my own than be swindled by a scoundrel like him. After our little tryst, it was both painful and embarrassing to see him around town. Even though I had behaved so poorly out of grief for my friend, I knew I had betrayed Eddie in some way, so yes, the day he disappeared was a good day for me." She slid out of the booth and picked up the basket of silverware. "Let me go get Huckleberry that bacon. The poor dear must be starving."

As she walked into the kitchen, I sat back in my seat and mulled over everything. It sounded to me like James Ripley was a real piece of work.

She returned with the bacon, and Huckleberry was on his feet ready to accept her gift. He spun around in tight circles of anticipation. She gave him the bacon and smiled.

"Losing Eddie changed your grandma, so you never knew the woman she was before Eddie passed. She felt guilty about not letting Eddie go to New York right out of high school. I know that was the reason that she encouraged both you and Stacey to leave Michigan and chase your own dreams. I think Emma Kay blamed herself for her daughter's death. If she would have just let Eddie leave when she wanted to, she would have never met James, and she might still be alive today."

Knowing that my grandmother lived with that kind of guilt for the rest of her life broke my heart.

Chapter Twenty-Nine

Chesney and I spent the first half of Monday preparing the barn and chicken coop for winter. It was a cold day, but we couldn't wait any longer. We had to put both the sheep and the chickens out of their homes so that everything could get a thorough cleaning, but we kept the sheep in the side yard by the barn. We still didn't know whether the bear was in Cherry Glen or if he had moved on, but I wasn't taking any chances with Teddy Bear and his ewes.

Diva's favorite thing to do each morning was leave the coop so she could terrorize other creatures on the farm. However, she was not in favor of having her castle invaded by humans with scrub brushes and soap. She barely tolerated us being in there for a few minutes to collect eggs. Going inside the coop under these circumstances was taking our lives into our hands.

Cleaning the chicken coop, in my opinion, was a much worse task than cleaning the barn. The ceiling was low and the corners were tight, but I would much rather do it alone than have Chesney in the coop with me. I didn't know if I could keep myself from telling Chesney what I had learned from her sister. What made matters even worse was, every time Chesney expressed how worried she was about Whit, I wanted to tell her what Whit had been doing with Rhett.

By my calculations, Whit had about three more hours before the twenty-four-hour waiting period she had forced me to agree to was up. I hoped that Whit would come forward with the information soon because my stomach was in knots wondering how Chesney would take it.

There was nothing dirtier than cleaning a chicken coop, but I was thrilled with the results when I was done. The walls shone, the windows sparkled, and all the nesting boxes were lined with fresh straw. As much as Diva was upset by the act of having the coop cleaned, I knew she was going to love the results.

I straightened the nameplate that Chesney had made for Diva's nesting box. "Diva the Chicken. Queen Bee. Top Hen. Dictator," it read. Right on every point.

I stepped out of the henhouse and found Diva standing outside, glaring at the door. "Your castle awaits, your majesty."

She gave me a beady look before she pranced into the coop. I knew it was getting a thorough inspection.

Shaking my head, I walked back to the barn.

In the barn, the five orange tabby barn cats sat together on a bale of hay and watched Chesney work. Esmeralda, who gave off the same queen energy as Diva, sat on the hay bale above the other cats. She always had to assert her authority. Huckleberry napped by the door. I had left him with Chesney while I cleaned, as Diva could barely tolerate Chesney and me being in her coop; she would lose her chicken brain if Huckleberry were in there too.

Huckleberry gave a great yawn and stretched as I scratched his belly.

I stepped into the barn, and it looked great. We had been working on it for a few days, and I was pleased with the progress. It was just about ready for winter.

"Chicken coop is all clean," I said. "Diva gave it her scratch of approval too."

Chesney dropped a shovelful of debris into the steel wheelbarrow next to her and then leaned on her shovel. "Wow, you must have done a great job if Diva liked it."

"I wouldn't say she liked it, because I don't think Diva likes anyone or anything, but she didn't rush at me with her talons after seeing it. I have to count that as a win."

"I would. The barn is just about done too." She pushed her bangs out of her face with the back of her hand. "I have to do a couple of more things, and then we are set for winter as far as the animals are concerned. There is a lot more work we have to do to get the fields and orchard ready."

How well I knew.

"After you finish the barn, take a little break, and if you can, make a list of everything we need to do to button up the farm for winter. Snow is predicted for later this week, so we need to stay on top of it."

"I'd love to!"

I knew she would. There was nothing that Chesney loved more than making a to-do list. I hoped that would put her in a good mood for when Whit talked to her. I also hoped that after I got home from town, Whit would have shared what she had been up to these last few months with her sister. I still didn't know what the last bit information was that Whit had to confirm before telling Chesney what she knew.

"What are you going to do?" she asked.

"I'm heading into town. There are a few people I want to talk to."

She adjusted her glasses. "Are you investigating Ripley's death?"

"I'm just asking a few questions."

She gave me a look. Chesney knew me well, which was why I needed to get away from the farm before she started asking uncomfortable questions. I was so afraid I might tell her what Whit said. A promise was a promise, and I had to keep the secret for at least two hours and twenty minutes more. I told myself I would do a little research in town, and when I got home, Whit would have told her sister everything that was going on. Then I would be able to breathe again. It sounded like a perfect plan. Too bad that none of my perfect plans ever turned out that way.

Forty-five minutes later, I was ready for my trip into town. I had one stop in particular in mind, and it should have been open by now since it was late in the morning.

As I was lifting Huckleberry into the cabin of the truck, the back door of the house opened, and Dad popped his head out. "Where are you going?"

I arched my brow. My father rarely cared about my comings and goings from the farm. "Town," I said.

"Good. I need a lift to the theater. Stacey had some kind

of meeting this morning and can't pick me up. She told me to get a ride from you. Let me grab my coat and script." His head disappeared back into the house.

Huckleberry and I shared a look.

Dad was back three minutes later. He set his walker on the back steps and very carefully lowered it to the ground before shuffling on the well-worn path from the back door to the driveway. "I wish I didn't have to rely on you girls for rides here and there. I'm perfectly capable of driving myself around."

I kept my mouth shut. It wouldn't do any good for me to remind him of the three fender-benders that he had gotten into before Stacey and I finally took away his license and truck keys for good. It wasn't an easy decision, but it had been the best way to keep him and everyone else on the road safe.

He reached the truck and handed me his walker to put in the back as he grabbed on to the passenger side door and lifted himself into the cabin. It took all my willpower not to give him a hand. I held back because I knew how insulted he would be and that he would be in a foul mood for the rest of that day over it. Dad wasn't one to recover from perceived slights quickly.

When the walker was stowed and he was inside of the truck, I closed the door and hurried around to the other side. At the rate I was going to reach the center of town, Whit would have most definitely told Chesney about their mother's adoption before I got back home.

I closed my door and started the engine. Huckleberry settled in next to my father's hip and gave a contented sigh. Dad fondled his ears. Dad might barely tolerate me a lot of time, but he loved my dog, and for me that went a long way.

Dad shifted in his seat. "What are you doing going into town? Usually on Mondays, you are crazed working on the farm. Don't you have a lot to do to prepare the farm for winter?" He wrinkled his nose. "It's already snowing off and on. I told you that you should have started getting the farm winter-ready before Thanksgiving, but you never take my advice when it comes to these sorts of things."

"There is nothing to worry about. We already have the barn and chicken coop done; those are the most important tasks. Chesney is making a list as we speak of everything we have left to do. It's well in hand," I said.

"You're lucky you have Chesney. You would never be able to do everything you have to for the farm without her. I wish that I had a Chesney all those years ago when I was running the farm solo. I would have been much more successful then."

I didn't say anything, as I saw no reason to discuss yet again why the farm had almost failed under my dad's care. It wasn't because Chesney wasn't there.

"If I were you, I would stay on the farm and help her," Dad said.

"I won't be in town long."

He sniffed. "I don't know about that. When you have an idea in your head, you're like a pug with a bone."

Huckleberry lifted his head.

"All right, Huck, I'll give you a bone when we get home later."

"What are you talking about? What idea do I have in my head?" I asked.

"I know you're not letting the Ripley thing go. You're going into to town find something to investigate. Does Sheriff Penbrook know what you're up to?"

"Milan trusts my decisions."

Dad shook his head. "Blinded by love."

I sighed. "Maybe it wouldn't be as hard for me to find out what was going on if you helped me," I said. "You were around when Ripley disappeared, and I wasn't."

"I don't know anything about it."

"Do you know anything about him? That might help me. I don't even know if he has any family."

He held on to his seat belt and turned to look at me. "What are you talking about? Of course you know that he has family."

"Who?"

"Norman at the general store is his nephew."

"What? Why didn't you tell me that before?"

He cocked his head. "I thought everyone knew that. Shiloh, sometimes I think you went to California and lost your mind. You don't seem to remember a thing about life in Cherry Glen from before."

I frowned. I remembered more than I wanted to at times, but I didn't bother to argue with my father about that.

"Were he and his uncle close?" I asked.

"They spent time together, I know that. They lived in the same house for a good amount of time."

I felt my neck tingle. This could be just what I needed to

lead me to Ripley's killer. If Norman and Ripley lived in that same house, Norman just might know what his uncle was up to at the time of his disappearance. Finally, I had somewhere else to look instead of at Grandma Bellamy, and I had my father, of all people, to thank for that.

The truck rolled down Michigan Street past Jessa's Place and the giant Sherman tank that was parked at the edge of town. I was still processing the conversation I'd had with Jessa the day before. I couldn't help but wonder if she had really told me everything that she knew.

I was just about to turn into the alley that led to the parking lot behind the theater when Dad said, "We are still a bit early for practice. Take me to the municipal building so I can surprise Connie. I'll walk over to theater after our visit."

"Walk? I'm not sure that a good idea, Dad." I gripped the steering wheel because I knew he wouldn't want to hear it.

He scowled at the windshield. "Shiloh Emma Kay Bellamy, do you think I am completely incapable of taking care of myself? I will use the confounded walker. It's less than a block."

"The road and sidewalk could be icy."

He glowered at me. "It's none of your concern. Connie will make sure that I can cross the street safely. At least she believes in my abilities, unlike you and Stacey."

"Stacey doesn't believe in you?" This was a surprise to me.

He sniffed. "She is always telling me to sit down and take breaks during play practices. She doesn't say that to anyone else. You both treat me like an invalid."

I winced. The last thing I want to do was make my father

think I thought less of him. That wasn't true in the least. Both Stacey and I worried about him. He had so many health concerns, and he was just a few weeks away from being eighty years old. We had good reasons to worry.

None of that mattered if we gave him the wrong impression. "I'm sorry, Dad. That was never Stacey's intent or mine. We know that you are very capable of taking care of yourself."

He examined my face as if to see if I was telling the truth. "Glad to hear it." He opened the cabin door and got out.

I held myself back from running to the other side of the truck to help him.

Dad held on to the passenger side door while I removed his walker from the truck bed and set it in front of him. He gripped the handles and shuffled forward.

The glass doors to the municipal building opened, and Connie came out. She wore the same outfit she always did to work: a long skirt, thick sweater, sensible shoes, and her eyeglasses hanging from a chain from around her neck. She had a set of keys clipped to her belt that was so large, I was surprised her whole body didn't lean to the one side due to the weight of it. They were on par with the keys of a nineteenth-century jailer.

"Oh, Sullivan, this is such a wonderful surprise. You're such a sweetheart to visit me today. I must tell you, the first day back in the building after a long holiday weekend is the hardest. You have made it so much better."

Dad grinned from ear to ear. "If I had known you were having such a challenging day, I would have had Shiloh stop so I could buy you some flowers."

She placed her hands on her cheeks. "You are the sweetest man."

My father blushed.

I looked from one to the other and felt like the proverbial third wheel. "I'm going to go to the general store for coffee now."

"Coffee." Dad snorted. "That's what you call you snooping now?"

"Oh?" Connie asked.

Dad shook his head. "Shiloh has it in her mind that she can solve the forty-year-old murder of James Ripley. Isn't that most ridiculous thing you ever heard?"

I grimaced. Connie Baskins worked for Chief Randy. How did I know that she wouldn't going to run to the police chief and tell him that I was meddling in his case? The death of James Ripley was difficult enough to solve without Chief Randy threatening to arrest me.

"I don't think that is wise. Chief Randy would not like it," Connie said. That was all the proof that I needed that she would go and tattle to the chief. I needed to get to the general store and find out what Norman knew about his uncle before the police chief put a stop to it.

"I really have to go. Dad, be careful when you walk to the theater." I waved to them and clipped Huckleberry's leash onto his harness.

"Oh, you're going to walk, Sullivan? I commend you for that. I'll walk with you. I can take my break when you head over. I would love to see how the stage was transformed over the last few days."

Dad beamed at her. "That is so kind. I don't know when I have had someone be so kind to me."

Connie looked over her shoulder at me. "I have your father now, Shiloh. Take my advice: don't get too embroiled in the death of James Ripley. He came to a bad end, and you don't want the same to befall you."

I jerked back. Her comment certainly sounded like a threat.

Chapter Thirty

Cherry Glen General Store was an institution in town much like Jessa's Place. They were the two businesses on Michigan Street that had survived the recession in Cherry Glen until its renaissance in recent years, with the help of Kristy's farmers market and Stacey saving Michigan Street Theater from demolition. A successful brewery in the old grain warehouse across the street from the municipal building and half a dozen little boutiques and shops up and down the half-mile stretch of downtown solidified Cherry Glen's new look. The small town was well on its way to becoming the backdrop of a feel-good movie.

Before a mega grocery store had opened on the highway between town and Traverse City, the general store was the place everyone in town went to buy what they needed. I remembered going there after school to pick up milk or paper towels for my grandmother. Today, the store was more of mix of soda fountain, coffee bar, and gift shop. However, if someone was in a pinch, they could still buy milk and paper towels there too.

Artisan wares from Michigan artists filled the front third

of the store. Intermingled through the colorful displays were café tables where people could sit and enjoy their coffee or ice cream, depending on the time of day.

Two young women sat at one of the café table, sipping lattes. Two strollers were parked beside them with sleeping infants inside. The women were in their early twenties. Had I still been in LA, I would have thought they were nannies taking their charges out for a walk, but in Cherry Glen, they were most likely the mothers of the babies.

I walked over to the old-fashioned soda counter, where Norman Perch was polishing glasses with a white cloth. He looked up at me and smiled. "Shiloh Bellamy, this is a nice surprise."

Norman was a rail-thin man with a gray ponytail and penchant for Grateful Dead T-shirts. This morning, he wore one such T-shirt. When I was a child, I had thought Norman was ancient. Now I realized he must have been in his sixties. Twenty years ago, he would have been close to the age I was now, but truth be told he always looked like he was older. Maybe the many outdoor concerts in his young life had aged him.

"What can I get you? A mocha? An iced vanilla latte? Cherry mocha? I have a new white chocolate turtle mocha that the young kids are going gaga over."

I hadn't had this many choices when it came to coffee since moving home to Michigan. It certainly wasn't LA, with a chain coffee shop on every corner. Jessa was firm that it went against her morals as a true diner proprietor to have any coffee drink available aside from regular coffee and decaf.

In Cherry Glen, if you wanted to find a cappuccino, iced coffee, or even just a latte, the general store was the place to go. Norman began to cater to the flavored-coffee lovers, and his business had picked up ever since.

"I'll take an iced latte with skim milk," I said.

He set the glass he had been polishing on the counter. "You're no fun at all. I am trying out new recipes. I was hoping that you would be my guinea pig."

"Maybe another time." I sat on a red vinyl stool at the counter. Huckleberry lay by my seat and promptly fell asleep; he had had a long morning of supervising cleaning.

I shifted on the stool. "I ate way too much on Thanksgiving, but now that I think about it, with Christmas on the way, you should add a peppermint mocha to your menu."

He snapped his fingers. "That's a great idea. I'll add it to the list. I should get on that too, because people are already flooding into town, doing their Christmas shopping."

I nodded. "We had a good turnout at the indoor farmers market on Small Business Saturday. Kristy was pleased and plans to do it again."

"Good to hear. You want the coffee to go?"

"No," I said. "You can put it in a glass. I'll drink it here."

He arched one of his silver bushy eyebrows and set to making my latte. As the machine hummed, I looked around the shop and thought about how I was going to bring up his uncle.

He set the latte in front of me in a frosted glass with a stainless-steel straw. "You're here to talk to me about my uncle James, aren't you?"

It seemed my worries about how to bring up his uncle weren't an issue.

I stirred my latte with the straw. "Is it that obvious?"

"I've been expecting you ever since I heard that James was found on your farm. I knew it would only be a matter of time before you showed up and started asking questions. You're always poking your nose into things, aren't you? And this one landed on your doorstep."

He wasn't wrong about that.

"I just found out he was your uncle," I said. "I had no idea until my dad said something."

He nodded. "It's not something I talk about a lot. He's not the kind of family member that you advertise. He wasn't the nicest of guys. Other than my poor mother, I can't think of anyone who missed him when he disappeared. The general feeling was relief."

"He was your mother's brother, then?" I asked.

Norman picked up a steel water bottle covered in peeling stickers from the back counter and took a long drag from it. As he screwed the cap back on, he said, "He was, and he was a bone of contention in my parents' marriage until he disappeared. My parents thought that he just left Cherry Glen for good. They would be shocked to know he's been dead all this time." He put the water bottle back on the counter. "I'm happy that my mother isn't alive to see it. She would have been crushed and blamed herself for not looking harder for him."

"And your father?" I asked.

"He's still alive and lives with my older sister and her husband in Traverse City. Before you ask, it won't do any good for you to talk to him. The poor old soul has dementia. He doesn't even know who I am when I drive out there to see him, which honestly, I don't do as much as I should. I know it's wrong to let it all fall on my sister, but I'm just not equipped for that."

I felt badly for Norman's father but was disappointed too. If he were in his right mind, I would have wanted to speak to him about Ripley. That was off the table now.

"When your uncle disappeared, how long was it before your parents realized he might not come back at all?"

"A few months. He was never officially declared missing. Chief Randy did look for him for a time as a favor to my mom. She had been his piano teacher growing up, and he always had a soft spot for her."

I blinked. Chief Randy played piano. This was an unexpected detail about the police chief. Not to mention that he had a soft spot for anyone other than his granddaughter, Hazel.

"I think he felt bad too." Norman began polishing glasses again.

"The chief did? Why?"

"He knew how much my mother loved her brother and how much my dad hated him. Chief Randy agreed with my father that Uncle James was bad news. He and my father tried to convince Mom to kick Uncle James out of the house for good. She just couldn't bring herself to do it."

I wrinkled my brow. It seemed to me that the police chief was more personally involved in James Ripley's life than I had known.

"When was this?" I asked.

"The summer before Uncle James disappeared."

I sipped my coffee. That would have been after Edna Lee died. Was that significant?

"As far as I know, Uncle James was the only topic that my parents ever disagreed on." Norman tapped his water bottle on the counter. "When my mother finally accepted that my uncle wasn't coming back, I never heard them argue again, but my mother was sad. I heard her tell a friend once that she failed her brother."

My heart hurt for Norman's mom. I certainly understood the strong desire to help your family but not being able to make a difference. And if the person you're trying to help doesn't want your help, you were even more at a loss.

"When did he go missing?" I stirred my coffee with the straw.

"Around Christmas." He nodded. "I was thirteen at the time, and my sister was already married and living in Traverse City. I remember because I was about to go to a haunted house with a group of friends, and Mom said that I couldn't go because she wanted us all to be there when Uncle James came home. I was so mad about it. I never cared much for my uncle, and I didn't want to miss a fun night out because of him."

"But he didn't come back that night."

He shook his head. "He didn't come back many nights, and it was right before New Year's that my mother went to Chief Randy asking for help. My dad was so mad about it. He said it was an embarrassment to the family bring it to light."

Her husband's opinion was likely the reason that she didn't file an actual missing person's report.

What surprised me was how embroiled Chief Randy had been in the case. He never once mentioned that he knew the family on a personal level. I really didn't know if it was noteworthy or not. As he said, everyone knows everyone else in Cherry Glen. That was true, but still I found this latest bit of news unsettling.

"What did James do for a living?" I asked.

He shook his head. "I don't know officially. My dad always said he was swindler. He was also looking for the next big idea and next big thing to invest money in. The problem was he didn't have any money. He would scrape up funds from who knows where or borrow it from my mother."

"Did he pay her back?"

"Not as far as I know. When my dad got wind of it, he blew a gasket. I'd never seen him so mad."

"When was this?"

He thought for a moment. "My parents' huge fight over Uncle James and money was years before his disappearance. I think I was in grade school. I don't remember exactly when, but I do remember the terrible argument my parents had about it. I really thought that they would get a divorce because of it."

"You said that he'd been able to scrape up money. Aside from your mom, do you know how?"

"I don't know exactly. Dad said we were better off not knowing. Even after my parents gave him money, he lived with us off and on. At the house I grew up in, there was a one-bedroom apartment over the garage. That's where Uncle James slept. He came and went all hours of the day and night."

"I heard that he worked on Broadway in New York as a showrunner."

Norman laughed. "Where did you hear that? He did live in New York for a while, but I believe he was just on the maintenance staff in a theater, and from what I remember my father saying, he didn't have that job very long at all."

I suspected as much.

"When he left for New York the first time, Dad was so relieved. He thought he was gone for good. He and Mom were happy then. Unfortunately, Uncle James came back. Except for that last time, my uncle always came back, and Mom always let him back in our lives."

Could Norman's father have killed his brother-in-law to remove him from his wife's life? It wasn't that far-fetched to believe. Norman's father had been upset with his wife when she reported Ripley missing. Norman's father would certainly be another suspect, a suspect that Chief Randy had completely ignored, but he was also an elderly man with dementia. It felt cruel to accuse him.

"Did your uncle have a girlfriend?"

"He always had a girlfriend," Norman said. "He had a way about him that was very charming. He was good-looking too. He always had the prettiest girls in town fawning over him. It was not a secret that Uncle James was bad news, but none of them seemed to care."

"Did you know my aunt Edna Lee?" I asked.

"Eddie? Sure."

"She was seeing your uncle."

He nodded. "She wanted to be an actress, and they had plans to go to New York. My father encouraged it because he wanted Uncle James to leave Cherry Glen and never come back."

I nodded. At least that was something that checked out with Jessa's story.

"But they never went," I said.

"No. Uncle James said they needed to save up money first. I think he meant that Eddie had to save up money because I far as I could tell, Uncle James wasn't doing anything to contribute to it. When Eddie drowned, Dad was so upset because that meant that Uncle James had no reason to leave Cherry Glen."

Norman's father was looking more and more like a viable suspect.

Norman sighed and set the glass he had been polishing down on the table. "I don't know what to do about the funeral arrangements."

"For your uncle?"

He nodded. "I'm next of kin and Chief Randy said that his remains will be released to me. I might just do a committal and spread his ashes at his favorite spot. I think that's what my mother would have wanted me to do."

"Where was that?" I asked.

"Herchel Pond."

The pond where my aunt died.

Chapter Thirty-One

I left the general store with a hot white turtle latte in my hand. Norman wouldn't let me leave until I tried it, and I had to admit that it was delicious even if it was so sweet that it made my teeth ache.

Up ahead of me on Michigan Street, I saw Chief Randy standing by my car writing on a notepad. I scooped up Huckleberry in my free arm and ran down the sidewalk.

I came to a stop about ten feet from the police chief and caught my breath. "What's going on?"

He arched one of his bushy silver eyebrows at me. "What does it look like? I'm writing you up a ticket for illegal parking."

"What?" I asked. "How? This is a legal spot."

He tucked his pen behind his ear. "I'm afraid you are over the line, and because of that, I have to give you a ticket. I may not want to, but the rules are the rules."

I looked down to where he pointed, and the bumper of my car was just a hair over the white line into the no parking area.

He ripped the ticket from his notebook and held it out

to me. "Now, if you want to take it to court, you can contest the ticket."

With no other choice, I took the ticket from his hand. I took a deep breath so that I wouldn't snap at him. Contesting the ticket would take more time and money than just paying it off, but that didn't mean that I was happy about it. Chief Randy knew my truck. Cherry Glen was small; everyone knew everyone else's truck. He specifically targeted me to give me a bogus ticket because he didn't like me. I was seething.

He snapped his notebook shut. "Sadly, this will be another point on your license," he said. "The speeding ticket I gave you a few years back is still on there too. Be careful. One more violation, and you could be in some serious trouble. I would hate to take your license away from you."

He wouldn't hate anything of the kind, and now I knew I needed to be on my guard, and watch my speed and where and how I parked. Chief Randy was gunning for me, but the question remained as to why. He didn't like me, that was clear, but I had never known him to go out of his way to make my life more difficult. What had changed? Was it finding James Ripley's bones?

He turned back toward the municipal building.

"Chief Randy, before you go, can I talk to you for a moment?"

He looked at me. "If it's about the ticket, you will have to take it up with the court system."

"It's not the ticket. I'd like you to reopen James Ripley's case."

He waved me away. "I am not going to let you waste my time with this nonsense."

"It's not nonsense," I argued. "You just can't blame a person for a crime because they aren't here to defend themselves. Is that really upholding justice?"

"Did I not tell you that your grandmother left a signed confession?" He raised his bushy eyebrows.

"I want to see it."

"Not going to happen."

"Then I will hire a lawyer to make you let me see it."

He laughed. "If you want to waste your time and money, that's your choice." He shrugged.

"I hadn't realized that you were so close to James Ripley's family."

He glared at me. "What are you talking about now?"

"I just had a nice conversation with Norman Perch, and he said that you and his father tried to talk his mother into kicking Ripley out of their home."

A red flush ran from the base of his neck to the very top of his bald head. "You have finally fallen off your rocker."

"That's strange because Norman specifically remembers you and his father having this conversation with her. He said it was the summer before Ripley disappeared."

"Why on earth would you believe what Norman has to say? The man has fried his brain smoking Lord knows what over the years."

I frowned. Norman never struck me as remembering something incorrectly. It was no secret that he had a history of marijuana use, and he would be the first person to admit it.

"Norman's mother was the sweetest woman that you ever met. She taught me piano for years when I was growing up. My only connection to the family was through the piano lessons, and I stopped those when I was in high school because I was more interested in playing football." He narrowed his eyes. "Are there any other questions that you have about my life story?"

I shook my head. "No, that was it."

"Let it go, Shiloh, if you know what's good for you. You keep this up and you will have a lot more than a parking ticket to deal with. Do you understand me?" With that, he went back into the building.

I stood there for a moment and felt a knot in my stomach. It seemed to me that Chief Randy was somehow involved in Ripley's disappearance. How closely he was connected was yet to be determined, but if he were directly involved, I could not help but worry what impact this would have on Quinn and Hazel. More than anything, I didn't want Hazel to be hurt.

Chapter Thirty-Two

When I parked in front of the oldest standing house in Cherry Glen, I hopped out to make sure it was perfectly placed by the curb. I had a feeling that Chief Randy had his officer out on the field just to monitor how I parked with the hopes of hitting me with another ticket.

Mayberly House was the former home of one of the richest men who lived in Cherry Glen, Jed Mayberly. In the early 1900s, he had started the granary that was now the local brewery. He and his family lived in Cherry Glen their whole lives. His ancestors were original pioneers in the area. As the story went, his great-great-grandfather came to Cherry Glen on a scouting trip, married an Native American woman, and stayed here. The family line finally ran out with Jed Mayberly's children, as they didn't have any descendants of their own, but there were still distant relatives who lived in the area.

I knew this all because of the countless lectures I had endured from my father growing up. It was funny that I could remember this story, but algebra was completely lost in the recesses of my brain.

The last direct descendent of Jed Mayberly left the house

to the town in his will, but by that time, the home was in disrepair. It had taken a Herculean effort to raise the money to restore it. I remembered selling candy and doing yard work when I was child to raise money for the house. It was a town-wide effort. That was over twenty years ago, and by the looks of it, Cherry Glen had forgotten Jed Mayberly and his home. The sign out front was crooked and the handrail leading up to the wraparound porch was loose.

The years had not been kind to Mayberly House. There was no *Open* sign on the outside of the house, and I wondered if I would even be able to go inside and search the town archives, which was my reason for being there in the first place.

I wondered if my father knew what a sad state the Mayberly House was in. I didn't believe he could have because he would have been up in arms over it. No one loved Michigan history as much as my father did.

I knocked on the door, but there was no answer after several knocks. I tried the antique doorknob, and to my surprise it turned. I let myself into the foyer.

The house smelled like just what I expected it to. It was a mix of must, stale air, and dried flowers. It was the same scent that seemed to permeate every historic home I'd ever visited.

There was a small side table along the wall with a guest book. A handwritten note by the guest book said, "Please sign." I did as instructed and took one of the shiny brochures off of the table. The people in the pictures looked they had just walked out of 1990s central casting.

Now what should I do? Was the tour of the house self-guided? Could I just walk around?

Before I could make up my mind to go look for the archives myself, I heard shouts from the parlor down the hallway.

I followed the noise.

"Do you want to save this place or not?" a sharp voice asked.

"Of course I do! Mayberly House is my life's work."

"Then start acting like it. This program is the one that's going to put the house back on the map."

"I don't think it was ever on the map," the second voice said.

"We are going to put it there and help my birds in the process."

As soon as I heard the word "birds," I knew where I had heard that voice before. Hedy Strong was in the building. Hedy was a naturalist and bird-watching guide in the area. I had gone on owl walks with her the past. Truth be told, I had gone on the walk with the hopes of finding a killer but had learned a lot about owls too.

"Hello," I called. I wanted to give plenty of warning I was there. Hedy was a punch-first-apologize-later kind of gal. I wasn't going to take any chances.

"Is someone out there? Matilda, did you lock the front door?"

"I don't remember doing it," Matilda said.

Hedy gave a dramatic sigh and came out of the room. She saw me standing there with Huckleberry like a couple of thieves creeping through the house. "Well, well, well, if it isn't Milan's girl."

"Milan's girl?" I asked.

She shook her knobby finger at me. "I know all about your little romance with my friend. I stay posted on such things."

I was sure that she did. Hedy was old friends with the Penbrook family. I was certain that she had heard from Mrs. Penbrook about Milan and me.

Another woman came out of the room. She was short like Hedy, but much thicker in the middle. Even with their difference in size, I could see the resemblance.

"Matilda, you will never guess who is here. This is Shiloh Bellamy, Milan's girl, who I was telling you about," Hedy said.

I really wished that she'd stop calling me "Milan's girl." It made me feel like I was a piece of property.

Matilda adjusted her glasses on her short nose. "She's pretty. I can see why Milan likes her, and you're right. She does look like she's from California."

Hedy clapped her hands. "Told you so."

Maybe I should get rid of my blond highlights to blend into the Michigan world better.

Matilda held out her hand. "Matilda Strong. I'm Hedy's sister, and it's so nice to meet you. What brings you to the Mayberly House?"

"I was hoping to use the archives," I said. "I'm looking into an incident that happened forty years ago."

Matilda eyes shone. "The archives! No one comes here to ask the use the archives unless they have a school assignment. When they do, they don't really want to be here." She paused and looked me up and down. "You're not here for a school assignment, are you?"

"I'm way past school," I said.

"What a delight." Matilda clapped her hands and then grabbed mine to pull me down the hallway.

I stumbled after her. "Is it okay if my dog is in here?"

She stopped and turned. "Oh, a pug? I just love pugs. I didn't even see him there; I was just so happy to have a real-life visitor. Yes, he can stay as long as he doesn't touch anything."

I grimaced and wondered how much experience Matilda had with dogs.

"This way. This way." She pulled on my arm.

Thankfully, Huckleberry followed me without question. He looked around the old house with wide terrified eyes. My father's farmhouse was a century old, but nothing inside of it was as ornate as the furnishings in the Mayberly House. Even the ceilings had carvings in them, and the ones that didn't have carvings were painted like the sky.

Matilda caught me looking up. "Jed Mayberly loved being outside, and when he wasn't outside, he wanted to feel that way, so he had the ceilings painted in this style. His bedroom on the second floor has a night sky so it would feel like he slept under the stars. There's so much to show you." She shook with excitement.

"Matilda, please calm down. You get so overexcited sometimes. This is why I don't let you on any of my bird walks. You would scare all the birds away!" Hedy said this as if it were a cardinal sin, and I almost jumped, hearing her so close behind me. I had no idea she'd followed us.

Abruptly, Matilda turned a corner and ran me right into the doorframe, knocking the air out of me.

"Oh, I should have told you about that sharp turn." She looked me up and down. "Are you all right?"

I nodded because I wasn't yet able to speak.

"Matilda, you're like a bull in a china shop. Yet another reason you can't come on any of my bird walks with me." Hedy sniffed.

"Yes, Hedy, you have made it clear where I stand on your bird walks. You don't see me asking to go on one, do you?"

While the two sisters bickered, I gathered myself and took in the room. It was a huge space, probably double the size of my cottage. Inside, there were shelves and shelves of archival boxes and old books.

"This used to be Jed Mayberly's study," Matilda explained. "But now it's used for the town archives. I would love to find another place to put the archives, so that we could restore this room to the way it was when Mr. Mayberly was alive. There just isn't enough time, money, or manpower to do everything that I want to do for the house. It is a constant battle to get any bit of help from town."

I could tell by the ceiling and the woven rug on the floor that this room had been as highly prized as all the others in the house, and maybe more so. The most striking feature was the fireplace, which had a hearth large enough for a full-grown man to stand in.

Matilda seemed to read my mind.

"Mr. Mayberly was always cold, and since he spent most of his time in here, he had this fireplace custom built so he could stay as warm as possible while he worked. Behind you is a hidden pocket door that leads into the parlor. When it was just the family here, the door would be open and the fireplace could easily warm both rooms on even the coldest night." She smiled. "Now, what was it you were looking for?"

"An article that would have been written in March forty years ago."

"Do you know the title of the article?"

I shook my head. "I don't even know if it exists, but I wanted to check."

"If you are looking for an article that is forty years old, that would be in the *Cherry Glen Daily*. Can you believe that Cherry Glen actually had a daily newspaper at one time? Everyone in town read it from cover to cover. It was the main source of conversation in the town. Mr. Mayberly was the person who fun—"

"Matilda! Stop!" Hedy shouted. "Leave the woman alone. You don't need to spout every single thing you know about the house. Shiloh came her for a specific bit of information.

"It's the computers in school, I tell you," Hedy said. "They think they can find every answer in the world in that little machine. Children can't even read cursive nowadays. It's disgraceful."

Matilda nodded.

"What is all in here?" I asked.

Matilda leaned against her desk. "There is just a wealth of knowledge here, and no one even knows about it. We have all of Mayberly's private papers, public papers from all the businesses that have been in Cherry Glen over the years, and of course, we have all the newspapers over the years all the way up through today. What was the subject matter of the article you wanted?"

"I would like to know everything you might have about Edna Lee Bellamy's drowning in Herchel Pond forty years ago."

Matilda placed a hand on her heart. "Everything?"

I nodded.

She jumped in place. "I didn't know that I would ever be asked about it. I have been waiting and hoping, and the day is finally here."

Chapter Thirty-Three

I glanced at Hedy, who rolled her eyes. What was clear to me was that the Strong sisters were passionate about the things they cared about. In Hedy's case it was birds, and in Matilda's it was archives.

"You have been wanting someone to ask you about Edna Lee?" I asked.

"Not Edna Lee specifically, but I was hoping someone would ask me about one of my death books."

I tensed up. "Your death books?"

Hedy flopped into the lone armchair in the corner of the room. "Matilda, you're scaring the poor girl. You make it sound like you're obsessed with death."

I looked from one sister to the other and wondered where I was. When I came into Mayberly House, I had not expected Hedy to be there, nor had I expected the archivist to jump up and down in excitement over my aunt's death.

Matilda put a hand to her chest as if she were trying to catch her breath. "I'm so happy you asked because I have death books for every person who died of suspicious causes in Cherry Glen. It's a bit of a hobby of mine."

"Death books?" I squeaked again.

Huckleberry looked up at me with concern. I debated scooping up the pug and fleeing Mayberly House right then and there.

Matilda nodded. "I think it's important to keep a public record in case anyone wants to look into one of the cases, and I want to do my part to help."

"Matilda is obsessed with true crime," Hedy explained. "It's all she reads, listens to, or watches. I don't understand it. There are plenty of problems in the world without digging up more from the past."

Ah. I suddenly understood. I had run into my fair share of super fans. They were the ones who called in outlandish tips or wanted to share a theory about what may have happened in a case.

Sometimes those tips and theories panned out, but most were duds. As a producer, I listened to them all in the hopes that just one would point my team in the right direction.

"Don't make it sound like it's just a little hobby, Hedy," Matilda said. "It's my life's work." She beamed at me. "You're in some yourself since you have been involved in a few of the murder investigations in town too. The more recent death books have more data, but I am doing my best to catch up the older cases too, as more and more information goes on the public record." She snapped her fingers. "Oh, I know why you're here; it's the discovery of James Ripley's bones in your family orchard. Yes, yes, that makes perfect sense. You wish to clear your grandmother's name. I just pulled James Ripley's death book this morning to update it. I have to tell you, adding to a death book that has grown cold decades ago is a thrill, and there is so much more to add to this one."

"He has a death book even though no one knew he was dead until this week?" I asked.

"He didn't technically have a death book, but since he went missing, I thought it was worth gathering the clippings and evidence that I had about him. Knowing who he was, I think everyone in town was convinced that he came to some kind of bad end. Some think he died, but others thought he just ended up in prison in another state or ran away to Mexico. He attracted trouble."

"I'd like to see Ripley's death book also," I said.

She clapped her hands. "This is the very best day." She pushed herself off of the desk and stepped behind it. "I was working on it late last night. It was a struggle to stop. Thankfully, I live on the second floor of the house, so I stumbled up to bed at two in the morning when I just couldn't keep my eyes open anymore."

Hedy clicked her tongue. "You tell me you can't stay up to go on my owl walks, but you stay awake to sort through papers?"

Matilda pulled out the desk chair, but instead of sitting in it, she looked at me. "Come, come, have a seat. Everything is here for you to see about Ripley. While you go through James's book, I will pull the death book about Edna Lee Bellamy. It might take me a little while. I will confess, I haven't looked at that one in a long time."

I smiled at her. "This is a good place to start. Just from

what I'm seeing, you have a lot here, and I have worked on cold cases before."

"You have?"

"I was a television producer in Hollywood for nearly a decade. I worked on home improvement and cooking shows, but most of my work was in true crime."

Her eyes shone. "You did? What shows did you work on?"

I named a few.

Matilda clutched her glasses. "I watched all of those. They are my favorites. Hedy, you didn't tell me we were in the presence of greatness."

From her chair, Hedy snorted in disgust.

Matilda's hands shook. "Everything I have done must look so amateurish to you. Oh dear, now I am so embarrassed for you look to at one of my books."

"Don't be. I'm impressed by what you have here. From what I can see, you're organized and dedicated to the facts."

She blushed. "That is the kindest thing that anyone has ever said to me." Tears came to her eyes. "Let me find Edna Lee's book."

Matilda scurried away, and I was happy to have a little peace and quiet for a few minutes while she searched. What I couldn't believe was how much she had been able to gather from the discovery of Ripley's remains, which happened just a few days ago. She had newspaper articles going all the way back to when he disappeared, but those weren't the only articles. There were even more from the police blotter from when he was alive. Ripley had been arrested for everything from assault to unpaid traffic tickets. The traffic ticket one stood out to me. Were they fair tickets, or had Chief Randy been targeting him too?

Not including the traffic violations, it was clear that Ripley had gotten into a great deal of trouble when he was alive. Norman had said that his uncle had been in trouble with the law, but it wasn't until I saw all these articles that I realized just how much.

I flipped through the pages. Matilda's death books were four-inch three-ring binders, and all the articles inside of them were neatly clipped and slid into acid-free plastic sleeves. They were organized in chronological order. Matilda was meticulous. I could have used her on my shows back in California. My notes and storyboards would have been a lot more orderly if she had been there.

I flipped through a few articles about Ripley's transgressions and stopped when I came to an unexpected article. It wasn't a mention of a traffic ticket or an arrest. It was the mention of a new business venture. The headline read, "Ripley Opens Survivalist School."

The article went on to say how Ripley was hoping that the school would teach children and teenagers to live off the land. He had bought a small parcel of land by Herchel Pond and hoped to start offering classes there.

Herchel Pond was the same place where Edna Lee drowned over forty years ago. This could not have been a coincidence. I frowned and checked the date in the article. It was over sixty years ago, which meant the survivalist school should have been well established when Edna Lee died twenty years later.

I frowned. That still didn't answer the question as to why Edna Lee had been there. She was an actor and used to the bright lights of stage and screen. She didn't strike me as a survivalist.

"Here. Here it is." Matilda placed a binder in the corner of the desk. "I know this one looks a lot thinner, but to be honest there wasn't much out there about her death. There was no sign of foul play other than your grandmother's letter to the editor."

I raised my brow and opened the book. The first article reported my aunt's death. The second was her obituary. I noted that the funeral services were to be held at Doreen Killian's church. This was a surprise to me. I had never known my grandmother to attend church there. In my lifetime she attended a Lutheran church just outside of town. Grandma Bellamy had never mentioned she went to Doreen's church, even as a child.

The third article was the letter to the editor that Matilda mentioned and was dated two months after Edna Lee's death.

"Edna Lee's Mother, Emma Kay Bellamy, Claims Foul Play" was the headline.

My grandmother wrote: "I know that someone was behind my daughter's death, and it wasn't an accident. The chief of police is protecting the culprit, and I can only believe that is because the guilty party has some information that Chief Randy doesn't want to get out. I won't stand for it and I won't give up until my daughter's killer is held responsible. Who is responsible, you ask? It's none other than James

Ripley. This should not come as surprise to anyone in Cherry Glen as he is the most notorious troublemaker in town, and I will stop at nothing to bring him to justice."

I whistled. Grandma Bellamy hadn't pulled any punches.

I could hear my grandmother say those words. She had been gone for almost twenty years, but I still could hear her voice in my mind. She had always been forceful and direct, and when she was angry, everyone knew it. In this article, she was angry. This was a declaration of war against James Ripley and also Chief Randy and his department. It made more sense than ever why Chief Randy disliked me on sight. We have butted heads over the years to be sure, but his dislike for me had all started with my family and my grandmother. There was no way he was ever going to give me a chance, and no wonder he and Doreen were so upset at the idea that Quinn and I had considered dating. They didn't want to be tied to the family of an enemy.

The next article was an interview with Chief Randy. It was clear that the reporter was there to get a reaction from the police chief after my grandmother's letter to the editor. "It comes as no surprise that Emma Kay Bellamy has made such a statement. She has been a troublemaker in Cherry Glen since she could ride a bike. I don't want to give her words that much attention, but what I can tell you is the Cherry Glen Police Department is dedicated to justice, and that is justice for all. Yes, James Ripley has been in trouble with the law in the past, but I am telling you there is no evidence that he was in any way involved in the death of Edna Lee. Stating the contrary is not only irresponsible but wrong.

I would advise Mrs. Bellamy to take care with her words or she could find herself in a whole heap of trouble."

The final article was another letter to the editor that my grandmother had written. In it, she vowed that she would never give up until there was justice for Edna Lee and that she feared no one—not even the police chief.

When I looked up from the book, I found Matilda staring at me.

I jumped.

"It's fascinating, isn't it? Now it's come full circle as Emma Kay has been found to be the killer," Matilda said.

"But she's not the killer," I said. "No matter how angry she was with someone, she would never take another human being's life. It's just not possible."

Matilda blinked at me. "But I have her confession."

My chest ached. "You have the confession?"

She nodded. "And according the Cherry Glen Police Department, it's all the evidence that they need."

"You mean according to Chief Randy."

"He is the police department," she said.

Hedy pushed herself out of the armchair that had attempted to swallow her small frame. "Matilda, you didn't tell me anything about this! Why didn't you say something?"

Matilda looked at her sister. "Because you have no interest in my death books. Every time I bring them up, you just pretend to listen, but I know from the look on your face, you're thinking of birds."

"I'm always thinking of birds." Hedy rolled her eyes.

"Exactly. How do you think that makes me feel to know

my sister has zero interest in any of my interests?" She sniffled.

"I could say the same thing to you. When was the last time you asked me about a bird?"

"Why would I? You talk about them incessantly. Bird talk has fried your brain."

I stepped in between them. "Ladies, please, let us focus on the situation at hand."

They both looked at me like they had no idea why I was there. I had a feeling they were in the middle of an old argument they repeated at least once a week.

"The confession," I said to their blank faces. "Where was it found? How did it come into the police's possession? And how did you get it?"

Matilda snapped her fingers. "It was with the bones."

"I can't believe that," I said. "If the bones had been there for decades, the paper would have decomposed by now."

"That's the interesting part. Whoever buried it with the body wanted it to be found because it was in a watertight metal tin."

The pain in my chest became a little worse, because this sounded remarkably similar to how my grandmother had buried her valuable stocks all those years ago under the front porch of my father's house.

But that didn't mean she wrote this confession or buried it with Ripley's body. It was just a coincidence, wasn't it?

"And Connie gave it to me. Unlike the chief, she sees the value of preserving Cherry Glen's history," Matilda said.

"Why would Connie send you anything on an active

case? She could compromise the investigation, not to mention get into a great deal of trouble."

"It's not an active investigation. It's closed and was closed as soon as the confession was discovered." She cocked her head as if she couldn't understand why I was so upset.

So much of this didn't make sense to me. I could see Chief Randy closing the case because of the confession, but wasn't it too early for Connie to be handing over the confession to Matilda?

Milan was at the scene the entire time the bones were being exhumed. He would have told me if a tin was found with the bones. Wouldn't he? Maybe he wouldn't have told me right then, but when I told him Grandma Bellamy was being blamed for the murder, he would have; I just knew it. This could only mean that the police chief hid this bit of information, or Chief Randy planted it. As much as I didn't like the police chief, I could not believe that he would plant evidence like that. He wasn't the nicest cop, and he made known who he liked and disliked, but I couldn't believe that he was so corrupt. I didn't want to believe that about Quinn's dad or Hazel's grandfather. I cared about both Quinn and Hazel, and it would crush them.

"Can I see the confession?" I asked.

"Yes, yes, of course, that's why I'm here: to make sure the residents have all the historical knowledge that they need about the town."

She rifled through a file folder and pulled out a single sheet of paper. She held it out to me. "It's not the original, of course. That's still in the police station, but Connie was kind enough to make a copy."

I took the paper from her hand and placed it on the desk in front of me. I was almost scared to read it, but I knew that I had to. I also reminded myself that Grandma Bellamy wasn't a killer and a simple piece of paper wasn't going to change my mind on that.

"James Ripley deserved to die for what he did to my daughter," the letter began. "This note is a reminder that, against all odds, my daughter received justice in the end. A life for a life. Emma Kay Bellamy."

I stared at the note. It was typewritten in an old-looking font. I frowned. Had my grandmother owned a typewriter back then? Computers were around then, but my family didn't get one until I was in high school. I tried to think back to the cottage where my grandmother lived. When I cleaned out the cottage, I didn't find a typewriter. There definitely wasn't a computer.

Grandma Bellamy was a farmer. Most farmers are very reluctant to throw anything away because it could always be used in a future season. Extra lumber was kept for projects, old paint cans were always on standby for touch-ups. If there had ever been a typewriter on the farm, it would still be there.

If this had been a handwritten note, I would have been more inclined to believe she wrote it. My grandmother loved to write notes and letters. Her penmanship was clean and distinctive.

"Does Chief Randy know Connie gives you evidence like this?" I asked.

Matilda's face turned red. "The police chief might not

think much of my death books, but Connie is a big supporter, and she is always helping me. After a case is closed, she sends me all the information she can find. What she sends me is not organized; it's always such a chore going through those notes. But this case wasn't as bad since I had had a death book on James for many years." She smiled. "It not often that a cold case like this is solved, and I like to believe that I played a part." She cocked her head. "Do you think this would make a good show? Can you pitch it to any of your old friends in Hollywood?"

I grimaced. The very last thing I wanted would be a true crime show blaming my own grandmother for murder.

I placed a hand to my forehead. It was cool, but that didn't change the fact that my head was spinning. Honestly, I didn't know what to think. A tiny part of my brain reminded me that Grandma Bellamy had never let me dig in that corner of the orchard.

"Has anyone else been here asking about Edna Lee or Ripley?" I asked.

"Yes!" Matilda's eyes sparkled. "A man is writing a book about Ripley's death. He interviewed me for it."

"When was this?" I asked.

"Just before Thanksgiving. He was back yesterday too. Such a nice man."

"Was it Rhett Lumberly?"

"Yes, do you know him from your true crime days?" Matilda asked. "How exciting."

I ignored her question and asked, "Did you show him the confession?"

"Yes, of course I did, and he made a copy of it too. He's going to use it in the book. Isn't that amazing? He's going to credit my death books too!" Matilda shook with excitement. "A book is great, but if Hollywood called I would be *very* interested in that!"

"I do have one more request," I said.

Hedy and Matilda nodded.

"Please don't tell Chief Randy I was here. And don't tell Rhett either if he comes back."

"We won't breathe a word," Matilda said.

"Not a word," Hedy agreed. "Because no matter who killed James Ripley, I think we can all agree we are happy he's dead."

Chapter Thirty-Four

"Hedy, how can you say such a thing?" Matilda cried.

"After the way he treated you and so many women, I can say whatever I want. I don't care if he's been dead all this time. It's good riddance, in my opinion. We don't need him here to waste perfectly good oxygen."

I raised my eyebrow. "How did he treat women?"

Matilda wrung her hands.

"He was a playboy," Hedy said. "He always had one or two girlfriends at a time, but he always told each woman that she was the one. It was disgusting. I can't believe so many women fell for it."

Matilda's face was bright red. "He was very charming."

"Charming?" Hedy snorted. "That is not the basis for a relationship."

"As if you have so much experience," Matilda snapped.

"I don't have any experience," Hedy shot back, "and that is on purpose. I would much rather go birding than waste my time on men."

Matilda bit her lower lip.

"And I certainly wanted nothing to do with James Ripley.

He had a reputation of being unkind to the women he was seeing," Hedy said.

"How so?" I asked.

"There were accusations of abuse."

It was what I was afraid she would say.

"Did anyone go to the police?" I asked.

"Chief Randy? Are you crazy? What good would that have done? He would have just dismissed us and told us we were overreacting. It's hard enough to accuse someone of something. It doesn't help if you're not taken seriously."

"Are you telling me a lot of the woman in Cherry Glen would have a reason to want Ripley to disappear?"

"I would be hard-pressed to think of one that didn't have a reason she wanted Ripley gone," Hedy admitted. "What really surprised me was when he disappeared there wasn't a parade. I think a parade would have just been the thing the town needed to celebrate such a victory."

When I left the historical society a few minutes later, my head was spinning. Outside of the Mayberly House, I shivered and stopped to zip up my coat. In the time I had been inside, the temperature had dropped by a good ten degrees.

Huckleberry lifted his paws from the porch and looked at them as if he wondered why they were so cold. I picked up the little pug and held him close to my chest.

Inside my truck, I turned the heat up full blast and looked at him. "Where to now?"

He gave a woof.

"My thoughts exactly," I said. "I need to talk to Connie Baskins."

I started the engine. I wasn't looking forward to this conversation with Connie. It was clear she had a problem with me. That could be my fault. I wasn't overjoyed when I found out that she was engaged to my father. I blamed that on being so taken aback by the news. I wished my father had told me about her prior to Thanksgiving, so it wouldn't have been such a shock.

As I drove down Michigan Street, town employees were wrapping the lampposts with green garland and white twinkling lights. I had been so caught up in James Ripley's death that I hadn't thought of Christmas at all. Chesney and I had an arts festival and Christmas parade where we were selling farm wares every weekend leading up to December twenty-fifth. That was what I should have been concentrating on… not who killed James Ripley nearly forty years ago.

I knew if I dropped it, it would all just go away. Townsfolk would whisper about my grandmother for a few days and then forget all about Ripley and his murder as they moved on to the next scandal to hit the town. Even my father thought I should let it go, but Dad never cared what anyone thought of him or anyone else.

I cared, and I couldn't just stand by and let my grandmother be labeled a murderer. I couldn't allow everyone to believe that Grandma Bellamy could have killed a person. Furthermore, I couldn't let the real culprit go free. Maybe it was all those years I spent working in true crime that made me like this. In any case, it was how I was now, and just as my grandmother wouldn't let Ripley off the hook for Edna Lee's death, I wasn't going to let Ripley's killer off the hook either.

That brought me to my biggest problem: the lack of suspects. Right now, the only suspects that I really had were my grandmother, who had passed, and Norman's father, who had dementia. Not even counting the confession, I could see why Chief Randy would accuse Grandma Bellamy of the crime.

The Strong sisters had said that Ripley had been a womanizer. Maybe I just had to find the other women he had scorned.

There was a small cluster of citizens in front of the municipal building. They were shouting and raising their hands. I parked a block away, clipped Huckleberry's leash onto his harness, and got out of the truck.

Huckleberry walked so close to me that I was afraid he would trip me with his leash. I scooped him up and tucked him under my arm.

As I drew closer, I saw that the crowd of ten or so citizens was around the mayor. Chief Randy and two other officers looked on.

"He's going to kill our pets!" a woman cried.

"He knocked over my trash can and made a terrible mess. Now, I have to clean up," an elderly man added.

"Please, please!" Sweat gathered on the mayor's forehead despite the cold. "The mayor's office is happy to take your complaints, but please speak one at a time."

Four more complaints about the black bear loose in town were hurled at him. I held Huckleberry a little closer to my chest, as if I expected the young bear to jump out from behind a lamppost or bench at any second.

The mayor wiped his brow with a handkerchief. He had been newly elected in the spring, and he looked like he was ready to quit. I imagined public service in a place like Cherry Glen would do that to a person. There wasn't enough money in the world to convince me to run for any political office.

Chief Randy stood a few feet away and had one hand on his Taser at his utility belt. I hoped he was doing that just as a show of force and wasn't thinking of actually tasing any of the people complaining.

"Please, please," the mayor said. "We understand how you feel, and we have park rangers from Sleeping Bear Dunes and other professionals in town actively looking for the bear. What I would tell you is to keep your trash cans in your garages and your pets inside until the bear is caught and moved to a safe area."

I held Huckleberry even closer. The last thing I would ever want to happen to him was to come face-to-face with a bear. Maybe it would be best to leave him back at the farm until this whole bear situation was handled.

"How do we know the bear won't come back after it's relocated? I saw a documentary that said they are very territorial. He might have claimed Cherry Glen as his territory!"

There was an audible gasp from the crowd.

The mayor, who wasn't even wearing a coat, pulled at his collar. "The people we have on the case are professionals. They will know what to do to make sure the bear is happily settled in a protected area."

"If they are so professional, why hasn't the bear already been caught? It's been days."

"Please," the mayor said. "I'm asking you for patience." He turned to Chief Randy. "Chief Randy, take it from here. I have work to do."

The police chief stepped between the mayor and the small crowd. "Now, that's enough. You don't have a permit to congregate here. I am asking you to disperse."

"A permit? We need a permit to ask questions?"

"If you have questions for the mayor, you can submit them through the mayor's office's website."

No one moved.

Chief Randy had his hand back on his Taser. "Go!"

Grumbling, the group broke up, but I didn't think that was the last that we would hear of complaints about the black bear in town.

After everyone was gone, Chief Randy and his two officers went into the municipal building. I waited a full six minutes in my hiding spot behind the tree before I went to the door.

I tried to open it, but it was locked. I set Huckleberry on the ground and cupped my hands around my eyes. I didn't see anyone or any movement on the other side of the glass.

I picked up Huckleberry and stepped back from the door. I frowned. It seemed the mayor, who had claimed to have an open-door policy for all his constituents, drew the line at bear complaints. Thankfully, I knew my way around the building pretty well, so I just walked around back to the parking lot, where I knew there was another entrance.

As I expected, the back door, which was for the staff, was unlocked. I let Huckleberry and myself inside. Huckleberry was getting heavy in my arms, but I was reluctant to put him down in case I needed to make a quick retreat. The back of the building went straight into the administrative offices for the town, and I knew I wasn't technically supposed to be there. However, I had a plan to say I needed to pay my water bill and got turned around. Never mind that the farm ran on well water, so there was no water bill to be paid. I would worry about that detail if it came up.

One of the doors along the hallway opened, and the mayor and Chief Randy stepped out.

"We have to get this bear. The townspeople aren't going to accept any more excuses. When was the last sighting?" the mayor asked.

"It was very early this morning by the high school."

"By the high school? We can't have it close to kids. Why didn't someone tell me? I need to be aware of this sort of thing." He pointed in the direction of the front of the building. "You saw what happened just now. They wanted to tar and feather me over the bear situation. As the mayor, I am always blamed for everything that goes wrong."

"It was close to four in the morning. By the time the team got there, he was gone. He must have moved on," the chief replied, not seeming the least bit concerned about the mayor's troubles.

The mayor sighed. "Just make sure that you get him, Chief Randy. I don't care how you do it, but I have to get these people off my back. I'm holding you responsible if anything at all goes wrong." He went into his office and slammed the door closed.

Chief Randy glared at the closed door before he stomped away.

I may not be a genius, but I guessed now would not be a good time to ask Chief Randy how exactly he found my grandmother's confession or, worse, suggest that he was one the who planted it.

Chapter Thirty-Five

I hurried down the hallway and went into the atrium, where Connie had her desk in the middle of the room. Her glasses were perched on the end of her nose, and their gold chain hung down on either side of her face. Her head bopped every time she typed a word.

"Hello, Connie," I said.

She jumped and knocked over a mug of coffee, spilling it onto her keyboard. She jumped up and coffee ran down her long denim skirt.

This was not the way to make a good impression on my future stepmother. I shivered at the notion of having a stepmother. This stepmother, in particular.

"Look what you made me do," she snapped. "Don't just stand there. Make yourself useful and get me some paper towels."

I set Huckleberry on the marble floor and told him to stay before I dashed off to the ladies' room for paper towels. When I came back a minute later, I found Connie standing over her trash can with her keyboard flipped over, shaking coffee out of the keys. I stepped behind the desk and was about to wipe up the mess on the floor when she snatched the paper towels from my hand and went about cleaning it up herself.

She set the remainder of the paper towels on her clear desk and flipped the keyboard upside down to let the last of the coffee drain from it. Something told me that this wasn't Connie's first rodeo when it came to coffee on the keyboard.

"Connie, I'm so sorry," I said. "Is there anything I can do?"

"What you can do is not sneak up on people like that. How did you get in here anyway? The front door is locked to keep the bear out."

I arched my brow. "You think the bear will come inside?"

"I don't know what that bear will do."

As we discussed the bear, Quinn came into the large room with a large carrier of coffees from the general store. I wasn't surprised to see it. He often bought coffee for his colleagues when he was on duty at the fire station, which occupied one-third of the municipal building.

Quinn stared at us. "What happened here?"

Connie sniffed. "Your friend made a mess."

Quinn chuckled. "Shi has been doing that her whole life."

I frowned at him. If he was trying to endear me to him, this wasn't the way to go about it.

Quinn removed one of the coffees from the carrier. "Here." He set it on Connie's desk with a smile.

Connie placed a hand on her chest. "You're such a gentleman. Kindness is always rewarded." She shot a glance at me.

Was she accusing me of not being kind? It wasn't like I startled her on purpose. I held my tongue from saying anything. I knew it would only annoy her more.

"What brings you here, Shi?" Quinn asked. "Are you one of the bear hunters?"

I picked up the end of Huckleberry's leash from the floor and wrapped it around my hand. "No. I have no interest in coming face-to-face with a bear."

"The crowd outside making such a scene about it is just looking for something to complain about," Connie said. "Today, it's the bear. Tomorrow it will be the choice of ornaments on the town Christmas tree. They're never happy. If the new mayor doesn't accept that, he is not going to make it in Cherry Glen."

"It's not easy to be a mayor of a small town," Quinn said.

"So true," Connie agreed. "I have seen so many mayors come and go over the years, and I can usually tell when one is about to bolt. It's only happened once, but I knew then what I know now about this mayor. He looks like a spooked horse."

"Don't you have to get those coffees to your coworkers?" I asked. "We don't want to hold you up."

He gave me a strange look, as if he were deciding whether or not I was speaking in some sort of code. I was, in a way, because I very much wanted to talk to Connie alone.

"They can wait," he said.

I pressed my lips together. "Connie, I was just at the Mayberly House."

"You were?" she asked. "It's such a nice little place. I know the mayor has it on his list of issues to manage this year. He doesn't see the value in it." She pressed her lips together in distaste.

"You have respect for history though," I said.

She sipped her coffee. "I do, but I don't know what you mean by that. Are you insinuating something?"

I shook my head. "I had a long conversation with Matilda Strong."

"Matilda Strong?" Quinn asked. "Hedy's sister?"

I nodded. "Hedy was actually at the Mayberly House when I was there. She is doing a birding program as a fundraiser for the house."

"I know Hedy is trying her best," Connie said. "But I don't believe that birding program is going to save the Mayberly House. Hedy needs to think bigger than that."

"Hedy is batty," Quinn said. "There's a good chance that her sister is the same way."

I frowned at Quinn. Why was he meddling with this at all? And why was he trying to make me look bad in front of Connie? I thought he and I had come to a truce.

"That is a rude thing to say," I said.

Connie shook her head. "No, he's right."

I looked back at her. "She showed me the death books."

Connie wrinkled her nose. "I think she shows everyone who goes to the house those books."

"I'm surprised that you seem to dislike the books, since Matilda said a lot of information in them have come directly from you."

She sniffed. "The Mayberly House has a close working

relationship with the municipal building. We all work for city government. I don't know why this would be headline news to you."

"Matilda said that Chief Randy doesn't like her death books and doesn't like it when you give her information."

"First of all, I only give her information on cases that are closed and/or the court case, if there is one, is already over. Second of all, Matilda doesn't know what she's talking about half the time. I would not look to her as a reliable source for anything."

I frowned. It was true Matilda was enthusiastic about her collection, but I didn't think she would purposely lie to me about Chief Randy's opinion on her death books.

"I was just surprised that you had already given Matilda everything about James Ripley's death. It's only been a few days," I said.

"Yes, I gave her copies of everything. The originals are still at the police station. I don't understand why you care."

"Because my grandmother was blamed for the murder based on a bogus confession."

Her face softened just a bit. "I can understand why you're upset. It's always shocking when we learn disturbing news about someone we love, but it's best to let that go now. You shouldn't let what happened all those years ago affect you. You didn't even know about your grandmother's involvement until this week. You see, it has had no real impact on your life."

"Have you told my father that you believe his mother is a killer?" I asked.

"How dare you! What happened forty years ago has nothing to do with the relationship I have with your father today."

Quinn looked down at his coffees as if he just realized that he didn't want to be there. "I'd better get these to the guys." He shuffled away.

To be honest, I was happy to see him leave.

The door to the municipal building opened, and a police officer came in.

Connie scowled at him. "What are you doing? That door is locked for a reason."

The officer held up the key. "The chief said that the people are calmed down enough now that he can unlock the door."

"All right," Connie said, but it was obvious she didn't like the idea in the least.

The officer hurried away. It was clear to me that he didn't want to get into an argument with Connie Baskins, and I didn't blame him. I wished I weren't arguing with her at the moment either.

A second later, the door opened again, and Milan strode into the room. He was in his brown sheriff's uniform, ball cap, and bomber jacket. He looked so official and handsome. My heart did a little flip.

Apparently, Connie wasn't moved like I was. "I knew we should have kept the door locked."

I was so grateful Quinn had already left to walk over to the fire department. The last thing I needed was the two of them to come face-to-face in front of Connie Baskins. I had no doubt in my mind she would run back to my father with a full report.

"Am I interrupting something?" Milan asked.

"Not at all," Connie said. "Shiloh was just leaving."

I sighed.

Milan raised his brow at me, and I shrugged.

Picking up Huckleberry, I walked to the door, and I heard Milan's footsteps behind me.

Neither of us spoke until we were outside.

"What was that all about?" Milan asked.

I unzipped my coat and tucked Huckleberry inside. The later in the day it got, the colder it became. "It's a long story. What are you doing here?"

"I wanted to talk to Chief Randy about getting a look at the confession you mentioned."

"You don't have to worry about that," I said. "I have a copy."

"What? How? He gave it to you?"

"Nope. Do you have time to go on a little field trip?"

He frowned. "I'm off duty, if that's what you're wondering."

"Good. Let's go in my truck because I know the way. I'll tell you everything I know and how I got the confession."

"Where are we going?" he asked.

"Herchel Pond."

Chapter Thirty-Six

The big freeze in Northern Michigan was really just beginning. Just the edges of the pond were frozen. There was still plenty of open water.

I stared at the pond and couldn't help but wonder how far out Edna Lee had been when she died.

"We're here," I said as I parked my truck in the small parking lot by the pond. It was the first time I had been to the pond since I was a teenager. Logan and I had come to the pond all the time to ice skate. Those afternoons on the pond were some of my favorite memories of high school. I could see Logan's face. He had one of those wide smiles that split his face in two. I had pictures of that smile that I rarely looked at anymore. It was so long ago, and when I saw pictures of Logan and me together, I felt like I was looking at two strangers. He was gone, and I was a completely different person. However, looking out at the pond, I could see his smile perfectly, and I could feel how it felt to hold his hand as I stumbled around the ice. Logan never stumbled.

"You okay?" Milan's voice was gentle.

I looked at him and wondered if I should tell him about

the memories floating around in my head. Who wanted to hear about their girlfriend's old fiancé? No one.

Even as I thought that, I heard myself say, "Logan and I used to come here all the time growing up. He was a great skater. He played hockey in the winter. I was terrible at it, but we always had fun here."

He nodded and said nothing. I was glad about that. It was what I needed from him.

"The last few days have brought so many memories back to me of my grandmother and of Logan. The memories of them both are so intertwined because they died so close together. I don't know if it makes sense."

"It does. You lost two people that you love within a couple of years of each other. Also, you were so young. It had to be a lot to digest."

"It was. I can't say I did a great job of dealing with it either. I just ran away to California." I stared out across the pond. It was so different from Lake Michigan, and not just in size. The Great Lake was in constant motion, like an inland sea, but Herchel Pond was as still as glass, reflecting the trees around us and the sky above, and projecting all of my most cherished memories across its smooth surface.

He reached over the seat and took my hand in his, giving it a kiss. "I think the truth is you're facing all of those memories now."

I realized that he was right.

Outside of the truck, Milan put his hands in his jacket pockets and looked out onto the pond. Outside of Michigan, I guessed this pond would have been called a lake. It was a quarter mile across and a half mile wide. There were spots when the water was as much as twenty feet deep.

The reeds and grasses that had grown all around the pond during the summer months had turned brown and bent over from the cold. Rose hips clung to multiflora roses. I took care to keep away from those, as the barbs on the stems were so sharp they could rip through denim like it was a piece of tissue paper.

It was no surprise there was no one at the pond that afternoon. Night fell early this time of year, and the temperature fell by the second. In the summer, people fished in the pond, and in the winter, they ice skated. The late fall was stagnant.

I walked up to the edge. The dry reeds and grasses crackled under my steps.

"Be careful," Milan said. He was a few feet behind me, giving me time and space with the memories rushing past my mind's eye like a VHS tape that had been fast-forwarded so much that the images were blurred and mere impressions.

He was kind to stand back. He was a good man, and I realized more and more what he added to my life. I cared about Quinn as a friend, and there had been a time that I thought that there was more to it. I realized now that wasn't true. We had just bonded over our shared grief for Logan. I needed a person who stood back when I needed a moment alone and held my hand when I was ready to accept help. That was Sheriff Milan Penbrook.

I walked back to Milan and wrapped my arms around him to give him a hug. "Thank you."

He looked at me, and his glasses slipped down his nose. It made me smile. He looked like a dumbfounded college professor, not a sheriff.

"For what?" he asked.

I carefully pushed his glasses back up the bridge of his nose. "For being patient."

He smiled.

"Now, I want to search James Ripley's wilderness school."

His smile grew into a chuckle. "Is that what we are really doing here?"

"How did you guess?"

With Huckleberry walking beside me on his leash, I led Milan around the pond. The good news was the ground was almost frozen. If it hadn't been, we would be just walking through mud. Mud was something that a person came to expect in rural Michigan during fall and spring. It was part of living the country life, but even though I was a farmer, I had never gotten used to it.

There were many times when I came in from the fields in the spring and I was covered head to toe in mud. It baffled me that there were so many people who paid for such skin treatments.

"When I was at the Mayberly House today, Matilda, who I told you about in the car, showed me an article about how Ripley had bought land by Herchel Pond and built a cabin there to live in. His plans had been to start a survivalist school." I pointed at a dilapidated cabin on the opposite side of the pond. "That has to be it."

"Cabin" wasn't the word that I would have used to

describe the building. It was much larger than that and looked more like a run-down barn.

"This cabin had to be here when you were a kid," Milan said.

"It was," I said. "Everyone thought that it was haunted, and kids would dare each other to go in there at night. It was just one of those silly town things."

"Did you ever go inside?"

"No," I said. "I was way too scared."

"You don't seem scared now. What changed?"

"I've seen a lot scary things in my life at this point. A haunted cabin doesn't seem like much."

Milan fell into step beside me. "Assuming that it is, we now know that he hasn't been in there for decades. What good does it do to search it?"

I pulled my stocking cap down over my ears. "I don't know, but I need another suspect for his murder. If I can just find one suspect, Chief Randy will have to reopen the case."

"I think you are overestimating the chief's eagerness or lack thereof to investigate anything."

The earth cracked and crackled under our steps. As we drew closer to the barn, it became more and more apparent what a terrible condition it was in.

The posts that had once held up the porch roof were toppled onto the ground. The roof itself was in pieces, scattered on what must have once been Ripley's front yard. Moss covered so much of the debris that we wouldn't have known what it was if we hadn't seen a shingle or two peeking out.

I picked up Huckleberry and tucked him into my coat.

There was no telling how many rusty nails or screws were lying around in all this mess.

Half of the front door was missing, and I gently pushed it open with the toe of my boot. It made a terrible creaking sound as it swung inward.

Milan and I peered inside. The interior was dark. The only light came through the open front door because the windows had been boarded up years ago.

"It's a wonder that they just didn't tear this place down," Milan said. "It's a wreck."

"I guess that depends on who is responsible for it."

"Whose name is on this land now?"

I turned to face him. "I don't know, but I do wonder if it could be Norman Perch as Ripley's nephew. I'll have to ask him."

"Are we going inside?" he asked.

"Of course." I stepped over the. I could barely see more than three feet in front of me.

Milan pulled a small flashlight out of his jacket pocket. He turned it on, and it was like the room had suddenly gone from black to high definition. The flashlight was small but powerful.

"You're like a Boy Scout. Always prepared," I said.

He smiled. "I'm a cop. The principles of being prepared are the same. I did leave my gun locked in your truck though."

I nodded. "There's no one here to worry about."

Huckleberry shifted around inside of my coat, and a second later, his head popped out. "I should have left Huckleberry in the truck too," I said. "I can't put him down. There are too many sharp, rusty objects in here."

"This place is a disaster, and I don't think it's just from the passage of time."

That was an understatement.

He shone his flashlight around. Every wall was spray-painted with fading graffiti and covered in stains and cobwebs. Cabinet doors hung from their hinges. "It's no wonder you all thought this place was haunted when you were kids."

I held Huckleberry closer to my chest, and he exhaled, like I was squeezing him too hard. I tried to relax, but I kept my pug close. The cabin was creeping me out.

"What should we look for?" I asked.

"I don't know that there is anything to look for," Milan said. "This place is rotted. We're lucky to be on a concrete slab. If we weren't we would fall right through the floorboards." He kicked one of the loose boards, and the most terrible smell filled the room.

I covered my nose with my right hand and used my left to cover Huckleberry's nose. "What is that?"

Huckleberry made a face. I was right there with him.

"It's some kind of dead animal," Milan said.

I held up my hand. "Don't tell me any more. I don't want to know."

"I thought you were a farm girl."

"Even if I'm a farm girl, it doesn't mean I like to see dead animals."

He nodded and kicked the board back over the animal.

"I think it's time to get out of here," I said. "There is no real sign of Ripley. Too much time has passed. Anything of value would have been stolen by someone by now." I started toward the door.

Milan reached out and grabbed my arm. "Wait."

"What?"

He pointed to the wall next to him. There were thick two-foot-long claw marks in the wood.

"Those aren't from a house cat," I said.

"No."

"Raccoon?"

"Not a chance."

There was a grunting sound behind us.

"Don't move," Milan said.

"Why?" I whispered even though I knew the answer.

"Bear."

Chapter Thirty-Seven

"What do we do?" I whispered.

It was a good question. The bear filled the doorway, which was our only means of escape. All the windows and the back door were boarded up. We wouldn't have enough time to rip the boards down before the bear attacked.

"I think the bear has been making this abandoned barn-cabin his den. He's not too happy we're here. Usually, they are more scared of us than we are of them, but we are in his space."

"Great," I said and held Huckleberry to my chest.

"I wish that hadn't left my gun locked in your truck," Milan said.

"You can't shoot him," I hissed.

"I wouldn't shoot him, but I certainly would use it to scare him off. Bears are scared of loud noises."

The boards cracked as the bear took one step into the cabin. In the light of Milan's flashlight, I could see a giant claw protruding from each toe on his huge paws.

I had never thought of black bears as big. When I thought

of a big bear, grizzlies and polar bears were the ones that came to mind. However, he looked plenty big in front of us as he stood on his hind legs. He had to be six feet tall.

"Hey, bear," Milan said. "Git! Git! Hey, bear!" He grew louder with each shout.

The bear looked at him as if he wasn't quite sure what Milan was saying.

"I don't know if that's going to work," I said. "I have a better idea." I took a breath and began singing "Jingle Bells" at the top of my lungs.

"That's actually horrible," Milan said.

The bear seemed to agree because he snorted. I didn't know if snorting was a sign of a bear about to attack or not, so I kept singing.

"*Jingle bells! Jingle bells! Jingle all the way!*" I sang at the top of my voice and completely off-key.

Milan put his free hand over one ear.

"Really? It's that bad?" I took a breath and kept going. At this rate I was going go hoarse and Milan just might go deaf.

"*All the waaaay!*" I sang.

The bear jerked his head back as if he smelled something bad, but I guessed it was his poor ears, not his nose, that had been offended. He took a step back and dropped to all fours again. I kept singing but could not help but wonder if that was worse. Weren't bears faster on all four paws? He might hate my singing so much, he could charge us.

"Sing louder," Milan said.

I gave "Jingle Bells" all I had. If I sang any louder, I'd lose my voice completely.

The bear began to walk backward, and then he turned and ran away.

Milan and I walked to the door and watched the bear tear off into the woods. We heard him crushing though brush. He was determined to get away, and I can't say I blamed him. I never wanted to hear myself sing either.

"Everyone's a critic," I muttered, but just to make sure that the bear didn't get any ideas and came back, I started singing "Jingle Bells" from the beginning again.

Milan held up his hand. "I think you more than scared him off."

I stopped singing. "What? You don't like my singing either?"

Huckleberry chimed in then and tilted his head back and howled at the moon, which was just beginning to rise over the pond as the sun set.

"Huckleberry," I said. "It's not *that* bad."

He howled again.

When the pug was quiet, Milan pulled his phone from his pocket and began dialing.. "Is that the only song you know?"

"No. I can take requests. I may not know the notes, but I always remember the words."

He shook his head and held his phone to his ear. "Hey, this is Milan Penbrook, Sheriff of Antrim County. We found your bear. No, no, he's not in my county. It's Herchel Pond in Cherry Glen. Right. We'll keep clear. We will head back to our truck and wait for you." He ended the call and looked at me. "Let me go out first."

"Sure," I said. I wasn't going to be a hero; besides, I still had Huckleberry in my coat. I wasn't taking any chances with my pug.

"Looks clear, but we shouldn't waste any time," Milan said. "We will fast-walk to the truck. If I tell you to run, you run. Understand me?" He looked me square in the eye.

I nodded. His gaze was so intense that I couldn't form words. I imagined this was much what he was like as the sheriff when he was on the scene of a domestic dispute or arrest. He always struck me as a mild-mannered man, almost academic, but I saw how serious he actually was about protecting others.

Thankfully, my singing seemed to terrify the bear into putting some distance between us, because we made it back to the truck without incident. When we were all safely inside the truck's cabin, I locked the door just in case. I wasn't taking any chances.

Huckleberry was so exhausted by the whole ordeal, he lay across Milan's lap and promptly fell asleep.

"There are bears around Torch Lake now and again. It's just part of living this far out in the wilderness. I will say I've never seen one that close-up before." He let out a breath. "It could have been really bad. I want you to be extra careful until the bear is caught and moved to better place for him."

This wasn't the first time in my life a bear had been spotted in Cherry Glen. It happened from time to time when bears wandered away from the national lakeshore. "Is the bear especially dangerous?" I asked. "Will they put him down?" I hated to even ask the question.

"They will only do that if he becomes a major threat, like

chasing or trying to attack someone. I'll talk to the rangers when they get here and make sure they know he's mostly docile."

"I mean, even though he might have been thinking about eating us, I still don't want him to be hurt."

Milan laughed. "You have a kind heart that way."

I stared out the windshield at the pond that was now illuminated in moonlight. It wasn't that late, but the sun had come and gone for the day. These short days were hard to stomach at times. When I lived in LA, I hadn't noticed or minded them as much. There was so much light pollution around me that it could have been in the middle of the night, and it would seem like midday. Out here, night was impenetrable.

The only light was the moon and the glow from Milan's cell phone as he checked messages. I knew he had to be checking in with his officers. As he said, he was never really off duty.

A cloud moved and the pond glowed. As I stared at it, I thought of what Grandma Bellamy must have thought of this place. I wondered if she ever came back here after Edna Lee died. She never talked about it with me, and I realized there was so much we never spoke about.

"What's on your mind?" Milan asked.

"I can't help but think how this place and what happened here changed my grandmother's whole life. My dad said that his mother and sister were opposites in so many ways. Grandma was the practical one. Edna Lee was the dreamer. In any case, it must have crushed her, but she never told me about it. I thought Grandma Bellamy and I were as close as a grandmother and granddaughter could be, but she never said a word of any of this to me."

"You were her granddaughter. She wanted to protect you."

I nodded. "And it would have been so painful for her to talk about, but Edna Lee was a huge part of her life. The longer I'm in Michigan, the more I learn about her, and the more I realize she kept from me. By not knowing the whole story, did I miss out on really knowing Grandma Bellamy before she died?"

Headlights hit the truck, and two park ranger SUVs and a police car pulled into the small lot.

Milan glanced at me. "Looks like Chief Randy is here too."

"Great," I said.

Milan and I got out of the truck, but I left Huckleberry inside just in case the bear was still around.

"Hey, Penbrook," one of the rangers said. "This was the place you saw him?"

Milan nodded. "From what we can tell, he's been using that old barn for shelter. It's not a bad place to be if you're a bear."

"But he's not in there now?"

"No, we made a lot of noise to scare him off." He glanced at me.

I was grateful he didn't tell the rangers that I broke out in an off-key rendition of "Jingle Bells."

"Where were you when you saw the bear?" the ranger asked.

"We were inside the cabin. From what I gathered, the bear was coming back home for the night and not too happy to find us in his place."

Chief Randy joined the group and stuck his thumbs into his utility belt. "What were the two of you doing inside that old cabin? It's unsafe. It should be leveled, if you ask me."

I spoke up. "Since it was James Ripley's cabin at one time, I wanted to take a look."

He narrowed his eyes at me.

The lead ranger glanced at Chief Randy and then at me and back again as if he were trying to figure out the tension between us. He shook his head. "If the bear has been living in that cabin, he's not likely to abandon it now. He'll be back. We will set up some trail cameras tonight to monitor the site and set up a humane bear trap at first light tomorrow. Hopefully, he will walk right into it, and we can move him with little trouble." He turned to Chief Randy. "Notify everyone in your town to stay away from Herchel Pond until the bear is caught."

Chief Randy nodded.

The lead ranger nodded at his coworker. "Let's get those cameras up."

They walked back to their vehicles, leaving me and Milan alone with Chief Randy.

He scowled at us. "I'm holding you responsible for letting the bear get away. How could you be so stupid? You're a police officer; where is your gun? You could have shot him, and that would have been the end of it."

"I'm not going to shoot a bear," Milan said.

"If I were here, I would have taken care of it. This just shows me what a weak backbone you really have." He glanced at me. "And that you would let *her* convince you to come out here on a wild goose chase is disgraceful to our profession."

Milan clenched and unclenched his fists at his sides. "I was not here as an officer. I came to the pond as Shiloh's friend. I should remind you if we hadn't been here, we wouldn't know where the bear was sleeping at night. The rangers have a much better chance catching him now that they know that."

"It's just like you to take credit where credit isn't due. Are you that bad of a shot? Is that why you didn't fire?" Chief Randy voice was taunting. He wanted to upset Milan, but I wasn't sure why. Was it just to get back at me?

"The animal is just looking for a place to live, and it's clear that he's much more afraid of us than we are of him. I'm not just going to shoot him."

Chief Randy sniffed. "I still don't know why anyone would elect you sheriff."

"Since we are from different counties, it shouldn't matter to you."

"It does because you keep showing up in my county. You have no jurisdiction here, and if you keep at it, I will report you to your superiors."

Milan balled his fists at his side. "I was off duty and spending time with my girlfriend."

"We all know that spending time with Shiloh Bellamy is far from an innocent act."

"What is that supposed to mean?" I asked.

"I wasn't talking to you," the police chief snapped.

"I'm talking to you, and I need to know what you know about my aunt Edna Lee's death."

He blinked as if he hadn't expected that turn in the conversation. That was fine by me; I was happy to catch him by surprise.

"What are you talking about?"

"Forty years ago, my aunt Edna Lee fell through the ice at Herchel Pond and drowned. You were the police chief at the time; what do you know about that?"

"It was an accident," he snapped.

"If that was true, why are you using it as a weapon all these years later to put the blame of Ripley's murder on my grandmother?"

"Because she would tell anyone who listened that she wanted Ripley to pay for her daughter's death. Ripley worked here at the pond. He was the one who found Edna Lee's body, but he wasn't responsible for her death. That is a false narrative that your grandmother started. I'm here to put an end to it."

"That may be true, but why bring my grandmother back up when we found Ripley's bones?" I glared at him.

"Because I have a confession." He shook his head at me. "How many times do I have to tell you this?"

"Oh, I've seen the confession, and I can assure you that it's too vague to really mean anything at all."

"What? How?" he sputtered.

"The Mayberly House has a copy," I said. "Since you prematurely closed the case, it is part of town history."

"That house is going to be the death of me. How did Matilda get it?" He balled his hands at his sides.

I wasn't about to throw Connie under the bus even if she wasn't the kindest to me when I asked her about it.

He glared at me. "It was Connie, wasn't it?"

I didn't say anything.

He shook his head. "She has been feeding Matilda information about cases since I hired her forty-nine years ago. There is no gratitude. And here I was just trying to help a woman who found herself in a little bit of trouble."

"Trouble how?" I asked. It was the last thing I expected him to say.

"The kind only women get into." He sneered. "But blame men like Ripley for."

What did he mean by that? I was about to ask him when he said, "I know Ripley wasn't here when Edna Lee fell through the ice."

"How could you possibly know that?" I asked.

"Because I had him in the jail sleeping off a hangover the morning Edna Lee drowned. He couldn't have been there or had anything to do with it."

I blinked. If this was true, why was the police chief just telling me this now? He could have said this anytime after finding Ripley's body.

"I told your grandmother that, but she didn't believe me. She thought I was lying to protect him. Why would I protect him? He got in so much trouble and was a constant thorn in my side for decades. He was horrible to my piano teacher, Mrs. Perch. I had no reason to help him."

Part of me wondered if the police chief could be lying. There had to be a reason that Grandma Bellamy had been so sure that Ripley was behind her sister's death. I needed to find out if Ripley had really been in jail the morning that Edna Lee fell through the ice. It would be easy for Connie to find out. That was if she was willing to help me anymore with this case after our disagreement earlier in the day. Perhaps I could appeal to her care for my father. Truly Dad wanted to know what happened to his sister too.

The rangers were walking back to us with their trail cameras.

"I'm done talking about this. James Ripley's case is closed." Chief Randy stomped back to his SUV.

Milan looked at me. "That went well."

"So well," I said with a sigh.

Chapter Thirty-Eight

The next morning, I was to meet Kristy and the other members of the farmers market planning committee at the market grounds. Kristy worked out of a trailer on the property, which had been the site of the old high school's parking lot. When the high school was torn down years ago to build a new one in another location, the parking lot had been left untouched. It became a weed-infested eyesore just a block away from the bustling Michigan Street that was revitalizing Cherry Glen.

That's when Kristy had the great idea for the farmers market. She built it from the ground up, and by the time I moved back to Cherry Glen, it was one of the most popular stops in town.

Kristy held the committee meetings in the trailer. The inside of the trailer was half office and half children's playroom. Her twins were on one side of the trailer playing with stuffed animals while our group of five sat close together on folding chairs.

"Shiloh," Russell Gershwin, a berry farmer, said as the meeting came to an end. "I heard that you came face-to-face with the bear, and here you are to tell the tale."

"Really?" Lance Poplar, a cattle farmer, said "Was he on your farm?" Lance was somewhere in his seventies, and he had been talking about retiring from farming for as long as I'd known him.

One the hardest things for a farmer to do was retire. The land and chores were a farmer's identity, but that didn't mean during rainy season, dry season, or just plain bad seasons that each and every one of us didn't think about quitting. It crosses every farmer's mind multiple times a year.

Very few actually gave up though, so I took Lance's complaints for just what they were: all talk.

"No, thank goodness. Diva is one tough chicken, but I don't think even she could stand up to a bear. I was at Herchel Pond. Looked like the bear was using that old barn-cabin there as a makeshift den."

Lance removed his baseball cap and showed off his mostly bald head. "That would make a mighty fine den for a bear. No one really goes out to the pond this time of year until it freezes over."

"Let's hope the bear is caught," Russell said.

"The rangers were confident they can trap him now that they know where he's sleeping," I said.

"Good. Good," Russell said.

"Tragedy has struck there before," Lance said knowingly. He looked at me. "I'm sure you know about that."

My pulse quickened. "You mean Edna Lee."

He nodded. "If you ever want to know what she looked like you need to look no further than your cousin, Stacey. She is the spitting image of Edna Lee. There are times I see Stacey, and I have to do a double take because I think it's Edna Lee. The biggest difference between the two of them is their personalities."

"How so?" I asked.

"I'm sure you know from firsthand experience that Stacey can be prickly at times. She can be so snippy it diminishes her physical beauty, if you ask me," Lance said.

I had thought the same thing more than once about my cousin, but I would never say it.

"Edna Lee was the opposite. She was as sweet as the day is long, and she never met a stranger. She always saw the good in people. She wanted to go to New York so badly, but your grandmother was convinced she would end up dead in a ditch because Edna Lee was too friendly. Your grandmother worried that she would trust the wrong person while she was out in the big city."

"Did she trust the wrong people in Cherry Glen?" I asked.

I felt Kristy watching me.

He shrugged. "There's no telling now that Edna Lee is dead. There is no one left to ask."

"No one left to ask" was the most frustrating part of this case, but I was more than thrilled that Lance had remembered so much about my aunt. It made me hopeful that I would be able to clear Grandma Bellamy's name.

"Do remember what my grandmother was like when she was young? She never really talked about her childhood or young adulthood to me. I'm realizing now how little I know, and I feel cheated when I could have just asked her these questions when she was alive. Now, it's too late, but I am eager to hear whatever you might remember about her."

Lance leaned back in his chair. I hoped that he wouldn't lean back any further. The folding chair wouldn't be able to take it.

"Emma Kay got married to your grandfather right out of high school," Lance said. "Jack Bellamy was a few years older than her, and he had just bought those four hundred acres that make up your farm today. I have to say, he was a good friend of mine later in life for a lot of years, and he would be so proud of you saving the farm. You should be proud of that too."

"And Edna Lee?" I asked.

"She couldn't be more different from your grandma if she tried. She had no interest in marrying a farmer. Believe me, many of them tried to catch her eye. She had dreams of being a star. I don't think anyone would be surprised that you and Stacey ended up in show business considering who your aunt was."

"Did she date anyone?" Kristy asked.

"James Ripley was the only one I ever knew of. The last few months before she died, when she wasn't working at the diner trying to make money, she was with Ripley. Everyone told her he was trouble, but I think she was attracted to him not just because he was handsome but also because he lived in New York City for a short time. It was the city where she wanted to be."

What Lance told me verified everything that I knew about Ripley and Edna Lee, but it still didn't answer the most pressing question. If it wasn't to visit Ripley, what was she doing out on Herchel Pond the day she died?

Chapter Thirty-Nine

Back at the farm, Connie Baskins's sedan was parked in my spot between the barn and the farmhouse. I frowned. It was still in the middle of the workday, so I expected her to be at the municipal building. Not to mention, my father wasn't home because I had taken him to play practice when I went into town.

I shared a look with Huckleberry; then I shifted the truck into park. He whimpered.

I went inside the house through the unlocked back door, and Huckleberry followed me. We stood in the mudroom just off the kitchen and were more than surprised to see Connie bustling around the kitchen in a frilly apron over her typical chunky sweater and long skirt.

"Hello?" I called.

She stirred a pot of chili on the stove. "Oh, Shiloh, I didn't expect you to burst in like that. You really should knock."

Knock? Knock? This was the house I grew up in. It was my father's house, which I technically owned since I had taken the farm over from him. All these thoughts flew through my head, but I didn't speak them aloud.

"What are you doing here?" I asked. "Dad is at play practice."

"I know that," she said. "I can take an afternoon off from work from time to time. Lord knows I have given the town most of my life. I have decided it's time to live a little. I'm even thinking of retiring. I'm over the age to do it. Certainly, after Sullivan and I marry in a few weeks, I will want to spend as much time with him as possible."

I bit the inside of my lip to stop myself from saying anything that might come off as rude. The truth was I wanted my father to be happy. My mother had been his one true love, and he had been a broken man since she died when I was small. It was just in the last few years that he started to build his confidence back. He got back into fishing. He started acting. He was happier. Why wouldn't this be the time he would attract a woman like Connie, who wanted to take care of him?

Also, why was I so resistant to it? I could use help when it came to caring for my father.

I cleared my throat. "I'm happy for you and Dad, I really am."

She looked at me as if she was trying to decide if I was lying.

"I'm sure Dad will love the dinner too. You're making one of his favorites."

"Thank you," she said in a clipped voice.

"I am sorry if you thought I ambushed you yesterday with all those questions about giving information to Matilda Strong at the Mayberly House."

She sniffed. "Yes, Chief Randy is not happy with me. I assume you were the one who told him where the information came from."

I nodded.

"I expected as much. You're so much like Emma Kay. She was a dog with a bone too."

"What do you mean?" I asked.

She shook her head. "I need to get back to making dinner."

I frowned. "My grandmother didn't approve of Edna Lee of being in a relationship with Ripley."

She looked up at me again. "I can't say I blame her. They were never going to work."

"Because Ripley was a womanizer; that's what I have learned about him. Could he have been cheating on Edna Lee?"

She narrowed her eyes at me. "How would I know?"

"Maybe it was in the police report. I would think the police would want to talk to any woman he might have been involved with when he disappeared because she might know something."

She turned back to the stove. "I know nothing about it."

I picked up Huckleberry and left my father's house feeling more confused than ever.

On the other side of the farm, I found Chesney in her kitchen making candles. The room smelled like beeswax, vanilla, and cherries. Even though it was cold outside, she had the window over the sink open. If she hadn't, the smell would have been too overpowering.

She smiled at me as she held a wick upright with her left

hand and poured wax into a clean mason jar with her right. "How did the meeting at the farmers market go?"

"Good. Kristy has big plans about making the market better than ever."

"Doesn't she always?" Chesney asked.

"Now she's talking about building a permanent structure to house the market all year long."

She raised her brow. "That would help us in the winter. We could sell our wares in one place and not traipse all over Western Michigan trying to make a buck."

"That's what I thought." I sat across from her at one of the kitchen chairs. "Do you need any help?"

She shook her head. "I'm almost done. I made fifty new candles, which should carry us through the coming weekend's craft fair. Anything else interesting happen at the meeting?"

"Lance knew my grandmother and aunt Edna Lee."

"Oh, did you learn anything new about Edna Lee?"

"Edna Lee and James Ripley were a couple." I went on to tell her everything that Lance had said.

She looked up from her hot wax, and her glasses slipped down her nose. "That would explain why she was at Herchel Pond."

"True."

Whit came into the kitchen. I raised my brow at her as if to ask her if she was finally going to tell her sister what she had been up to these last several months.

"Chesney, can I talk to you?" Whit's voice was meek.

I started to stand up. "I'll head back to the cottage so that you two can talk."

"No," Whit said. "You can stay, Shiloh. I want you to stay."

Chesney looked at both of us. "What's going on?"

Whit took a breath. "I know I have been distant lately, but that's because I was working on a project."

"What kind of project?" Chesney asked.

"To find our family."

Chesney frowned. "Our parents are gone. We don't have any more family."

"I mean Mom's birth family," Whit said.

"Mom said it was closed adoption."

Whit nodded. "I know, but I hired a private investigator to see if he could find out who mom's birth mom was, and maybe from there we could find even more family members."

Chesney's mouth hung open.

"Who is it?" I asked.

Whit glanced at me. "Connie Baskins."

"What?" Chesney and I shouted at the same time.

"Are you sure?" I asked.

She nodded. "Rhett was able to track down the original birth certificate."

"Who was her father then?"

She shook her head. "We don't know that. That line was blank, but Rhett said there was evidence that she was seeing someone a lot older than her. Maybe that's why she kept it a secret. And this was over fifty years ago. She wasn't married. It would still be frowned to have a child out of wedlock at that time."

"Where was your mom born?" I asked.

"At the hospital at Traverse City," Whit said.

"That's so close to here." Chesney placed a hand on her cheek "This is a lot to take in."

"I know. I had my suspicions it was Connie for weeks, but I didn't want to say anything until the investigator confirmed it. It took a lot longer to do that than I thought it would."

An idea tickled the back of my brain from something Chief Randy said about when women got in trouble and blamed men like Ripley for it. I thought it was just another of his offhanded sexist comments. Maybe it was that and something else too. Was I crazy to guess James Ripley was the father of Connie's child? If he was, Chief Randy knew. He had hinted to me. Why?

"Connie is at my father's farmhouse making him dinner. Are you going to confront her?" I asked, not ready to tell the girls my suspicions just yet.

She shook her head. "She left the farm. When I drove up the road, she was going the other way. I was so shocked to see her after what I learned."

"If she gave her baby up for adoption, maybe she doesn't know it was our mother," Chesney said.

"She knew. It was a private adoption and Connie picked the family." Whit rubbed the back of her neck.

"So, your grandparents knew Connie was the biological mother?"

She shook her head. "No, they only knew that they had been picked by the mother and she lived somewhere in Michigan."

"*Somewhere in Michigan.* She lived right here in Cherry Glen," Chesney said.

"How old would your mom be today?" I asked.

"She'd be fifty. She had me when she was young," Chesney said. "She and my dad got married when they were twenty or twenty-one."

"This all started as a project for school," Whit said. "And it's turned into something so much bigger. I have a meeting with Connie tonight at the municipal building under the guise of a project for one my government classes. I told her that I had to interview someone in town government, and since she's the person in town who's worked the longest in civil service, I wanted to talk to her." She looked us both in the eye. "I'd like you both to be there."

Chapter Forty

When Whit, Chesney, and I walked into the municipal building together that evening, Connie Baskins appeared to be surprised to see all three of us.

She looked from Whit to me. "What are they doing here?"

"I wanted them to be here for this conversation," Whit said.

Connie frowned. "For an interview for class?"

Whit shook her head. "I want you to tell Chesney and me what you know about our mother."

Connie paled. "Your mother? I don't know anything about her at all."

"Aren't you our grandmother?" Whit asked.

Connie gasped. "You have lost your mind."

"I asked Rhett to help me find my family, and he came up with you. It's all there." Whit placed a file folder on Connie's desk.

Connie didn't touch the folder. She wouldn't even look at it. "It was supposed to be a closed adoption."

"It was," Whit said. "But we were able to find enough evidence to prove you're our biological grandmother."

Connie looked at me. "I can understand why you and Chesney are here, but what is she doing here?"

"Shiloh is like family to us, and I wanted her to be here," Whit said.

Connie pursed her lips together. "I did what was best for your mother."

"We know that," Chesney said. "But after she died, why didn't you come forward and tell us? You knew we were young and alone."

Connie pressed her lips together. "You were better off without me."

"Because you didn't want them to start asking uncomfortable questions about who their grandfather was?" I asked.

Connie stood up and glared at me. "What are you talking about?"

"Isn't James Ripley their grandfather, and you didn't want anyone to uncover that?"

She glared at me and walked around the desk.

"Did you get rid of Edna Lee because you were afraid that Ripley would leave you for her, and he was never willing to leave with you?"

"She was all excited when she came to the pond to meet James. They were going to leave for New York that night." Connie narrowed her eyes.

"But he wasn't there," I said. "He was in jail from the night before. You would know that because you were already working at the municipal building. Ripley's arrest would have gotten your attention. What were you doing at the pond?"

She glared at me. "I was waiting for her. When he was in

jail, I went down there to talk to him. No one else was there. I pleaded with him to take me back. I did everything that he asked me to. I left Cherry Glen to have the baby. I gave my daughter away for him, so we could be together. Over the next ten years, he had so many relationships with other women, but I waited patiently. He always came back to me when he broke it off with the other women. It wasn't until he said he was going to New York with Edna Lee that I knew he was never coming back, and I gave up everything that I could have had with my child for nothing. I loved her from afar." She looked at Whit and Chesney. "It broke my heart into a thousand pieces when your mother died. Truly."

"Did you kill Edna Lee?" I asked.

"I didn't kill her. I just wanted to warn her about the man that James really was. She didn't believe me and ran out on the ice on her own accord. She wasn't far in when the ice gave way."

"Did you try to help her when she went into the ice?" I asked.

Connie looked away.

"You just let her drown?" Whit asked, as if she couldn't believe someone she knew could be so cruel.

Connie was still not looking at us. "James came to the pond and found me there. He had just been released from jail again. I was in shock over what had happened to Edna Lee. I didn't want her to die. He said it was my fault she was dead, but if I did what he asked, he would keep it a secret."

Tears were in her eyes. "He told me to leave him alone. He said that he never wanted me to so much as look at him ever again. If I did, he would go to the police."

"I tried my best to do what he wanted. I spent the following months watching him chase women, and I just couldn't take it anymore. He was all I had in the world. I gave up my baby so I could be with him. If I couldn't have him, no one could, so I came the pond one night to give him one more chance." She looked at the marble floor.

"He said he was done with me and planned to go the police the next day and tell them I killed Edna Lee. I had no choice but to shoot him."

"How did he end up on my farm?" I asked.

"I told your grandmother that he killed Edna Lee and that he attacked me too, so I killed him in self-defense. She was so certain that he killed her daughter, she agreed to help me bury him on your land."

My heart hurt to hear my grandmother was involved in at least the cover-up of the murder.

"That's all I need to hear," Chief Randy said, stepping out of the shadows.

On the drive from the municipal building, I called the police chief and told him what I suspected about Connie. As to be expected, he didn't believe me at first, but he agreed to hide in the lobby so that he could hear the conversation. I really thought he only agreed to do it to hear me be proven wrong. How surprised he must have been when he heard Connie's confession.

Connie stared at him—and then she took off running for the door.

"Stop!" Chief Randy called.

She didn't stop and went outside.

Chief Randy radioed his officers so that the chase could begin, even though I had no idea how far Connie could get on foot. However, that didn't matter. Connie came running back into the building. Her eyes were as wide as saucers.

"What is it?" I asked.

"The bear is on the sidewalk. I'd rather be arrested than eaten by a bear."

"Good call," Chesney said.

Epilogue

Christmas in Cherry Glen was special. On Christmas Eve, Kristy had organized a farmers market that ran the entire length of Michigan Street. Snow fell in giant puffs, and Chesney and I were doing a brisk business.

Whit, my father, and the others who were part of Michigan Street Theater walked up and down the road in costume and in character for *A Christmas Carol*. Dad shook his chains at tourists as Marley. Young children ran away from him with gleeful shouts. I was happy to see Dad so at ease. I was afraid that when he learned of Connie's part in Edna Lee and Ripley's deaths that he would go back into a depression. However, he seemed relieved.

"She wanted me to marry her," he had said. "This gets me off the hook."

I felt the most for Chesney and Whit. Whit had been so hopeful that she would have more family. She found it, but it certainly wasn't what she expected. She learned the lesson that sometimes the best family is the one you chose.

As for the bear, after the incident at the municipal building, he was finally caught and taken to the Sleeping Bear

Dunes. I wanted to thank him for catching a killer, but I never got a chance. I hoped that he lived his best bear life in the park.

I saw Milan walking down the street toward our booth looking as handsome as ever. He was there to see me and it warmed my heart. I could not have asked for better partner in life. He grinned when he caught my eye and gave me a little wave. I waved back.

"What's next for Bellamy Farm?" Chesney asked after our latest customer stepped away from the booth.

I smiled. "Whatever we dream up together."

She grinned. "That sounds like a plan."

**If you've enjoyed *Natural Barn Killer*,
read on for an excerpt from
Crime and Cherry Pits, another cozy
Farm to Table Mystery!**

If Penelope Lee Odders clicked her pen one more time, I might have jumped into the Grand Traverse Bay. Penny Lee, as she preferred to be called, was a woman about sixty years old who fancied herself a hard-hitting reporter covering the annual National Cherry Festival in Traverse City for a newsletter called the *Sweet Cherry News*.

"Now," Penny Lee said as she looked down at her notes and her gray curls fell over her eyes. "What happened in Los Angeles that made you want to come back to Michigan in the first place? Man trouble? Lawsuit? Tell us all." She brushed her hair aside.

I ground my teeth; Penny Lee had asked me the same question about my life in Hollywood a myriad of ways in the last hour. Maybe I was slow on the uptake, but it seemed to me that she was much more interested in my past than my present as owner and organic farmer at Bellamy Farm in Cherry Glen, a small town thirty minutes east of Traverse City.

Penny and I sat on folding chairs on a dock overlooking the gorgeous blue of the bay. Against the dock, the bay began as sky blue and deepened into a vibrant navy blue as it emptied into the deep waters of Lake Michigan. The July morning sunlight, which beat down on our heads, reflected off on the water like crystals and shone on the countless sailboats that made their way out on the lake for the day. My little pug, Huckleberry, sat under my chair in the shade. Huckleberry had been born and raised in LA, and although we had lived in Michigan for just short of a year, he still looked continually confused about how he ended up in the middle of the north woods.

The edge of the dock would have been the perfect spot to sit and reflect on the fact that I had made the right decision to leave my job as a television producer to move back home to save the family farm, but glancing at the woman with frizzy gray hair and pointy nose across from me, I had a brief moment of doubt.

I stood up. "Penny Lee, I'm really grateful to you for this interview. The National Cherry Festival is the biggest event in Michigan, and I know that you must have so many people to talk to and so much to cover, so we should probably stop now as the festival opens"—I consulted my smartwatch—"oh, in ten minutes!" I squeaked. If I want to be at Bellamy Farm's booth at opening time, I had to go now.

Penny Lee stood up and smoothed the wrinkles in her prairie skirt. "I suppose you're right. I'm sorry we had to end before we were able to get to the meat of the matter."

The meat of the matter? What on earth was she talking about? When I agreed to this interview, it was to talk about my farm, our cherries, and the organic baked goods and products that I sold. After many months, the farm was no longer just getting by but making a modest profit as a working farm.

"Thank you for your time," I said. I couldn't believe that I was thanking her, but good manners were so ingrained in me by my grandma Bellamy, it was impossible to not say thank you even in the most uncomfortable situations. Tugging lightly on Huckleberry's leash, I stepped around her to walk up the dock.

"One last question," she called to me.

I closed my eyes for a second and, against my better judgment, said, "Yes, what is it?"

"How long have you and your cousin Stacey Bellamy been fighting over your late grandmother's money?"

"No comment." I stomped away, and my little pug galloped after me to keep up.

I was fuming as I hurried through the festival to reach the Cherry Farm Market, where Bellamy Farm had a booth for the very first time in its over seventy-year history. As a Michigan cherry grower, to have a booth at the Cherry Farm Market at *the* National Cherry Festival was a major feather in our cap. It was something that we could use to promote the farm on social media and in advertisements. To be at the market, your cherries have to meet the highest level of excellence, and my farm director, Chesney Stevens, and I worked tirelessly to bring the farm's half-dead orchard back to life.

Even though we were accepted into the festival by the slimmest possible margin, I knew that each year the farm would improve dramatically, and in a few years, I could see Bellamy Farm being one of the most popular organic cherry booths at the Cherry Farm Market. Or at least that was the dream.

As Huckleberry and I walked through Open Space Park, where the majority of the festival was held on the edge of the Grand Traverse Bay, I glanced at the smaller of the two stages on the lookout for my cousin. She had been avoiding me in town, but I hoped that during the festival, we would have a chance to talk about what to do with our grandmother's stocks. I had to make Stacey understand that I didn't want to keep the money from her. However, for her to receive any money at all, she had to give her consent to the distribution of the inheritance as a legal heir. Just thinking about it gave me a headache. The argument had been going on for months.

There was no sign of Stacey on the stage as I walked by, but I saw Whit Stevens, Chesney's younger sister, next to a silver and red university trailer parked to the right of the stage. From what Whit had said, the trailer was used a green room of sorts when actors were between scenes.

Whit was dressed all in black and had a headset around her neck that was almost hidden by her streaked, bumblebee-bright yellow and black hair. Whit was a college student and worked as the stage manager at the Michigan Street Theater. It was no surprise to me that she had this job at such a young age. She was just as hardworking as her older sister.

Whit folded her arms across her chest as she spoke to a young man about her age. He had longish brown hair that he continually flipped out of his face with a flick of his head. Whatever he was saying to Whit, she didn't appear too happy about it. My curiosity was piqued, but I knew it was none of my business, nor did I have the time to snoop.

A man bellowed at me, shaking me from my thoughts. "Out of the way!"

I glanced over my shoulder to see a short plump man carrying a giant cherry-headed mannequin on his shoulder. The man's face was as red as the cherry man he carried. I scooted to the side of the park trail, scooping up my ever-faithful pug, Huckleberry, in the process.

The two of us stood there for a long moment watching the bobbing cherry head disappear in the sea of cherry red around us. The color literally was everywhere.

The festival was spread across the entire downtown area, with the carnival rides along East Grandview Parkway, the large music performances at the Bayside Music Stage, and the small acts, the Shakespeare performance, and Cherry Farm Market in Open Space Park.

There were so many things going on that I didn't even notice twelve-year-old Hazel Killian running toward me until she called my name. Her long ponytail flew behind her head like a flag, and her knobby knees moved like pistons on a locomotive. "Shiloh! Shiloh!"

I waved at her.

She pulled up short when she reached Huckleberry and me. She bent over and gulped for air like she had just finished a marathon.

I rubbed her hand. "Hazel, what's wrong? Are you sick? Are you breathing?"

She was still bent over and held one finger in the air in the universal sign for *hold on*. I waited for her to collect herself.

She stood up straight. "Where have you been? Chesney is freaking out. The festival is about to open, but you're not at the booth."

I studied her face, looking for the truth in her statement. It wasn't that I thought she was lying, but she did have a tendency to exaggerate. I highly doubted that Chesney Stevens freaked out about anything. My young farm director was just about the coolest customer there was, and there wasn't anything at the booth that she needed me for. She could do everything I could and twice as well.

Not wanting to make a big issue out of it, especially after my less than pleasant conversation with Penny Lee, I said, "I'm heading that way now."

SHILOH'S
Quick Farm Tips

The easiest way to make candles is with an old jar or cup to hold the wax. I like to use old teacups that I find at secondhand stores. Reusing mismatched teacups is a great way to help the environment, and it turns them into something beautiful. Here's how I make my teacup candles.

MATERIALS

- Teacups
- Candle wax
- Wooden pencils
- Candle wicks
- Essential oil for scent
- Crayons for color
- Hot glue gun and glue

DIRECTIONS

Glue the metal circle of the wick to the bottom of the teacup with hot glue.

Wrap the top of the wick around a pencil and lay the pencil across the teacup's rim.

Melt wax in a double boiler or in a dedicated Crock-Pot that you only use for crafting.

If you would like to add color, break up a crayon that is the color of your choice and melt it with the wax.

Add a few drops of essential oils to the melted wax for the desired scent. I, of course, love anything cherry scented.

Pour hot wax into the teacup. Be careful to keep the wick in the center of the teacup. The pencil lying on the rim will help with that.

Let wax harden.

Trim wick and enjoy!

Acknowledgments

First and foremost, I want to thank my readers who have told me how much they enjoyed the Farm to Table Mysteries. I have loved writing this series for you, and I love highlighting Michigan cherry country in the books. If you ever have the chance, I highly recommend you go and visit the Traverse City area. You won't be disappointed. I can't wait to go back.

As always, I have to thank my amazing agent, Nicole Resciniti, for all she has done for this series of books and for my career as a whole. I also thank my editor, Anna Michels, and the whole team at Poisoned Pen Press and Sourcebooks for all they do to get my books into the hands of readers.

Thanks, too, to my reader Kimra Bell for her close read of all my works.

Love and gratitude for my husband, David Seymour, who is there every step of the way with every book I write. I could not do this work without his unwavering support.

Finally, thanks to God for not only allowing me to have a farm but to write about one too.

About the Author

Amanda Flower is a *USA Today* bestselling and Agatha Award–winning author of more than fifty mystery novels. Her novels have received starred reviews from *Library Journal*, *Publishers Weekly*, and *Romantic Times*, and she had been featured in *USA Today*, *First for Women*, and *Woman's World*. In addition to being a writer, she was a librarian for fifteen years. Today, Flower and her husband own a farm and recording studio, and they live in Northeast Ohio with their adorable cats.